Titles by Natasha Madison

The Only One Series
Only One Kiss
Only One Chance
Only One Night
Only One Touch
Only One Regret
Only One Mistake
Only One Love
Only One Forever

Southern Series
Southern Chance
Southern Comfort
Southern Storm
Southern Sunrise
Southern Heart
Southern Heat
Southern Secrets
Southern Sunshine

This Is
This is Crazy
This Is Wild
This Is Love
This Is Forever

Hollywood Royalty
Hollywood Playboy
Hollywood Princess
Hollywood Prince

Something So Series
Something Series
Something So Right
Something So Perfect
Something So Irresistible
Something So Unscripted
Something So BOX SET

Tempt Series
Tempt The Boss
Tempt The Playboy
Tempt The Ex
Tempt The Hookup
Heaven & Hell Series
Hell And Back
Pieces Of Heaven

Love Series
Perfect Love Story
Unexpected Love Story
Broken Love Story

Faux Pas
Mixed Up Love
Until Brandon

DEDICATION: TO LOVE.

Finding it. Fighting for it. Keeping it.

THE ONLY ONE SERIES

ONLY ONE Night

ONE

MANNING

"PUSH, PUSH, PUSH," I say to my son, Jaxon, who skates beside me. Holding his hockey stick in his left hand, he skates around to the other side. He looks over at me and smirks when he gets around without falling this time. "Good." He skates until we do three whole turns.

He stops by the bench where he put his water bottle when we got on the ice. Chest heaving, he takes off his glove and unsnaps his helmet to get a drink of water. I grab my own bottle and squirt some water in my mouth. "I'm going to set up the cones," I tell him. "Then I want you to take the puck and zigzag through them." When he nods, I feel my whole chest expand. This right here, this special time with him, is worth everything.

Unlike my son, who started skating as soon as we could get skates on him, I didn't start skating until I was six. I would alternate between forward and defense and usually didn't know which position I was playing until

I was told which side of the bench to sit on at the start of the game. When I turned twelve, my father convinced me to stick to defense. It also helped that I was growing like a weed as well as honing my skating skills and increasing my speed. I grew five inches in one year and was already six foot two at fifteen. By the time I turned nineteen, I was six foot five. I wish I could say I was drafted number one overall, but I was drafted number forty-nine to Nashville.

Three years later, I finally made my NHL debut. That was also the year I met Murielle at an after-party. I wasn't a big shot when we met, but as I started climbing the ladder and making a name for myself, the shy girl started to change. I don't think I can pinpoint the exact time, but I knew the minute I saw it. She had just given birth to Jaxon and refused to let my parents stay in our house because I could "afford" to put them up in a hotel. That was the first fight we had, and it just went downhill from there. First, she hired a night nurse to get up with Jaxon if he would cry, then she hired a housekeeper. After that, it was a cook. And now, I can't even tell you what she does all day. I also don't care.

"We have another hour left," I tell him. "I have an event to go to tonight." He nods his head. My son looks just like me, which makes Murielle even happier. His blue eyes are exactly like mine, and his brown hair is just a touch lighter. "Just like his daddy," she always says, making me cringe. I've spent the past four years trying to get her to divorce me. Four years of convincing her that we aren't good for each other, and four years since

I moved out of our bedroom. Four years of me living in hell. The only thing that keeps me from moving out completely is Jaxon.

For the next hour, he pushes himself harder, and when we walk out of the arena, he does it with a huge smile on his face. "I'm going to show Caleb my tricks tomorrow." He gets into the back seat of the SUV, and I wait for him to buckle in before closing the door.

"You have practice tomorrow," I tell him, and he nods. "Then you have a game next week, but I'm going to be on the road." I hate missing his games, but when I'm home, I'm in the stands cheering him on. At first, it was rough because people would hound me for pictures and autographs, but I would just smile and decline. I was here for my son, and they always understood that. But then Murielle would push me to take pictures, and we would end up in another fight. A fight that would have to wait until Jaxon got on the bus before I laid into her. I would never fight with his mother in front of him. I never wanted him to feel like he had to choose one parent over the other. Sadly, I was the only one who thought like that.

"Can we have a boys' night tomorrow?" he asks, and I smile at him.

"That sounds like a great plan," I say as we pull up to our house. I park the SUV and then wait for him to get out. I always walk with my hand on his shoulder. We open the door, and the house is eerily quiet as we walk through the grand foyer to the kitchen, where he opens the double Sub-Zero fridge. He grabs an apple and then looks to see what the chef left for the day. The sound of the basement door opening causes me to look over, and I see Murielle walking up with her trainer. He doesn't even make eye contact with me as he walks out of my house. Last year, I caught them going at it on the weight bench. I don't know what she expected from me, but I can tell you what she didn't like. She didn't like me turning around and walking out of the room.

"Hey, guys," she says, coming back from the front door, and I just look at her. "Did you guys have fun at the rink?" She walks to the sink and washes her hands. Her brown hair is tied on top of her head, and all the hard work she does in the gym keeps her body in perfect shape. That, and the many visits to the plastic surgeon. Her tits are done, her ass is lifted, her lips have been injected, and there is so much Botox in her face that, at times, I don't even know if she's smiling or frowning.

"Yeah, Dad showed me a couple of tricks," Jaxon says to her. I walk over to him and take out a meal for him, knowing he doesn't know which one he should pick. He looks up at me. "I want the chicken."

Nodding, I walk over to the stove and put his meal in the oven to warm. "Go shower," I tell him, "and it'll be done when you come out."

He walks out of the room, coming back two seconds later to grab a couple of snacks from the pantry, stuffing them in his pocket while he holds the apple.

"Don't leave the wrappers in your bedroom!" Murielle yells after him.

"What do you care?" I say. "It's not like you walk around cleaning up."

"I don't want him to live like a pig," she says, leaning her hips against the counter. "What are we doing tonight?"

I laugh at her. "*We* are not doing anything." I grab a couple of things out of the fridge and start to make a protein shake. "I have a dinner."

"Should I come with?" she asks, and I just look over at her. "I'm just asking if you need me to accompany you."

"Murielle," I say. "I don't know how many times I have to tell you. I don't want you by my side. Aren't you miserable living like this?" She folds her arms over her chest, pushing up her tits, and I see the hickey that she now has. "Don't you want to just live your life happy? Be able to do whatever it is you want to do without me?" I don't wait for her to answer me. "I mean, you just had sex with your trainer in the basement. Where my kid plays."

"I have needs, Manning," she says, her voice not even rising. "You obviously won't entertain them, so I have to get it elsewhere."

"I'm not entertaining them because I don't feel like that anymore. We've spoken about this for the past four years. You keep holding on to this marriage for what reason, exactly?" I start the blender. "So you can have the title of captain's wife? What does that do for you?"

"I've sacrificed my whole life for you. To make sure you had everything you needed."

I have to laugh at this. "What exactly did you sacrifice? I never stopped you from doing anything. In fact,

I encouraged you to go back to school to get a degree or get a fucking hobby. All you cared about was wearing my jersey to the games. All the perks that came with being my wife got under your skin, so now here we are."

"What about Jaxon?" she asks. "How do you think he'll feel about having divorced parents and going from one house to the other?"

"You obviously don't know your son," I say, pouring my protein drink in my glass. "You think he doesn't know we live separate lives? He knows I live on the other side of the house. He's smarter than you think," I say. Spinning, I walk out of the kitchen, leaving her with those words. After I climb the winding staircase, I turn right to go to my room. I walk into the bedroom and make my way to my en suite, locking the bathroom door. I had to start doing that after I walked out one day and found Murielle naked, getting ready to join me in the shower.

After I shower, I walk into the closet, grabbing a blue suit and white button-down shirt. I run my hands through my hair, slide on my silver Rolex watch, and then make my way down the stairs. I find Jaxon playing his Xbox in the living room. "Hey there, kiddo," I say, and he looks over at me. "Are you alone?"

"Yeah, Mom said she has a migraine," he says, and I look up at the ceiling.

"Do you want me to stay with you?" I sit next to him, and he shakes his head.

"I'm okay." I mess his hair up and bring him to me, kissing his head.

"Well, you call me if you need anything," I say, and he nods without looking away from his game.

I walk out of the front door and call Murielle on her phone. She answers right away. "Can you at least try to parent while I'm gone?"

"He's fine," she huffs out. "He ate, and he's playing his game." I shake my head. "I'm in the house. It's not like he's alone."

"Whatever," I say, disconnecting the phone and getting into my black Range Rover SUV. I slip on my gold aviator glasses and put the address to the restaurant in my GPS.

The phone rings on my way there, and I see that it's Becca, my agent. "Hello?"

"Hey," she says. "I know you have the meeting tonight with the people from Hauer." She mentions the big hockey equipment chain that sponsors me. "Just so you know, this restaurant is a supper club."

"Ugh," I say with a groan. "What, why? Why would they do this?"

"I know, and I just searched it," she says. "Anyway, I booked you a room in the adjoining hotel just in case you get wild and let loose tonight."

I chuckle. "The last time I let loose was . . ."

"Next to never." She laughs. "Yeah, I know. Anyway, I got you the suite. The key will be delivered to the hostess desk for you."

"You think of everything," I say.

"No, I just don't want you to get caught drinking and driving, and lose all the money that I make off you," she says. It's my turn to laugh. "Anyway, I have to go. Have fun and let loose. Just, you know, don't make it onto *SportsNet*."

"I'll try my best," I say, parking the SUV in the valet spot and disconnecting the phone. I get out of my SUV, and the valet guy notices me right away. "The keys are in the SUV," I tell him, and then I take a deep breath and walk toward the door.

TWO

EVELYN

"YOU'VE BEEN HOME for a week, and you already have plans on Saturday night," my sister-in-law, Veronica, says over the phone with a laugh. "And you didn't know if you should move back home."

I laugh as I walk through my new house; the smell of paint still lingering. "I've been gone for fourteen years," I say as I make myself a green tea. "Who comes back home at thirty-two?"

"Well, I know we are all glad you came back," she says, and I smile.

"I have to be downtown at seven," I say. "Remind me again why I agreed to this."

"Well, she's one of your best friends, so it's only normal you would be her bridesmaid," Veronica reminds me, and I roll my eyes while I sip my hot tea, walking back to my bedroom.

"I mean, remind me again why I thought a bachelorette party was a good idea?" Entering the en suite bathroom, I turn on the bath. "The last thing I want to do today is get all dressed up and go out."

"You need to get out there," she says. I hear the water running in the background and then hear the plates clink together. "Drink a bit, dance a lot, and if you end up going home with a guy, we can call everything a win-win."

I laugh now. "I have never in my life had a one-night stand. Not even in college, so I doubt I'll do it in my thirties."

"How are you getting there?" she asks.

"I was going to drive, but then I thought about it, and I'm just going to take an Uber. I think she said the girls are renting a room in the adjoining hotel, but I'm not sure I want to stay out all night. Besides, if I get home drunk, it's always better to wake up in your bed in the morning."

"Okay, well, can you promise me one thing?" she says, and I almost groan. "Have fun."

"I will. Kiss the kids for me," I say and hang up. I put my phone down on the white marble countertop and then change my mind, opting to take a shower instead of a bath. If I take a bath, I'll want to slip into my pjs, and that will be the end of the night for me. Sliding off the robe I was wearing, I step in and close my eyes.

Never in my wildest dreams did I think I would come back home. When I turned eighteen, I packed up my room and left to go to school in Chicago. Since I was a little girl, it was my dream to move there. I don't know what it was, but I just thought if you lived in Chicago, you had made it. I was caught up in the hustle and bustle of Chicago and loved it in every sense of the word—from walking down the Magnificent Mile to getting out on the lake each weekend.

I pushed myself hard in school, and it's where I met Dex, Joshua, and Ally. The four of us took to studying together. My relationship with Dex grew without us even knowing. Then we found out Joshua and Ally also started dating, so the four of us were always together. We all got jobs as soon as we got our master's degree. We each built our portfolios until we decided to take a leap and start our own financial firm.

We were growing so fast we had to hire people, and it was my dream come true.

Until I walked in on Dex and found him balls deep in Joshua while Ally sat on his face. The three of them were snorting coke off each other.

They didn't even notice I had walked in or out. When he came home five hours later, he was shocked to see my bags at the door. I asked him one question before I left: How long? It was the only answer I really wanted to know, and I was shocked when he said it's been since we all started hanging out together. I mean, it was right under my nose the whole time. I walked out and then came back to pack the rest of my stuff.

It was a bit sticky since the four of us owned a company together. I sold them my shares, and now I'm basically starting over, though not from scratch. Luckily for me, my family works in finance, so I just joined their financial firm. My father was over the moon when I asked him about it. My brother, Timothy, was even happier. He hated Dex, so my returning was a win-win for him. I also left with my portfolio, and most of my clients had agreed to follow me.

As soon as I flew into town, I bought my house. I had already chosen it online, but the minute I stepped in the front door, I knew it was for me. I made sure that the house had a new coat of paint on the walls before moving in, so when I went furniture shopping with my mother and Veronica, my whole house was furnished in a matter of three hours.

Stepping out of the shower, I grab my white plush terry cloth robe and slip it on, then wrap my hair in another towel. I walk toward my walk-in closet and go through my clothes. The dress code is pink and black, so I choose a blush pink skirt with a long-sleeved black wraparound silk top. The sleeves cut all the way down the sides and tie at the wrist in a bow. I walk back to the bathroom to finish getting ready.

My long auburn hair is down to my waist, and I leave it down, curling the ends. My makeup is done dark, making my green eyes pop. The lipstick is nude, and when I slip on the pink skirt, I forget how short it is. I mean, it's not short enough that my ass hangs out, but it's definitely not the length that I'd wear to work. I slip on my black bra, and then slide my arms into the wraparound shirt, tying it around my waist into a bow, just like at the wrists. I make sure that I'm secured into the shirt, so no boobs slip out. I grab my YSL heels and walk over to the bed when I hear my phone ringing from the bathroom.

I get it right before it goes to voice mail, and I see it's Jeanie, the other bridesmaid. "Hello," I say, and I can hear the music in the background.

"Hey!" she shouts. "Just letting you know we are going to be heading to the restaurant in a couple of minutes." They had the whole pre-party before the actual party, but I was waiting for a delivery and had to opt out of it. The truth be told, I wasn't in the mood, and I knew that Stephanie understood.

"Perfect," I say. "I'm slipping on my shoes right now, so I should be there in about thirty minutes."

"Sounds good," she says. "I'll text you when we get there." She hangs up, and I slip my foot into my shoe. The strap goes over my toes and then ties around my ankle. Once both shoes are on, I take a final look in the mirror, then grab the matching YSL purse and order an Uber.

I remember to spritz my perfume right before he gets here. Walking out of the house, I feel the warm air on my legs, and the wind is blowing just a bit. I get into the car, saying hello to the driver, and I scroll through Instagram while we make our way downtown.

I see pictures from the pre-party, and I smile when I see that we are all practically dressed the same. Only Stephanie is dressed in white. She has a rose-gold sash around her that says "Bride-to-be."

I finish applying my lipstick right before the Uber comes to a stop. Opening the door, I thank him. As I walk toward the front door, a black Range Rover parks in valet, and I can see a man walking around the SUV.

When my phone beeps in my hands, I glance down at it and then look up to see the door in front of me. I'm reaching out to open the door when a massive hand covers mine, and I look up into the most intense blue eyes I've ever seen. His brown hair looks like he just ran his hands through it. "I'm sorry," he says in his deep voice. His plump lips are surrounded by a beard.

I look down at our hands holding the door. "I'm sorry, I wasn't even watching where I was going," I say, and both our hands fall from the door. "My phone rang, and I should have been paying attention to where I was going." I look up at him and notice not only how tall he is but also how he fills out his suit. His white button-down shirt isn't buttoned all the way to the top, and you can see a bit of ink coming out from his collar.

"Please," he says, putting out his hand, and I open the door. He grasps the top of the door to hold it open, and I feel him at my back.

"Thank you," I say over my shoulder, and he just nods at me. I walk to the hostess, whose eyes light up as soon as she sees the guy behind me, and I want to roll my eyes. I get it, he's hot and handsome, and he smells good from what I can tell.

"Mr. Stevenson," the woman says before I even start to talk. "I have your key right here." She hands him a white envelope, and he takes it from her, holding it in his hand.

"I don't have a key," I say to the hostess. "I'm not sure if I should or not." I laugh, looking over to him and seeing him chuckle now. "At least I wasn't told I needed a key."

"I think only the cool kids get the keys," he says, finally smiling at me.

"Is that it? I'm definitely not a part of that club." I look from him to the woman still ogling him. "I'm here with the party under the name Stephanie," I say before I'm forgotten while she takes care of the guy behind me. I look down at my phone. "They are in the back," I say, looking over her to see if I see them. When I spot them, I hold up my hand when Jeanie looks over at me. "I found them." I look over at the man. "Guess I can get in without the key." I laugh. "Have a great night."

"You, too," he says. "Find me if you get stuck and need a key," he jokes, and I walk away from the hostess stand, feeling his eyes on me the whole time.

THREE

MANNING

"FIND ME IF you get stuck and need a key," I try to joke with her, and she throws her head back and laughs. Looking toward the back and walking away from the hostess stand, I'm not even going to pretend that I'm not watching her.

My tongue almost hit the ground when I grabbed the door handle at the same time as she did. I saw her walking, but all I could see was her legs. Her tan legs in those shoes were suddenly the sexiest thing I've ever seen a woman wear. I thought she was going to stop, but she didn't, and we both reached for the door at the same time. Then she looked up at me, and my feet were stuck on the ground as if I wore concrete boots. Her green eyes popped, and her auburn hair looked almost as if it were silk.

"Um, Mr. Stevenson," the hostess says, blinking her eyes, and I look at her. "If you will follow me, I will show you to your table." I nod, looking back at where I saw her disappear. She's hugging girls now, and her smile lights up her whole face. I turn back and follow the hostess as she leads me past the busy bar area. The brown granite bar has glass shelves behind it lined with bottles and decorated with hanging lights. I see a couple of people look over at me, and some recognize me. The guys always nod, and the women stare. We walk past the glass wine cellar, containing bottles and bottles of wine stacked all the way to the top. She stops next to it and opens the glass door. "This is the private room," the hostess says, and I nod as I walk in.

"Manning." One of the guys gets up from the round table and walks over to me. "Good to see you."

"Andrew." I put my hand out to shake his. Andrew is the CEO of Hauer, a company he started ten years ago. "Nice to see you."

"Thank you for coming," he says. "I know you hate doing these things."

With a laugh, I put my hands in my pockets and look out the glass door at all the tables being set up and taken. This is the place to be on a Saturday night. It helps that the tables are cleared off at ten to make way for the dance floor. There is another bar right outside our private area. "I don't hate them." I chuckle. "I just prefer not to do them." It is no secret that I am super private. I don't do Instagram, I don't do Facebook, and I don't do Snapchat. Basically, I don't do anything on social media. I have a Facebook page that Candace, my social media girl, handles. If I have to be honest, the only reason I have it is for my sponsors. If it weren't for them, I wouldn't even be on there.

"Let me introduce you to the team," he says, pointing at the other guys sitting at the table, and I nod my head as he makes the introductions. I listen to them talk and then look over to see if I spot her sitting at her table. I keep looking over, trying to find her, and finally, I do. Smiling, I shake the men's hands and turn when the door opens. Miller walks in with Ralph behind him.

I stand aside with my hands in my pockets as Andrew introduces them to the guys I just met. I take the time to look over at the table of ten girls. They're holding up their glasses of champagne now, and they toast what I think is a bride. I mean, she's wearing a veil and a sash. She sits at the end of the table facing where I am, so I see her laugh now with her head thrown back before she drinks the whole glass. She then snaps her fingers and dances, stopping when the waiters come over to her, and she orders something from him. He smiles at her and then walks away, and I watch him go to the computer. He talks to another waiter and motions to the table with his chin. I know exactly what he's saying.

"Have you been here long?" Miller says from beside me, and I look over at him.

"A couple of minutes," I tell him with a shrug. "Did you guys drive here together?" I ask, meaning him and Ralph, and Miller nods his head.

"I dropped off Layla at their house, and I'll pick her up on the way there." Miller was the most sought-after NHL star that there was. He was on the cover of *GQ*, and he had women flock over to him. But he had his sights set on Layla for forever, and when she finally caved and bought a date with him at the charity auction, it was only a matter of time until he made her fall for his charm.

"Would you like something to drink?" I hear the waitress, who must have come in when we were talking, ask me.

"I'll have a soda water with lime," I say, and she nods her head. Miller and Ralph, who just joined us, order the same. I'm not a drinker, to begin with, but I stick to a clean diet during the season.

"I've never been here," Ralph says, looking around, and Miller laughs at him.

"Why am I not surprised?" Miller says, shaking his head.

"Is this your old stomping ground?" Ralph asks him. I take a second to look back at her, which makes me all confused. Why do I care where she is? Why do I suddenly want to know her name? I'm not going to lie; as a professional athlete, I am surrounded by women all the time. Women who just want to say they fucked an NHL player and don't care if you're married or not. I see it all the time—players who have a girl waiting in every city. I haven't been with anyone in four years. Four fucking years but no one would believe me if I told them. Only five people know about Murielle's and my true relationship—Ralph, Miller, Candace, Nico, and Becca.

"I've been here a couple of times," Miller says. "What's cool is that on the weekends, they have a DJ that comes in, and they transform an outdoor seating area into a dance floor. Those tables over there"—he points—"slowly start to move, and this whole place becomes a dance floor. The booths on the end stay, but you have to pay extra to be in there." He points at where the redhead is seated. "It's a fun place."

Andrew comes over to us. "Before we start, can we get a picture of the three of you?"

"Sure," Ralph says and looks at me. "I have to put this picture up on Instagram, or Candace will have my ass." He mentions his wife, the social media expert.

I stand in the middle as the captain with my two assistants flanking me. "This is the first time in our company's history that we have the captain and his assistants both working with us."

He snaps a couple of pictures and puts it on Instagram with the tagline:

Making History

"Shall we sit down?" Andrew says once he finishes with his phone. I walk over to the table, grabbing a seat with a view of the restaurant. That's not normal for me. I usually like to sit with my back to everyone, so no one can snap my picture without me knowing.

"Since when do you want to look out?" Miller says, sitting next to me.

I don't answer him before I shrug and sit down. The waitress comes back with our drinks, and I take it, but then look back over at her. Why am I so curious about her? Every single time I look over at her, she's laughing about something, and it lights up her whole face. "What's up with you?"

I look over at Miller. "You've been acting weird since we got here."

"What are you talking about?" I ask, taking another sip of the water. "I'm fine."

"You seem distracted," Ralph says. "Is everything okay at home?"

"Well, if you're asking me if Murielle is still there, the answer is yes." I stop talking when the waitress comes over and takes our orders.

As the waitress opens the glass door to leave, I notice the music is now playing, and the sound is getting louder.

Conversation during the meal centers on how we can better the equipment they have for us. The developers all take notes of the things we want done. "I would like for my stick to be just a touch lighter," I say, and they all look at me.

"You hold the record of the hardest shot from the All-Star game last year," Miller says.

"One hundred and eight point five," Ralph says, eating a piece of his steak. "You broke Karlson's ankle last year when he tried to block the shot."

I laugh. "That was not my fault. Who gets in the way? That's what they have a goalie for."

"You play defense," Miller says.

"Yeah, and Karlson was playing forward. Would you get in the way of a puck?" I ask, and they shake their heads.

"I mean, not yours," Miller says, laughing. "No way in hell would I even attempt that. But with anyone else, I don't see the danger. You broke the Jones stick with that one-timer," he says, talking about the time I took a shot and the goalie tried to block it with his stick. The part that got in the way of the puck broke off.

"Anyway." I roll my eyes. "Last year, my stick was good, but if we can get it just a touch more flexible, I think it would be the stick to beat."

"I'm going to test a couple of things out this week in the lab," the man, whose name I think is Daniel, but I'm not sure, says. "I'll have a couple of samples available within the next two weeks."

"I wouldn't mind a couple of samples," Miller says, and the rest of the meal is spent talking about things he would like to have done for him. I only notice the outside once I look up. The lights have been dimmed now, and some of the tables have been moved.

I start to panic when I don't see her, which makes me even more confused. I don't think I've ever felt the need to talk to someone like this before. When I spot her, I see that she is still laughing, and she is drinking a glass of wine. From the looks of it, the table is having the best time. Someone must have said something really funny because the redhead hits the table, and I swear I can hear her laughter. Something inside me clicks; I just don't know what it is.

FOUR

EVELYN

I TAKE A sip of my wine and set the glass down next to my plate. I am the first to admit that this night is becoming one of my favorite nights in the longest time. It could also be the champagne and the wine talking.

When I got here, I was forced to put on a penis necklace. "We better be getting cheesecake for dessert." I look over at Jeanie, who downs another glass of wine. "Oh, or apple pie with ice cream."

"You just ate two appetizers, and then your whole meal, plus the extra mac and cheese you ordered."

"It had lobster in it," I say. "One does not say no to mac and cheese with lobster."

She throws her head back and laughs. One of the bridesmaids clinks the glass with her spoon. "If I can have everyone's attention," she says, and I take a sip of my wine. "We are going to go around the table …" She has to shout to even be heard over the music being played in the restaurant. I look around to see that some of the tables have been moved, making way for a dance floor.

Looking out the back window, I see the outdoor space is filled with hanging lights, providing a soft glow to the garden of greenery all around. The DJ is set up at the corner on a stage of sorts. They have booths outside where people sit and drink, but some are up and dancing already. I get my glass of wine and take another sip, then turn my attention back to the other bridesmaid as she sits down.

"What did I miss?" I ask Jeanie, who leans in and whispers.

"No fucking clue, I was watching one of the waiters." I look over at the guy she is trying to eye fuck, and I suddenly think back to the blue eyes I've been thinking about this whole time.

I mean, I've been thinking about them and then forcing myself not to. When I walked away from him, I felt his eyes on me. Only when I got to my table and went to say hello and hug Jeanie did I look back at the door and see that he was, in fact, looking at me. I turned back two seconds later, and he was gone. I searched the restaurant, but I can't find him anywhere. I mean, I can't find him in my part of the restaurant, but he could still be on the other side. Or maybe he's in a special part of the restaurant that you need the key for. I grab my glass of wine and take a sip, putting it down.

"I have to go pee," I say, grabbing my purse and scooting out of the bench seat. Luckily, I'm on the end.

"I can come with," Jeanie says, and I shake my head.

"No, I'll be fine," I say, smiling at her. My heart is extremely light from all the smiling and laughing I've done tonight. I forgot all about moving away and why I had to move back. Being with my friends feels like I never left. I walk back to the front and look around for signs to the bathroom. I can't find any, and when our waiter spots me, he comes over.

"Can I help you with anything?" he says with a smile. He's been blatantly hitting on me all night. "I told you before that your wish is my command."

I smile and look down, my hair falling to the front. "That is very kind of you," I say as I tuck the hair behind my ear. "I'm just looking for the bathroom."

"Follow me this way." He turns and walks toward where the hostess was. The restaurant is packed, and I have to zigzag with him as we turn and pass a huge glass wine cellar. I finally spot the dark hallway.

I look to my right and spot my table. "I guess I took the long way," I tell him as we pass the bar. "Thank you," I tell him. Walking toward the darkened hallway, I pass the guys' bathroom and then open the door to the women's.

Two women walk out. "They play for the Dallas Oilers. Their captain is sex on a stick," one of them says as I move aside for them to walk. Their hips sway a little bit too much, but they are both almost six-foot, so I guess they can pull off walking like they are on the catwalk. Entering the bathroom, I see a woman sitting down next to a table with everything you think you'll need. I smile at her and walk to one of the stalls, going in and sitting down. When I finish and get up, I do my drunk test. If I can still touch my nose without giggling, then I'm good to drink a bit more. I want to be tipsy, just not drunk.

I walk out of the stall, going over to the sink and washing my hands. The woman gets up and hands me a brown paper towel. I smile at her, thanking her, and when I'm done, I take my lip gloss out and apply another coat. I hand the lady a five-dollar bill and walk out of the now empty bathroom. I'm closing my purse as I walk to my table and run smack into a chest. "Oomph," I say right before two hands hold my arms. When I look up, I'm staring at the same blue eyes from earlier tonight. "Oh my god," I say. "That's twice tonight." He just looks at me.

"You have a thing with not looking where you're going." He lets me go now, and I laugh.

"I was actually just closing my purse," I tell him. "It's all good." I place the purse under my arm. He just looks at me and tucks his hands in his pockets. The bathroom door opens, and a guy comes out. He looks at me and then at the blue-eyed stranger.

"Sorry," he says, and I move aside.

"Well, I'll let you go," I say, smiling at him. The wine plays a huge part in my courage for this conversation. "I have to ask."

"What is that?" he says, and I can almost see a smirk on his lips.

"Was the key to a secret room?" I look at him, and it's his turn to put his head back and boom out a laugh.

"Okay, I take that as a no." I look past him. "Well, it was good bumping into you again. I'll try to watch where I'm going from now on." I nod at him, and all he does is stare at me, giving me tingles in my hands and just a bit of flutters in my stomach. Okay, fine, a lot, and when I walk past him, I get a whiff of his cologne, and I swear it's the hottest thing I've ever smelled in my life.

My legs are shaking, and it has nothing to do with the bottle of wine I've been drinking and everything to do with the man who just eye fucked me. Or maybe it was just me, and he was looking at me with pity. I swing my hips as I feel his eyes on me, and when I finally do get back to my seat and sit down, I make the mistake of looking over at him and find him watching me. His hands are still in his pockets, making his shoulders look huge. Maybe he plays football.

"Are you okay?" Jeanie asks, and I look away from him. "You look flushed," she tells me. I raise my hands to my cheeks, and they feel like they are on fire. I look back now to where he was standing, but I don't see him anywhere.

I grab my glass of wine and down it in two gulps. "I'm fine," I say with a smile. The waiter comes over with a tray full of shots.

"Okay, ladies," he says. "Time to get this party started." He walks around the table, giving each of us a shot. "Okay, can I have the bride come over to me?" he asks. I get up to give her space to walk out, and it's only then that I notice most of the tables have been taken out.

Stephanie walks over to the waiter and stands with

him. "This song is for you," he says and nods to the DJ watching him. The song "Run the World" starts playing, and we all laugh. "To not remembering tonight," he says, lifting a shot, and we all follow him. I take the shot, my eyes closing when the hot liquid goes all the way down, the blue eyes haunting me. Opening my eyes, I look around to see if I can spot him.

"I hate tequila." I hear one of the bridesmaids say as the waiter hands me another shot.

"I don't really think I should," I say, and he just smiles at me.

"You need to stop thinking and let loose." He winks at me, and nothing happens to me. There is no flutter in my stomach or racing of my heart like when the blue-eyed stranger looked at me.

After he walks away, I pour the shot into an empty glass, then pick up a glass of water and take a couple of sips. I look over and see the dance floor is starting to get crowded. A song comes on, and the whole table gets up and starts to dance right next to our table. I feel eyes on me, but when I look around, I don't see anyone looking at me. It must all be in my head.

We dance up a storm, and when I get back to my seat, I sit down and drink the glass of water in front of me. I look over to see the bottle empty. I look around to see if the waiter is anywhere, and when I don't see him, I look at Jeanie and point at the bar, and she just nods her head.

I walk through the crowd and make my way to the bar. It's full in the front, so I walk over to the side near the bathroom. I lean against the cool bar, looking at the two bartenders going nuts. I feel eyes on me. I look over to the right, and there he is, leaning against the bar in the dark. I turn now, looking at him. "Fancy meeting you here," I say, trying to sound funny, and he just chuckles. "Well, I guess the saying is true," I tell him, holding my hand up to get the bartender's attention. He sees me and nods his head, coming over to us.

"What can I get you?" he asks me.

"Can I have an apple martini and a bottle of water," I tell him, and then he looks at the blue-eyed stranger.

"I'm good," he says, and his voice is smoother than it was before.

"No problem, Captain," the bartender says and turns to walk away.

"So, what is the saying?" he asks, and I look at him.

"There is never a third time without a second," I say, and then I look up and think about it. "I think that's how it goes." I try to focus, but my head is spinning.

"Actually," he says, and I lean into him just a bit, turning my face so my ear is in his direction. He leans in just a touch now to make sure I can hear him. Except he gets so close, the smell of him makes all my senses go haywire. I don't even know what he has to say. His face is coming so fucking close to me that I could probably feel his beard on my ear if he wanted to get even closer. "It's never two without three."

FIVE

MANNING

"IT'S NEVER TWO without three," I say, my lips as close to her ear as I allow myself. I watched her dance, and she walked over to the bar, not seeing me.

I leaned on the bar, propping my elbow up, looking at her. When she walked out of the bathroom, and I had to hold her up, my heart was beating so fast in my chest. I could have sworn it was the bass coming from the DJ. But I was too far for that. My mouth went dry when she looked up at me. Her eyes were brighter than before, and the minute she saw it was me, her cheeks turned a light pink.

"I think that is the same thing I said," she says, laughing at me, and the bartender comes over with her drink.

"I got it," I tell him, and he just nods at me, walking away to go serve someone else. He called me Captain before, and I waited to see if she reacted, but she didn't even bat an eye. Did she really not know who I was?

"Thank you," she says, grabbing her martini and bringing it to her lips. "So does this mean I get two more drinks?"

"I don't know." I lean in to make sure she can hear me. I hate that the music is getting louder and louder, but then again, I love that she has to lean in to hear me.

"Do I need a special code word or something like that?" she asks, mirroring the way I'm leaning on the bar. Someone comes in behind her and nudges her, and she has to move closer to me. "Do you come here often?" she asks and then laughs. "God, that was so lame. It's like Pick-up Line 101." I laugh now, looking around to see the guys still in the room. Ralph is writing something down with the guys. Miller is sitting in his chair with his phone in his hands. I stepped out for a second, telling them I wanted to come get a water, and no one even batted an eye.

"Are you trying to pick me up?" I ask, my hands getting clammy. I have no fucking clue what the fuck I'm doing right now.

She tilts her head to the side and takes another gulp of her drink. "No. Do girls usually try to pick you up?"

"It's been known to happen." I tell the truth.

"Obviously," she says, rolling her eyes, and now I put my head down and laugh. "A little bit full of ourselves."

"Not at all. It was an honest question. Are you trying to tell me that your waiter wasn't trying to pick you up?" She looks at me shocked now, her mouth opening and then closing.

"How did you . . .?" she says, looking around, and

then she sees the guys in the room behind me. "You were watching me."

I smirk now, looking around to make sure no one is watching us. She gets bumped again, and this time, she gets really close, so close that my hand comes out and goes to her hip to stop her from flying onto me. I mean, I don't mind if she does, but she's going to want to know why my cock is so hard over a fucking stranger. "Do you have a name?" I finally cave and ask her.

"I do," she says, looking up at me with a smile. "I mean, at least there is a name on my birth certificate." I wait for her to tell me her name. "I'm Evelyn," she says, holding out her hand. I stand now, holding out the arm I was leaning on. My hand grips her hand, and I can swear I feel electricity go through my veins.

"Nice to meet you, Evelyn," I say.

"Usually," she says, while our hands still move up and down, in the longest shaking of hands I've had in my life, "when a woman gives a man her name, it's customary for the man to reciprocate."

"Is that how this goes?" I joke with her, and she drops her hand. I want to grab it back.

"I'm Manning." I put out my hand for her, and she grabs my hand again and shakes it. "It's nice to meet you, Evelyn." When I say her name, my stomach does something weird.

"Manning," she says, and I can now picture her saying my name while I bury my cock so deep in her. I need to get away from her because this is crazy. My cock has not been this hard in forever, actually.

"Well," she says, finishing her drink. "I should get back to the girls."

"Have a great night, Evelyn," I say, and she smiles and looks up at me. If I could, I would wrap my arm around her waist, pick her up, and kiss her lips. My heart thumps in my chest; my stomach feels upset.

"It was a pleasure to meet you, Manning," she says. "Thank you for the drink." She turns now, and I watch her disappear in the crowd until I look over and see her hands up in the air as she dances with her friends. I watch for a couple of minutes and then turn to walk back into the room.

I open the door and walk over to my chair. "Who's the chick?" Miller says, looking at me. I just stare at him. "The redhead."

"What?" I pretend not to know what he's talking about. I pick up my empty glass of water and hear Miller snicker beside me.

"Shit. Is the calm, cool captain shaky?" he says, and I glare at him.

He puts his hand to his mouth to hide his laughter.

"I mean, she's hot." I grip the glass in my hand, and I swear if I hold it any tighter, it's going to smash in my hand. Miller reaches over and grabs the glass out of my hand. "You need to simmer down there, buddy. I'm happily taken. Besides, Layla would skin my balls alive."

"Okay, I'm done," Ralph says, and then I look at him. The Hauer guys walk out of the room to check out the club. "What did I miss?"

"Captain Cool over here"—Miller points at me—"was

chatting with a redhead, and she got under his skin."

"She did not get under my skin," I tell him off, shaking my head. "We met when we walked in together, and then I was getting water at the bar. I bought her a drink," I say, my mouth getting dry, and I look for our fucking waitress.

"You bought her a drink," Miller says in shock.

"That is like rule 101 in trying to pick a chick up," he says, and I just look at him. "Ask Google," he says and picks up his phone.

I snatch the phone from his hand and toss it back on the table. "Hey, don't be mean to my phone because you are all sexually pent up over a chick."

"You need to stop talking," I say with my teeth clenched.

"Miller," Ralph says warning him, trying not to laugh. Miller looks at me, leaning back in his chair.

"What's her name?" he asks me, and I don't want to tell him. I don't want to tell them anything. It's nothing.

"You did ask her for her name," Ralph says, his eyes going big. "You don't just buy a girl a drink without knowing her name." He gets up now and looks down at me. "I'll be back."

"Where are you going?" I ask him.

"I'm going to go stand with the guys and see if I spot her," he says, and Miller jumps up to follow him.

"I'll point her out."

"Stop!" I shout right before they walk out of the room. "Seriously. She has no idea who I am."

Miller shakes his head. "No fucking way. Everyone

knows who you are."

"I know," I say, getting up now. "The bartender called me Captain, and she didn't even bat an eye."

"Maybe she's fucking with you," Miller says, and I clench my fists now. I glare at him, and he puts up his hands. "Or not."

"Let's go get a drink at the bar," Ralph says and pushes the glass door open. Our waitress finally appears out of nowhere.

"Can I get you guys something to drink?" she asks, and then I hear the DJ come out.

"We have a special crew tonight." I look over to where I know she's standing, and she is drinking a glass of wine. Her chest rises and falls, and her eyes meet mine. "Stephanie," he says, and she puts her glass down, breaking the eye contact with me and claps her hands. "This one is for you, girls." I wait for it, and he starts playing "Single Ladies." The dance floor makes space for her party of girls. Her hands go into the air as she sings the words. My hands go into my pockets as everybody's eyes go to them.

"That's her." I hear Miller beside me tell Ralph. Her hips sway to the music as the girls all sing the words. More people move in, and just like that, my view is obscured. The guys grab a drink from the waitress, and I look at her with a nod.

"You need to stop staring at her," Ralph says from beside me, and I look at him. "It's not just a stare. It's a creepy stalker look you have on your face."

I don't know what he's saying. Miller looks at Ralph.

"Shall we take off?"

"Yeah," he says, looking at me. "You leaving?"

"Soon." They both share a look of shock. I'm usually the first one out of events. I dip in and dip out so fast that it's like I was never there. "Don't."

The guys walk over to Andrew and shake their hands. Ralph walks over to me, slaps my shoulder, and then squeezes it. "Be careful." I just nod at him.

Miller is next. He slaps my stomach. "Go get 'em." I shake my head and watch them make their way out. They are stopped twice, and I even see Miller just hold up his hand to say hello, not stopping for pictures. He definitely has changed. The old Miller would be in the middle of that, making sure everyone got a picture.

I turn back to the crowd, standing with Andrew, who talks to the guys. My eyes find her again; it's magnetic. She sings along with the song, and she must feel my eyes on her because she looks over at me. She winks at me, making me laugh, then walks back to her table. Grabbing a shot and taking it, she then takes her glass of wine and chases it down.

I stand here with my hands in my pocket and my heart hammering in my chest, wanting to go over to her. I want to talk to her. I want to hear her say my name one more time. If only for tonight. If only for one night. I see her walking around, and it looks like she's going toward the front door. *She's leaving*, I think to myself. My chest tightens as I see her head disappear. I turn toward Andrew to say something to him and see that he's at the bar having shots.

I'm about to walk out with the hopes I can catch her one last time. I am about to take a step forward when I see her walking toward me from the other side. She stops in front of me, her eyes on mine. "Why are you watching me?"

SIX

EVELYN

"WHY ARE YOU watching me?" I ask him, and my heart beats so fast and loud in my chest, I don't think I would be able to hear him answer. My knees get a little weak from looking at him. He has to be the most handsome man I think I've ever seen in my life. I can't seem to stop looking at him or for him. The pull to him is beyond my control.

This whole time, he's been watching me from afar. I know this because I've also been watching him. From when I walked away from him before, I've been dying to go back to him. To talk to him, to touch him, to see his smile, his smirk, his laugh. He is all that and a bag of chips.

I'm waiting for him to answer when a waitress comes over to us, asking if he would like anything to drink. She stands there looking at him. "Scotch," he answers her. "Neat." He looks at me, his eyes turning a deep blue.

"And an apple martini."

"Vodka," I say. "Grey Goose, cranberry." She nods and walks away. "Does this mean you have to buy me another one?" I ask him, moving closer to him while someone tries to walk around us. His hand comes out again and goes to my hip. His touch shoots through me. This has never happened to me, and I wonder if it must be the shot of tequila I just had. I really just did it so I could psych myself up. *This was stupid*, my head screams at me. This whole thing is absolutely insane. If someone told me this story, I would think they have lost their marbles.

I met this man three hours ago, maybe five. But ever since then, all I can do is think about him and his lips. His beard, wondering if it is soft and how it would feel between my legs. His smooth voice, the way he said my name. The way he held my hip, his thumb moving softly up and down. My senses are all on alert around him. I swear I can feel him staring at me, and even at that, I can't help looking over at him to see if he is watching.

"What do you want, Evelyn?" he asks, leaning down, his face so close to mine all it would take is me to turn just a bit, and his lips would be on mine. He stands up, and now I stand closer to him, so close that there is no space between us. My hands are at my sides, but I want to reach up and hold his hips. I want to hold his hips and tilt my head back and have him kiss me. The music is still playing in the background, but I'm lost in him. I can only see him, and it's frightening that this man has this hold over me.

I get on my tippy toes to get closer to him. "That is a loaded question," I say, swallowing down the lump in my throat. "What do you want from me, Manning?" I watch him as I ask him this. Two can play this game. He's driving me crazy. I wait for him to answer. The seconds feel like hours. I see him swallow as his Adam's apple moves. I'm about to grab his jacket with my hands, but the waitress comes back over and interrupts us.

"Here we go." She hands me my drink with almost a leer and then hands Manning his scotch. "Is there anything else you need?" she asks him, and I want to shout at her to get off his dick. Besides, I'm standing right here. His dick is already taken care of. I mean, if he wants. Just thinking that way, I know I should not drink this. My mind is playing tug-of-war with my heart and my vagina.

"We're good," he says to her, and she walks away.

I hold my drink up. "To three." I smile at him and wink. He holds up his scotch glass to mine, the glasses clinking, but with the noise of the music, you can't hear it. It almost feels like the world is spinning around us, and the two of us are the only ones standing still.

"You," he says, looking at me, "are trouble with a capital T." He brings the glass of scotch to his lips. "It's written all over you." I laugh now, taking my own sip of my drink.

"Why do you say that?" I ask him, and he looks around. He does that a lot. I tilt my head to the side, and I have to wonder what the hell I am doing. I'm playing with fire. I'm so out of my comfort zone right now. I'm also way, way out of my league. This man can have any woman he wants. I know it, and he knows it. Fuck, the waitress even knows it, yet he's standing here playing cat and mouse with me, and I just hope to fuck I can still stand at the end of it.

He takes another gulp of his scotch. "You." He shakes his head. "You just make me think of things I shouldn't be thinking about," he says, looking down at me. He lifts one of his hands, and it looks like he's going to touch my face, but he catches himself and puts his hand in his pocket. My body is now aching for his touch.

"And what things are you thinking about?" I ask, taking another sip of the cool crisp drink. My mouth is getting drier and drier each time I look at him. My knees shake just a bit, but I hold steady. "Who knows." I lean into him and get as close to his ear as I can. "Maybe we're thinking the same thing."

His eyes gloss over when he takes another sip of his scotch. "How often do you do this?" he asks. Any other time, I would be offended, if not insulted. But let's face it, I'm coming on strong, which is not anything I would do any other day.

"Define do this?" I ask. Someone walks behind me, and I have to step closer to him, and at this point, our chests touch. "If you're asking about me flirting, it's been a while." I take a sip of the drink and look at him. "If you're asking me about having a one-night stand." I shake my head. "Never." He swallows now, looking down at me. "What about you, Manning? How often do you do this?" I have never been this brazen or this cut-throat to get a man.

"Never," he says, taking another drink, and I have to wonder if this is his liquid courage also. "Never had a need to. Never wanted to."

I laugh now. "So full of himself," I say, and someone else bumps into me now. His hand comes out of his pocket, and he places it at the base of my lower back. I can feel his hand through the silk of the shirt. The dance floor starts to get so cramped that you can't even move. "So, tell me, Manning, why now?" He looks over at the crowd, scanning it. "Are you with the FBI?" I ask, and his eyebrows pull together.

"What?" he asks, laughing.

"You keep looking over at the room, so it tells me that you are either in the FBI, a police officer, or you're in the witness protection program, and you shouldn't be here." He throws his head back and laughs. "Or linebacker for a football team." I laugh now. "I almost went with wrestler but . . ." I wait for him to look at me and take the last sip of his drink. "So tell me, Manning, why now?"

He leans down now, and my breath hitches in my chest. "You make me want things I shouldn't." His breath comes out, and I shiver in his arms. "You make me want to do things I shouldn't," he continues. "It's a lethal combination." I turn my head just a touch, and my lips are so close to his, it would take nothing to kiss him.

"Is that so?" I say, licking my lips, and then the words are out of my mouth before I can even take them back. "Show me."

It happens so fast I don't even know it's happening. He stands straight, and I feel his cock on my stomach. He grabs my glass and puts it down in a plant beside us. He grabs my hand and pulls me as he makes his way back to the bathroom, and my head is going all over the place. Is he going to fuck me in the bathroom? I know I'm going all YOLO for this guy, but banging in a men's bathroom stall is not something that I would do. My head spins with the idea of where he is taking me when I see him opening a door and pulling me inside. I only get a little bit of a glimpse in the dim lighting before he presses me against the door. "One chance, Evelyn," he says, his teeth clenched. "One fucking chance to say no."

His hands are against the door by my head. I finally put my hands on his chest and pull him to me. "Stop talking, Manning," I tell him, and he growls before his lips smash onto mine. His mouth opens on mine, and I can taste the scotch on his tongue. My eyes are closed now as I breathe him in, as his tongue ravishes my mouth. His hands come down, and he buries them in my hair. I arch my back, wanting to get closer to him.

He lets go of my lips and kisses down my cheek, bending his legs to kiss my neck. My hands go to the door, and his hands come out of my hair. I hope they cup my tits because my body is ready for him. He groans when my hand comes down and goes around his neck. "Manning," I whisper. He lifts his head back, and his mouth is attacking mine now. His hands go to my ass, lifting me off the floor, and I wish the dress had more stretch. He bends his head again, sucking on my neck this time. "Manning," I say, and I want him to lift my skirt so I can wrap my legs around his hips.

His mouth comes up now, and we look at each other, our chests heaving. "Come with me?" he asks, and I just look at him. Bending my head now, I nip his bottom lip before sucking it into my mouth. His tongue comes out, and I suck it into my mouth. We are both frantic to touch each other; his hands move off my ass and to my hips and back again. "Come with me?"

My hand goes to his face as my thumb wipes his bottom lip, and he sucks it into his mouth. "Yes," I whisper. "I'll come with you." I have no idea where he is taking me. I have no idea about any of this. The only thing I know is I would give anything for only one night with him.

SEVEN

Manning

"Come with me?" I ask her, my heart thumping so hard in my chest. My chest is heaving as if I just ran a marathon. I dragged her into a supply closet, for fuck's sake. I snap, and I probably have lost my fucking mind.

Anyone could have seen us. Anyone could have taken a picture, and then what? But even knowing all this, the only thing I could think of was tasting her, kissing her. If I got anything from tonight, it was to have her in my arms.

"Yes," she whispers, my hands still on her ass. "I'll come with you." She tilts her head to the side, and I kiss her again, the earth feeling like it's shaking under my feet. I move one of my hands from her ass, all the way up to her back, and then grip her neck in my hand, bringing her closer to me. I've never had this happen, never had the need to just take what I wanted. Never had the tempt-ation like I did this time. But the best, the motherfucking best, was she had no idea who I was. She wasn't doing this because I was Manning Stevenson, the captain of the Dallas Oilers. She was doing this because she wants me.

Her tongue slides with mine and turns around and around. I can taste the cranberry juice on her lips, and I suddenly want to lay her out and devour her whole body. I let go of her lips when I hear voices coming closer to the door. Both of us look at each other while we try to steady our breathing.

"Where are we going?" she asks.

"I have a room here," I say. "My . . ." I was about to tell her my agent got it for me. "My assistant made the plans." She looks at me now, and her lips are plump from my attack of them. "Not that I do this." I want her to know that I didn't get the room just to take someone to it. "Just in case I had a couple too many drinks."

"Okay." She leans in now and licks my bottom lip with the tip of her tongue and then slides it into my mouth, and we both groan. My cock is fighting me to get out and sink into her.

"We should get out of here," I say when I let go of her lips, but then go to suck on her neck. "I have to say good-bye to the guys," I say, and when I look at her, her eyes are closed with her head against the door. Her chest is rising and falling, and the things I want to do to her are now adding up in my head. "Evelyn," I say, and her eyes open slowly. "Do you need to say good-bye?"

"Yes," she says softly. "I need my purse, and I need to tell the girls."

I let her go but not all the way. My hand grips her hip.

"How about I say good-bye to the guys, and then you meet me?" I want to walk with her, but I can't take the risk. Not for myself, but for her. She doesn't need to be plastered across some fucking newspaper.

"What is your room number?" she asks, and I shrug, making her laugh.

"I have no idea," I say, reaching into my pocket and getting out the key.

"Seven twenty-six," I say, looking at the writing on the key card. I take out one key card and hand it to her. She raises her hand and takes it. "Evelyn," I say, loving the way her name feels on my lips.

"Yes, Manning." When she says my name, I want to kiss her again, but I also want to get the fuck out of this supply closet before someone catches us.

"I'm really glad you came tonight," I say, and she smirks.

"If you play your cards right . . ." She puts her head back and bites the side of my jaw. "You'll make me come in more ways than one."

This fucking woman has me ready to snap, literally. If I didn't give a shit, I would throw her over my shoulder and drag her to the room. "Now let me go out first, and then you come out," she says, making sure she looks okay, and then she stops and looks up at me. "Um," she says, unsure, and my stomach sinks, thinking she's going to change her mind. "I wasn't planning on doing this tonight." She uses her hands in a circle. "So my bra and panties are different colors."

I throw my head back and laugh. "Noted." I lean in

and kiss her lips softly. "Now get out of here so I can see for myself how they don't match." Her hand goes to the handle of the door, and I grab her hips before she opens it. I press my cock to her back. "And just so everything is clear. I plan on spending the night making you come." Her head falls back to my chest, and I swear she wiggles her ass.

"Noted," she says, opening the door and slipping out. "I'll see you soon, Manning," she says right before closing the door. I wait a couple of seconds before opening the door again. Thankfully, I walk out to no one, and when I get to the bar, my eyes find her right away, and I see she's saying good-bye to her friends. I see Andrew, and I thank him for everything he's done.

I walk out of the restaurant and toward the hotel entrance with my head down the whole time. I'm not going to make eye contact with anyone. The valet guy looks like he is on his phone while he waits for people to arrive. "Welcome," the doorman tells me when the glass doors slide open.

"Thank you," I tell him, making my way into the lobby. I look around, trying to find the elevator without having to ask anyone. The front desk attendant raises his head and nods at me when I make my way past him and toward the elevators.

Standing to the side of the two elevators, I am almost hidden from any eyes. I can see the door where she is supposed to enter, and my heart speeds up as I think about her.

What the fuck are you doing? my head asks me, and

for the first time in my whole life, I answer. "Doing something I want to, for me." I look down at my phone and see that it's almost midnight. Putting my hands in my pockets, I look around, and I can still hear the music from next door. Raising my hand, I look at the clock and see two minutes have passed. I start to pace in the little space. *Maybe she changed her mind*, I think as my heart sinks. Maybe she didn't feel what I felt. So many things are running through my head, so many doubts, and all doubts are pushed aside when I hear her laughter. My eyes snap to the door as the doorman makes a joke with her.

"Thank you," she says as she walks in. I can watch her now, and I see the valet man is looking at her, and so is the doorman. *She is fucking beautiful*, I think. Beautiful is not even a strong enough word. Her hips sway as she walks and says hello to the front desk attendant. Her long auburn hair sways, and I make a mental note to wrap it around my hand sometime tonight.

She looks around, and when she spots me, the smile on her face gets even bigger. She walks my way, and I press the up button. "Hi," I say, and I want to bend down and kiss her, but I know they are looking this way.

"Hi," she says, looking at me from the corner of her eyes.

"I thought you changed your mind," I say nervously.

"No." She shakes her head. "I just had to make a pit stop."

My eyebrows pinch together. "I went to get essentials," she tells me and then mouths out, "Condoms." I want to smack my hand on my forehead. I didn't even think about condoms. Obviously, I never carry them with me because, well, I haven't had sex in four years, and if anyone has seen *Friends*, they know those things expire.

"Good call," I say as the elevator pings, and I let her walk in first. She presses the number ten, and then seven. I wait for the doors to close before going to her.

"Why the number ten?" I ask, pushing her against the back wall of the elevator.

"I didn't want them to know that we're together. I'm just praying they aren't on duty when we do the walk of shame," she says, giggling. The elevator stops and opens. I grab her hand, walking out, and I scan the numbers as fast as I can and literally pull her to the end of the hall.

I turn to her, and she just looks at me. "How drunk are you?" I ask, knowing she had quite a few drinks tonight. "I don't want—"

She puts her finger on my lips, stopping me. "Sober enough to walk here without falling," she tells me, putting her palm on my chest, and I can feel her touch through my shirt. "Drunk enough to do this." I look at her hands as they move down my chest to palm my cock. "And drunk enough to ask you to try lots of things."

"Last chance," I say through clenched teeth when her hand moves up and down over my cock.

"Do you want to use my key?" she asks, but if she has to get her key, that means she has to let go of my cock, and I'm not ready for that to happen.

I reach into my pocket, and I literally have to close my eyes while she moves a touch faster. "Evelyn," I whisper.

"Manning," she calls my name. I step away from her small hand and open the door. I drag her in, not turning on any of the lights. The door closes behind her, and I push her against it. Her purse drops to the floor while I bend down and devour her mouth. She wraps one arm around my head and the other around my neck. I pick her up now, and she lets go of my mouth long enough to say, "Wait."

I stop moving, my cock hard as a fucking rock, my heart beating so fast in my chest, and my hands itching to touch her. "I need to . . ." She drops her hands from me to go to her hips, where she ever so slowly lifts her skirt higher and higher until it's around her waist. The only thing I could think is I've died and gone to heaven. She stands there in the smallest lace thong I've ever seen.

"Now, where were we?" she asks, and then she comes to me. "You were lifting me," she tells me. "And I was finally going to get to wrap my legs around you." I push her hair away from her face. "Kiss me, Manning." She puts her head back, and I bend down, taking her mouth. Our tongues are fighting with each other to get deeper into the kiss. My hands go to her waist, and I lift her against the door, her legs wrapping tightly around me. My hands go to her bare ass, and I have to let go of her mouth as we both groan.

"Fuck," I hiss out, my cock looking to break out of my pants. I close my eyes to try to focus, but her mouth is now on my neck. She sucks in, and all fucking bets are off. "I wanted to take my time." I try to tell her, but she just moves her hips up and down on my cock.

"Manning." She moans out my name. "I want you to take a condom out of my purse, and I want you to fuck me against this door," she tells me, her legs going tighter around my waist. My hand goes around her waist as I bend down to pick up her purse, seeing the condoms out of the purse from when it fell. I grab the one and tear the corner with my teeth. The whole time, she rubs up and down on me and moans each time. I undo my belt and buckle. Pushing down just a touch, my cock springs out, and she looks down, and I look back up at her as she licks her lips. "Later," she says as I roll the condom down on my cock, "I'm going to suck that cock for hours."

I can't answer her because my cock is going to explode any second. She slips her hands between her legs and pushes her panties to the side, and now it's my turn to lick my lips. "Later," I say, pushing her into the door with my hips, "I'm going to eat that pussy for hours." I grab her hips and slam her down on my cock. I put my hands under her legs now on my forearms. She wraps a hand around the back of my neck as my mouth finds hers, and I fuck her harder than I've fucked anyone in my life. With each thrust, her pussy squeezes me tighter and tighter. The sounds of our skin slapping together along with our pants fill the room.

"Manning." She says my name right before she comes on my cock, and I'm right after her.

"Evelyn." Her name is a whisper as I bury myself in her and come.

EIGHT

EVELYN

MY EYES FLICKER open once and then close again. Soft light comes into the room, and I look at the clock on the side table right next to the empty condom wrappers, seeing it's just past seven in the morning. I look over on my other side and see Manning.

He's lying on his stomach, not wearing anything under the white sheet resting on his plump ass. He's facing the other way, so the only thing I can focus on is the tattoo covering his left shoulder. A tattoo I traced with my tongue last night.

I look down at the sheet covering my naked body. One of my legs poke out from under the sheet, and when I move it, I wince. I haven't had a workout like this in a long time. Oh, who am I kidding? I haven't had sex like this in my whole fucking life. I slip out of bed, trying not to wake him. Neither one of us wanted to close our eyes because we didn't want to waste any time. I slip out and tiptoe to the bathroom, not turning on the light until the door is closed. When I do, I squint at the brightness of the light and then make the mistake of looking in the mirror.

My hair is a mess from our shower. The makeup I tried to wash off while in the shower still lingers. I stop looking at that and see the love bites all over my body. I have five on one tit. Are those teeth marks? I look down and see his teeth marks on my hip. I smile and then look around to see if I can spot a towel, but all of them are on the floor and wet from when we started in the bath only for me to ride him, and the water went everywhere.

Slipping out of the other bathroom door into the seating area, I see more destruction there. I follow the trail of clothes, bending to pick them up. I place the clothes on the couch and then slip into my skirt and bra since my thong is shredded. I clean up the empty condom wrappers; we used all eight.

After I said good-bye to my friends last night, a sudden thought about protection had me running into the bathroom. I took all the condoms the lady had on her stand, leaving her a fifty-dollar tip. All she could say was good luck. Little did I know how much I would need it. I find my shirt and put it on. I sit down and wince again, closing my eyes but rushing to put on my shoes. Opening my purse, I take out my phone and order an Uber. My eyes fly to the bucket of empty champagne in the middle of the coffee table. Two robes lie on the floor beside it.

"I'm going to order something sweet," he said to me *after he bent me over and had his way with me right after*

the bathtub overflowed. He walked over to the phone naked, and I just took his body in. He was per-fucking-fection. Nothing could compare to his body. His ass and thighs were thick, and his abs were on fucking point, but the best was his long and thick cock. I licked my lips, and he looked over at me and smirked. "Like what you see?" he asked me.

"More than you know," I answered him, and he ordered strawberries, chocolate, and champagne.

"Twenty minutes," he said, hanging up the phone. "Is there a robe in there?"

I grabbed the two hanging in the bathroom and walked to him. "It's a shame to cover up," I told him, and he bent his head down to take my lips again. His kisses woke my body up, and I got on my tippy toes.

He grabbed a robe from me. "If we keep this up, I'll be balls deep in you when they get here." His arms slipped into the robe.

"I see nothing wrong with that." I winked at him as I slipped my arms into the robe. Going to the couch and sitting down, I said, "We have twenty minutes. Want to play a game?" He sat down next to me. "Would you rather stay in or go out?"

"I'm a homebody," he said without thinking twice. "You?"

"Me, too. I mean, I like to go out, but to me, preparing dinner together is just as romantic as going out." I leaned in. "Besides, you can always get naked in the middle of it." I winked, and my brain called me a hussy. I leaned forward and waited for his kiss. His tongue

slipped into my mouth, and I got lost again in him. I sat back down and waited for him to ask me a question.

"Would you rather get up early or stay up late?" He grabbed my legs and pulled them on his lap.

"I'm okay with either," I answered, and my body shivered as he rubbed my legs. I couldn't stand it, so I got up and straddled him, kissing him again.

"I usually have to unwind after work," he said, "depending on what time I get in. Would you rather spend the day inside or outside?"

"That depends." I leaned my head on my fist on the couch. "If I'm on a beach, I'd rather spend the whole day on the beach. If I'm up north and there is snow falling, definitely inside by a fire."

He looked at me and smiled. "That is my exact answer."

I just looked at him. Even knowing this was a one-night stand, I wanted to know so much about him, yet I knew I didn't have a right to it. His mouth now found mine as we kissed. "What is your biggest fear?" I asked him with my own heart pounding in my chest.

"That one is easy," he said, pushing my hair away from my face. "Ending up with someone who isn't the one." His voice trailed off, and I didn't have time to answer him because the knock on the door interrupted us. I watched him walk over to the hallway, and I sat there in shock. This man who I just met had the exact same fear as me.

The phone buzzes in my hand, and the memory of last night is gone. I get up and look over at the dark room, seeing him in the middle of the bed in the same position. "Bye, Manning," I whisper and walk to the door. Stopping before I walk out, I open my purse to take out an elastic and tie my hair in a high ponytail.

I mean, there is nothing I can do that doesn't say this is my walk of shame and I spent the whole night with cock. I open the door, and my heart sinks for leaving, but it's a lot better than the awkwardness of the morning after. I mean, I'm assuming—I've never done this before, so I don't know what the rules are. I walk down the hallway and press the down arrow button when my phone beeps that my Uber is there.

The elevator door pings, and I get in, pressing the L button. The whole time, I feel a sense of dread, but I try not to think about it as I walk with my head down. The doorman opens the door for me. "Have a great day," he says, and I smile at him, looking for the Honda that is supposed to be waiting for me. I spot him and raise my hand, and he drives over so I don't walk too far. I get in and slam the door behind me.

"Good morning," I say and put my head back on the seat. He mumbles good morning and then makes his way to my house.

I close my eyes, and all of a sudden, I'm back in the hotel room as memories of last night come crashing to me.

The minute I pushed his jacket from his shoulders, I couldn't wait to get his shirt off him. But he had other plans. "All night, I've thought about these bow ties," he said, taking the one around my waist and pulling it loose, opening the shirt down the middle.

"Even better than I thought," he said, taking his index finger and opening my shirt all the way. My black demi push-up bra barely covered my pebbled nipples. "Fuck," he hissed, and his eyes were mesmerized by it. He traced the swell of my breast with his finger until he slipped it into the bra to touch my nipple.

"Evelyn." He said my name and then bent to take one in his mouth. Biting it, he then sucked, repeating the same thing to the other one. I looked down at myself when he finally let me go, and all I could see was my shirt hanging open and my bra cups under my tits, pushing them higher. I watched as he looked down at me.

"You have too many clothes on," I told him, and my hands went to his shirt. I tried to undo the button, but it got stuck, so I just ripped a couple off. I thought I was ready for what was under his shirt, but I was not. His abs were on point, and I could see the ink sticking out just a bit. I moved the shirt and traced it with my finger. "I'm going to lick every single inch of you," I said out loud, and he groaned when I pushed the shirt off him. "I just don't know if I should start with your chest or your cock."

He wrapped an arm around my waist, and I expected him to carry me into the hotel room, but he didn't. He just put me down on the table in the hallway. Before I even had time to think about the coldness on my ass, he was on his knees, and his mouth was on me. My hand went to pull his hair as I lifted my ass up and down on the table. All I could do was watch while his tongue fucked me. He looked up at me as he bit my clit and then sucked it into his mouth. I watched him fuck me with his tongue while I pulled his hair as I begged him to make me come. I'd never in my life felt this way.

"Excuse me, miss." I hear the driver say, and I open my eyes. "We have arrived."

I look out the window and see we are in the driveway of my house. "Thank you," I say, getting out and making sure that I cover myself since my thong is in my purse. Not like I can use it again, but still.

Unlocking the door, I step in and put my purse on the table at the front door. Closing my eyes, I can picture myself on the same table again, just in a different room. Moaning his name, begging him to fuck me.

I bend down to take off my shoes, and when my legs scream, another memory comes to me.

After coming on his tongue, he stood, and I pulled him back to my lips. I tasted myself on him, and it was the sexiest fucking thing I've ever tasted in my life. "I thought the scotch tasted good," I told him when I let go of his lips, and he looked at me, his blue eyes almost a dark, deep blue. I got off the table, and my panties fell onto the floor at that point. "But I have to say, me on your tongue tastes even better."

"Evelyn." Every single time he said my name, I wanted to make him say it over and over again.

"That's one for me," I told him, and my hands went to the button on his pants. I undid the button. "Time for you to catch up," I said, and I had never wanted to suck a cock more in my life. I was on my knees before he could

stop me or move. His zipper came down, and I came face-to-face with the most beautiful cock I'd ever seen in my life. Long, thick, hard, and fucking perfect.

I open my eyes, and my whole body is awake now. It's begging me to go back to the room for relief. It almost cries out when instead of going to the door, I walk into the house. I walk over to start the coffee machine, then go back into my bedroom to take off last night's clothes.

My head is full of images of last night. His smile, his laugh, the way he said my name when he was balls deep in me and came over and over again. When I had his cock in my mouth, and his eyes were looking into mine. I can still feel his kisses on my lips, and I raise my hand to feel them.

It took me thirty-two years to find the man whose kisses I would never forget. It took me thirty-two years to have the best sex of my life. It also took me thirty-two years to have the best one-night stand I'll ever have. Also, it's the only one-night stand I'll have. It also took thirty-two years for me to meet someone who can make my toes curl.

I slip on a pair of panties and then a long shirt, walking out to make my coffee. "Today," I tell myself as I make my coffee. "You have today to think about last night and this morning, and then you forget about it." I scoff. "Fat chance of that happening." With my coffee cup to my lips, I know he's going to be in my dreams, and he's going to be the star of many nights I spend with my trusty friend.

NINE

MANNING

I OPEN MY eyes when the phone rings and look at the brown wall. I close my eyes again. "Evelyn," I say and reach out for her as the phone stops ringing.

I find the bed empty, and I push up on my elbows, looking at the spot where I left her. The last time I saw her was when I picked her hips up and slammed into her at around five a.m. After not having her for forty-five minutes—forty-five fucking minutes—I craved her again.

The phone rings again, making me sit up and walk to the living room area. Looking around, I see my clothes on the couch. The bathroom door is closed. I walk to the couch and take my phone out, seeing that it's Murielle.

I look at the door and then back at the phone, wondering if I should answer it. How the fuck do you explain to the woman who you spent the night with cherishing that you have a wife? The thought makes my stomach sick.

The phone stops ringing. "Evelyn," I say and look down when the phone pings in my hand.

Murielle: Your son would like to talk to you.

I exhale and walk to the bathroom door knocking once. "Evelyn." I say her name again and then hear nothing. The silence is fucking eerie. I look around to spot anything that is hers, and my heart picks up speed when I don't see anything.

I ripped her panties over by the door when I devoured her. Fuck, she tasted like heaven. And she didn't shy away, she pulled my hair, and my cock stirs when I think of how she got on her knees.

"Time for you to catch up," she said right before her mouth took my cock into her mouth to the back of her throat. I couldn't move; it was fucking glorious. All I could do was watch her try to take me into her mouth. I watched her move her mouth up and down my cock. "Your cock," she said. "Best looking cock." I didn't know what to say. "Tonight," she said as she twirled her tongue around the head of my cock, "I'm going to ride this like a fucking rodeo queen." It's the last thing she said to me before I told her I was coming. I was expecting her to jump off me but not my woman. She took me, all of me.

My eyes move to the table that holds two empty cans of whipped cream next to a plate of strawberries. It was around three a.m. when I got up and ordered the strawberries and cream. Right after she rode me like the fucking rodeo queen she was. It was also our round three at that time. I look around, and I don't even see any condom wrappers. I open the door, but I don't know why I'm shocked it's empty.

I look at the wet towels on the floor that we used to mop up the bubble bath that overflowed. I spot a lone condom wrapper on the counter and pick it up as my phone rings again in my hand.

"What?" I bark.

"Is that any way to speak to your wife?" Murielle's voice comes through, and my cock suddenly goes down. "You didn't come home last night."

"I thought you said Jaxon wanted to talk to me." I don't even bother answering her question. She's spent half of last month sneaking in at six a.m., not that I cared. Fuck, I was hoping she wouldn't come home at all.

"Someone is cranky this morning," she says.

"I'm hanging up so unless Jaxon wants me," I say, and she huffs out. It's time to buy him a cell phone.

"Hey, Dad," Jaxon says, coming onto the phone. "What did you want?" he says, and I shake my head. "Mom said you wanted to talk to me."

"Did she?" I say, my stomach sinking. I fucking hate when she uses him as a fucking pawn, and I've told her that more than once.

"I did." I lie to him. It's one thing for me to hate her, but I'm not going to turn him against his mother. She can do that all on her own. "I was just confirming we are still having a boys' day."

"Yeah," he says. "What time are you going to be home?"

I look at myself in the mirror. "Soon," I say. "Love

you." I wait for him to answer and then hang up. I look at my chest and smile. Her teeth marks next to my nipple look like they're going to bruise, and I think about when she gave it to me.

"Evelyn." I said her name as she stood at the sink, trying to wash the makeup from her face. I knew she was beautiful, but without the makeup, she was exquisite. Walking over to her, I placed my hands on her hips, and her eyes met mine in the mirror. Without her heels, she reached the middle of my chest. The way she looked at me, I knew she wanted me just as much as I wanted her.

"Manning." When she said my name, I knew at that moment I would never forget the way she said my name. She turned in my arms, and I bent to kiss her lips. Her lips opened for me, and her hands landed on my chest as we kissed each other. She let go of my lips.

"How?" she asked me. "How do I want you already?" I looked at her, my thumb coming out to touch her soft cheek, and I could see little freckles.

"I have no idea," I said to her as I picked her up and put her on the counter. I grabbed a condom and rolled it down my cock. "But if you find out the answer," I said, "you have to tell me." I rubbed my cock up and down her slit. "I fucked you seven minutes ago, and I want you again," I said to her as I sank inside her. Both of us moaned as she put her hands behind her to hold herself up. I fucked her slow, and she hated every single second of it. She begged and pleaded with me to fuck her faster. She begged me to fuck her deeper, and when I just smirked at her, she leaned forward and bit my chest.

"Manning," she said, frustrated at this point because I was just playing with her clit with my cock. "I need you," she said, and she knew that the minute she said that, I would snap. Picking up her leg, I put it on my shoulder, and she knew it was coming. I started pounding into her.

I shake my head of the memories and walk into the bedroom, looking at the bed. The covers are on the floor, the pillows scattered everywhere, and the only things left on the bed are two pillows and the sheet. I look over at the side table, spotting the rest of the condoms all piled together. I pick them up and throw them in the garbage.

I walk back to the couch and grab my boxers. "How did I not hear her leave?" I almost kick myself. I mean, we stayed up all night fucking each other. When we weren't fucking, we were laughing and then telling each other what we wanted to do next. I slip my pants on and then slide my shirt on. I find three buttons missing when I start buttoning it. Thinking about it makes me smile. Fuck, everything about her makes me smile.

The way she wasn't shy to ask for anything. The way she smiled right before she took what she wanted. The way she moaned out my name. The way she looked at me over her shoulder. The way she touched me softly, the way she cherished me as much as I cherished her. I shrug the jacket back on, and my stomach sinks.

I just had the best night of my whole fucking life. I just had the best sex I will ever have. She literally fucked my brains out, and I love every single second of it. She made me fucking feel free, and all I have is her name. I don't even have a last name. I don't even know where she lives or what she does. I take one look around the room again, and my heart sinks when the door shuts behind me, the click of the lock making it so final.

I hand the valet my coupon, and he nods at me when he brings me my SUV. "Good luck, Captain," he tells me, and I don't know if he's talking about the game or finding the girl. I mean, how many Evelyns could there be? I put my sunglasses on as I make my way home.

I park in the garage and walk into the house, hoping that I don't get spotted before I change. Where I was free last night, stepping foot into this house is like walking back into a jail cell.

"Well, well, well." I hear Murielle and look over as she leans against the doorjamb of the kitchen. She is wearing a robe that is hanging open, and you can tell she isn't wearing a bra. "Look what the cat dragged in," she says, lifting her cup of coffee and bringing it to her lips to take a sip.

I don't even bother answering her. I just turn and start to walk to the stairs. "Well, if that isn't the walk of shame, I don't know what is." She snickers, and I stop and look over at her.

"Trust me, Murielle. Nothing I did last night was shameful. Can you say the same?" I don't even bother waiting for her to answer. Instead, I walk up to my bedroom and undress. I step into the shower and wash away the smell of her. I don't want to, but I know what it will mean for me if Murielle even catches a whiff. It will just be another noose around my neck.

I close my eyes as the water runs down my shoulders and over my back, and it's a mistake because the minute I close my eyes, I think of her. She smiles at me and looks up at me, asking me to kiss her. As soon as I think about her, my cock is rock hard, and I take it into my hand. I swear he moans when it's my hand and not hers. I jerk myself off to the memory of her sucking my cock. Her name is on my lips as soon as I come.

I walk out of the shower and wrap a towel around me before anyone sees the marks. "Evelyn." I call her name softly, and for just one minute, I hope she knows I'm thinking about her. I hope she knows that what we did last night is going to stay with me forever. I hope she knows that for only one night, she gave me the world.

TEN

EVELYN

I HEAR THE alarm, but I don't want to get up. I don't want to leave the dream I'm having. I don't want to open my eyes and see the bed empty beside me.

My hand slips out of the bed, and I know this is the last moment I will have with the memories of last Saturday. It's during the quiet moments when I still see his face above me, on top of me, all around me. My hand hits the button, turning off the alarm. Rolling over in my bed, I open my eyes, and just like that, he's gone.

This week has been brutal. I've gone over that night again and again. I wouldn't change anything that happened with the exception of one thing. I would have woken him up before leaving and told him good-bye.

I flip the covers off and slip on my slippers, walking to the kitchen to start my coffee. Once it's finished, I walk back to my bedroom to get ready for work.

After finishing my shower, I look in the mirror and

see that the little marks from last week have faded. He will only be a figment of my imagination now. My black pants hug my hips with a relaxed fit in my legs. I go through two shirts before I decide on the black silk long-sleeved that wraps around with beige stripes. I grab my black Louboutins and my black Gucci purse before picking up my phone and walking out of the house.

I stop at Starbucks before making my way over to the office. Parking in my spot right in front, I walk in, smiling at Tonya, the receptionist. "Good morning," I say, and she smiles back. "Happy Friday."

"I take it they didn't give you the casual Friday memo." She looks me up and down, and I just stare at her.

"Are you saying I didn't have to wear the most uncomfortable pair of shoes I own?" I joke.

"I mean, you look fabulous as always," she says, and the phone rings, so I walk away while she answers it.

Making my way to my office next to my brother's, I say hello to everyone there. I stop at my brother's door, and I see him at his desk already. His button-down shirt is rolled up at the sleeves, and I know he's wearing jeans. "Morning, asshole," I say, and he looks up and sees me.

"Oh," he says when he sees me dressed up. "Casual Friday."

"Fuck you," I say, walking to my office and turning on the light. Putting my purse on the filing cabinet that I have against the wall next to my desk, I pull out my chair and boot up my computer.

My father started this financial planning firm when he

graduated from college. My brother followed in his foot-steps, and when he joined the practice, they brought on consulting and investment management. The staff went from three to twenty-seven and is now at over fifty.

My father always wanted me to join the firm and never let me know he was upset when I didn't come back from Chicago. He would drop hints every single time I came home to visit, or he came to visit me. He even tried to convince Dex to join him.

Now that I'm here, he has decided to retire. Or semi-retire, he's calling it. In other words, he's handing me his clients for now, and then he wants to travel the world starting next year.

"I could have sworn I mentioned it to you," my brother says, walking into the office, and I was right about the jeans. He is two years older than me, and we have always been very, very close. He made sure everything was ready for me when I finally moved here. He and Veronica are my ride or die people.

"Lies, Timothy." I use his full name, and he laughs. "All lies."

"How about I make it up to you by cooking for you tomorrow?" He sits on one of the chairs in front of my desk. "Caleb has a hockey game at eleven, so how about you spend the day with us?" He mentions my eight-year-old nephew.

"I might be able to forgive you if you grill me a steak and baked potato," I tell him, knowing it's the only food he actually knows how to cook and do it well.

"I can invite Mom and Dad," he says, taking out his

phone and typing something. Then he looks at his calendar. "Shit, I have hockey tickets tomorrow."

"Fun," I say sarcastically. "That's fine. How about we do lunch, and maybe I can take my nephew to see a movie and have a sleepover?"

"Ooh." He looks up. "That would give Veronica and me some alone time."

"Ew," I say. "Ew, ew, ew." He laughs, getting up.

"Lunch works but let's do a family lunch on Sunday. It can be your welcome home meal." He walks to the door.

"We've had that five times already." I remind him of all the dinners we've had since I got here. "Besides, I have a bridesmaid fitting on Sunday, so . . ."

"Oh, that's right. How was the bachelorette party?" he asks. Manning's face flashes in my head, but it's not just any face that I see. Nope, it's the one with him pounding into me as his hair falls onto his forehead.

"It was uneventful," I finally say, swallowing the memory. My phone rings, saving me from talking more about the weekend.

My father peeks his head in about thirty minutes later, and now I don't feel as bad since he's dressed in slacks and a button-down with a sweater over it. "Hey there, sunshine," he says, and I smile. "We have five meetings today."

"I just saw my schedule," I tell him, getting up to hug him. "You are not messing around with passing on the baton," I tell him, and he hugs me tight. I turn back to my desk, grabbing a legal pad and a pen. "Let's get a head start," I tell him, and we walk to the conference room with his arm around me.

The five meetings go smoothly; all his clients were comfortable with the switch. I mean, semi-comfortable. At least they want to see what I have to offer. I reassure them that I have their best interests at heart and promise to send them my plan of action, so that gets them on board.

When the last client leaves at four, I'm ready to burn these shoes.

"That went better than I expected," my father says, walking back into the conference room with me. "He was a hard nut to crack, to begin with." He mentions his oldest client. "But you have him eating out of the palm of your hand."

"No." I shake my head. "The fact he is going to make more money is what got him eating out of my hand."

My father throws his head back and laughs. "Money. It makes the world go round."

I look at him. "True story. I knew coming here would be almost like starting over, and I'd have to prove myself to all of your clients." I smile at my father. "And to be honest, I was excited about the challenge. This is going to push my portfolio out of the water with all these different clients. Who knows, I might be the most sought-after person at this firm." I clap my hands. "Tim would die." We both laugh now.

"How are you settling in?" he asks.

"Good," I say, and he just stares at me. "Okay, fine." I throw up my hands. "It's an adjustment, but I have to admit I'm happy to be home. This is where I want to be. I want to meet someone and for them to be close to my family. I want to be able to go shopping with Mom." He smiles. "I'm just happy to be home." I smile. I don't add that I might have found someone who he would love because I don't even know this man's last name.

"Any news from Dex?" Just the name makes my skin crawl. It also shocks me that I haven't thought about him this whole week. Not once did he enter my mind. Not once did I wonder if I did the right thing. Not once did I miss him.

I shake my head. "It's a done deal. The contracts are signed and money transferred, so I have nothing else to say to him." I didn't tell my parents what happened. The only one who knows is Veronica. I couldn't even tell Tim, knowing he would have beaten his ass to the ground.

"These things happen," he says, frowning. "People grow apart."

"Yeah," I say. When I called them, I just said that we had grown apart and wanted different things. Our path was at an impasse, and I had to go one way, and he had to go the other. Tim sort of knew it was bullshit, but he didn't press me. My mother also wasn't sold on the explanation, and she let me have my moment. My father was the only one who fully bought it. "Well, you never know. Absence can make the heart grow fonder."

I don't bother letting him know that no amount of absence will make my heart grow fonder when it comes to Dex. "I'll be fine," I tell him, getting up. "Now if you'll excuse me, I have some work to do."

"It's almost five o'clock," he says. "If your mother finds out you are working this late on a Friday . . ."

"Well, I'm not going to tell her." I wink at him. "I'm not going to stay late," I reassure him. "I'll bring some of it home to do." I lean down and kiss his cheek. "I might swing by on Sunday afternoon."

I walk out and go to my office, seeing that most of the people have gone home. I see Tim's light off in his office before walking into mine. I don't know how long I sit at my desk before my cell phone rings.

"Hello?" I answer when I see it's Tim calling.

"Hey, where are you?" he asks, and he sounds out of breath.

"I'm at the office. Why?" I put the pen down.

"I need a huge favor," he says. "I'm stuck about two hours away. Veronica is with a patient, and Caleb is at hockey practice."

"Okay," I say.

"Can you go get him? He gets off the ice in twenty minutes," he says, and I stand, going over to my purse. "He usually comes out in thirty-five minutes."

"Where is the arena?" I ask.

"It's about twenty minutes from the office, depending on traffic," he says. I'm already walking out of the office and getting into my car.

"I'm in the car now," I tell him. "Send me the address, and I'll go right over."

"Thank you." He huffs out, "I owe you."

"This list is growing more and more," I say, and he

laughs as he disconnects. I wait for him to send me the address, and then I make my way over there.

When I pull up to the big gray building, I grab my purse and walk in. I see a staircase right in front of me, and when I walk past the staircase, I see a white brick wall with another staircase. When I get to the second staircase, I look down the right hallway and the left hallway, but they both look the same. A television screen hangs there, and I see four areas.

I call Tim, and when he answers, I ask, "What rink is he on?"

"His team is called the Hawks, so check the screen," he says. I look up and see that he's on the second rink. "You can watch upstairs if you want or stay in the lobby, and he will come out."

"Okay," I say and hang up. I'm about to go upstairs when I hear the sound of kids coming from one of the hallways. I look down and see kids coming out in different shirts.

"Auntie Evelyn." I hear him calling me and look down to the right, seeing him come off the ice with his teammates. He talks to the boy beside him and then walks over to me. "Auntie Evelyn," he says, running over to me on his skates.

"Hi there," I say. Opening my arms, I hug him and then feel the wetness. "Gross," I say to him, and he laughs. He takes off his helmet, and I see his wet hair matted to his head. "You stink. Like cheese and feet." Both boys laugh when I tell him this and scrunch up my nose.

He looks over at the kid that is with him. "Jaxon, this

is my aunt Evie."

"Hello, Jaxon." I smile over at him, and he waves at me.

"I'm going to get changed. Can I have a slush?" Caleb asks, and I nod my head. "Go get changed, you two, and if it's okay with your mom," I say to Jaxon, "we can go get a slush."

"My dad is picking me up," he tells me, "and he plays hockey."

"Oh, fun," I say to him. "Go get changed, and we can ask him when you come out." They both turn around and run back to their changing room.

I send Tim a text.

Me: The package is safe and sound.

I put my phone in my purse, never expecting what is to come.

ELEVEN

MANNING

"I CAN'T WAIT to get home." I hear Ralph beside me say, and I look over at him. "Road trips are the worst."

"I don't mind them," I tell him, getting off the bus and walking toward the plane waiting for us. The soft drizzle of rain coming out. Ralph, Miller, and I walk together. "I mean, I miss Jaxon, but I get away from Murielle, so it's a vacation." I walk up the stairs first, and the two of them follow me. After I store my bag, I sit down in the seat, and Ralph sits next to me. I grab my phone out of my jeans pocket and send Murielle a text.

Manning: I am going to take Jaxon out for dinner after his practice.

Murielle: Sounds good. I'm in the middle of planning stuff with the Oilers foundation. Wish I could join you.

I ignore her whenever she says shit like this and look out the window. "Longest week of my life," Miller says from behind me. "I can't wait to see my woman," he says, and for the first time, I'm actually jealous of what he has. I'm fucking jealous of going home to the woman you want to go home to instead of the one who makes my stomach turn to stone. The one who just won't let me be. The one who stays married to me for the fucking perks of being the captain's wife. The one always invited out. The one who is always the center of attention. The one everyone wants to be. Not for me, but just to be the captain's wife. Instead, she sticks around, ruining both of our lives, and there is nothing I can say to her, no amount of pleading will get her to leave.

The last time I brought it up, she took off with Jaxon for two weeks, returning only after I promised not to bring up divorce again. He was six, and it's been two years. I thought I could tough it out. I thought it would be okay, but now, now something inside me has woken up. The need to be happy. The need to be wanted for me. The need to just fucking live my life.

This week, my mind has been all over the fucking place. My dreams are of Evelyn each night. The memory of those hours plays over and over again. The sound of her laughter, the sound of her voice, the sound of her breath hitching right before she lets go.

"We play tomorrow night," Ralph says, and I nod.

Miller pipes in from behind me. "Any big plans this weekend, big guy?" he says, and I just glare at him.

When I walked onto the plane on Sunday morning, Miller was the only one here. One look at me and he pointed at me. "You had sex," he said right away, and I looked at him, shocked.

"How the fuck do you know that?" I avoided his eyes as I stored my bag. My heart hammered in my chest, and my mouth was suddenly dry. I wondered if Murielle would have been able to tell. I wondered if she knew. The fear of her ruining the one thing I have in my life that she can't touch.

"You didn't walk in with a chip on your shoulder." He smirked at me, and I tried to ignore him. But he was Miller, and there was only so much ignoring you could do. "Plus, you have a bounce to your step, which makes sense since your balls have been drained." I looked at him, not even sure how to answer him. "Was it the chick from the restaurant?" I glared at him, and he threw his head back, letting out the biggest laugh I'd ever heard from him.

"Where the fuck is everyone?" Ralph said when he walked in and looked around, only spotting the two of us. "What are you two talking about?" He looked at us, storing his bag.

"Captain here got his rocks off." I swore through my teeth and sat down, thankful people had started arriving so he couldn't say anything else.

"No plans so far. I know that Jaxon has a game to-morrow morning, and I'm hoping I can go to that," I say, looking out my window as the plane takes off. I usually make his weekend games when they are early enough. "I'm picking him up at practice tonight when we get in." I look at my watch. "Then I'm going to take him out to eat."

"You going to go out after the game?" Ralph asks, and I just look at him. "You never know, she can be going back to see if you show up." I shake my head.

"It's better this way," I tell him, feeling the pit that I have in my stomach. The plane lands twenty minutes later than scheduled, and I run to my SUV, tossing the bag in the back seat to make my way over to the arena. The parking lot's full when I get there, and I see that I'm late.

I walk into the arena and look around the lobby. Glancing at my watch, I see I'm ten minutes late. *Fucking traffic*. I spot a couple of parents from their team. "Hey, guys," I say, walking past them and going up the back stairs to where the restaurant is.

I look around, my eyes scanning the room, and then I see her. My heart starts to speed up in my chest, and it feels like it's going to pound out of my chest. What is she doing here? Right now, I couldn't care less because she's here. She's breathtaking and beautiful and so much more than what I remembered. Her hair is still loose, and I wonder if it's as silky as I remember. I wonder if she's thought about me. I wonder if she regrets walking out on me. I have so many questions, but the only thing I know is that now that she's in front of me, I'm not going to waste time.

I watch her as she hands my son a slush and smiles at him. I walk to her, and she must feel eyes on her because she looks up, and for the first time in my life, my heart stops. Literally, the world could crumble around us, and I'd be okay with her there with me. Her eyes go big when she sees me, and I smile as I make my way to her. I see her mouth my name, and I can hear it in my head.

"Daddy," Jaxon says when he spots me, and her mouth opens now in shock, her eyes flying to me and then back to Jaxon. "That's my dad," he tells her, and she has no words. She just nods at him.

"He plays hockey." I hear Caleb say, and I stop in front of them. The smell of her brings back every memory from that night. And I mean every memory plays in my head on fast-forward.

"Hey, buddy," I say, bending down and kissing Jaxon's head. "I missed you." I look back up at Evelyn, who just blinks. "Hi," I say softly. "I'm Manning, Jaxon's dad," I say to her, holding out my hand.

"I-I'm," she says, stuttering now and not sure how to act. "I'm Evelyn. Caleb's aunt," she tells me, sticking out her hand, and when I shake her hand, the heat feeds my soul. The touch makes my body come alive, and I want nothing more than to bend and kiss her hello. I want to wrap my arms around her, bring her to my chest, and just hold her there.

"It's great to meet you," I say, our hands still in each other's hand. I'm not ready to let her go just yet. Maybe I'm afraid that this is a dream, and when I let her go, I'll open my eyes, and it will be over.

"Can we go play in the arcade?" Jaxon asks, and I'm about to say yes to get them to leave us. I'll give them all the tokens in the world to just leave us alone. But instead of savoring in the moment of seeing her again, my eyes see the one person I don't want to see.

"Evelyn," I say her name, dropping her hand. I want

to say so many things before it happens. My heart pounds in my chest, my palms getting sticky, and my neck starts to tingle.

It happens like a freight train crash. The one you slow down to look at, and I suddenly feel like I'm floating out of my body. "Hey there, you two." I hear her voice, and I don't have time to do anything when I see her in front of me, and she kisses me on the lips.

"Welcome home, baby. Missed you," she almost purrs out, and I think I'm going to be sick. The burning in my stomach moves up to my throat. "Sorry I'm late. Did you just get here?" she asks with a smile, bending to kiss Jaxon's head. "Someone needs a shower," she says and finally looks at Evelyn, who stands there with her mouth hanging open. I see her eyes going from me to Murielle and then back to me again.

I want to tell her it's not what it seems, and it's just a farce. I want to tell her I've spent the past week thinking about only her. I want to tell her that I want another night. I want anything she will give me. But the universe has other plans for me right now. I feel Murielle slip her arm into mine, something she usually does when I'm talking to a female she doesn't know. "Hey," she says to Evelyn. "I'm Murielle." She smiles at Evelyn, holding out her hand. "Jaxon's mom."

TWELVE

Evelyn

"I'M MURIELLE." SHE puts out her hand. "Jaxon's mom." I stand here shocked, to say the least. My heart beats so hard in my chest that I think everyone will be able to hear it. Heat rises all the way to my neck, and I feel like I'm going to faint. I feel like I'm having an out-of-body experience. I feel like the earth is crumbling under my feet. This can't be happening to me. This can't be true. It can't be. But then I look up and see him, his eyes, and I know. Everything we did was a lie. Everything I felt was a lie, and everything he said was a lie.

In a matter of three minutes, everything came crashing down. Everything I built up was destroyed. I felt eyes on me as soon as I handed Jaxon his slush. Looking up, I thought it was a figment of my imagination. I thought that it was my mind playing tricks on me. It couldn't be.

But as he walked closer to me, it finally sank in that this was real. He was real, and he was in front of me. He was wearing black jeans and a white shirt with a black jacket. He was even hotter than he was in the club. But not hotter than he was naked.

I'm sure the expression on his face mimicked mine. He was in just as much shock to see me, and when he stuck his hand out and I touched him, my body suddenly woke up, remembering his touch as it waited for more. I wanted to look up at him and for him to look down and kiss me. I wanted him to put one hand around my waist and bring me close to him. I wanted to tell him I was sorry about taking off on him without saying good-bye. I wanted to tell him I've been thinking about the blue-eyed stranger all week. I wanted to tell him all that, and then everything changed. Just as fast as the overwhelming feeling I had of seeing him, came the devastating blow that he wasn't all that I built up in my head.

I stood there speechless as she kissed his lips, the same lips I felt every night in my dreams. I stood there as she wrapped her arm around his, and I couldn't help notice the way she clung to him with her big diamond rock on her finger. My head was spinning as I took all of it in.

He had a wife. He has a wife.

I slept with a married man. I slept with someone's husband.

The thoughts made me want to throw up, but I pushed it down. I would not give him the satisfaction of making a fool out of me twice.

"Hi." I forced myself to smile. "I'm Evelyn, Caleb's aunt." I shake her bony hand, taking a minute to look at her. She is taller than me, her breasts are definitely fake, her lips injected, and not one frown line around her eyes or her forehead. She is lean, and you can tell she works out and not just like I pretended to but for real. Her black eyes are perfectly styled; she is perfectly put together.

"Oh, you're Tim's sister," Murielle says, letting go of my hand. I pull my nephew to me, and I want to get the fuck out of here.

"I am," I say to her, then look down to blink away the tears threatening to escape.

"Veronica was talking about how excited they all were that you were finally moving back home." The whole time she talks, she doesn't let go of Manning.

"Yes, I'm very happy to be back home." I look down at my nephew who thankfully doesn't seem to notice anything is wrong with me.

"Are you ready to go, buddy? Your mom and dad are waiting for us." He nods his head at me. "I hope it's okay I bought Jaxon a slush." I look at them or better yet at her, avoiding the blue eyes that I want to forget.

"More than okay," Manning says, and I make the mistake of looking at him. My chest feels like it's shattering right down the middle, but then the anger slowly builds up in me. "Thank you so much for staying with him."

I just nod at him, not sure I can say anything, I swallow down the lump in my throat. "Say good-bye."

"Bye, Jaxon," Caleb says and then looks at me. "Can Jaxon come to the movies with us tomorrow?" I stand here, not sure what to do or say. It's one thing to know he's married and to know that I know who he is and to see him. It's a whole other ball game to try to be friends with this asshole.

"Oh, Mom, can I?" Jaxon asks, and I look down at the boy who I now see looks just like his father. Why didn't I see it before?

"We have the hockey game tomorrow night," she tells him, and his shoulders go down.

"That's okay." I look at Jaxon. "How about we do it another time?" He smiles at me, and if I didn't hurt before, I hurt now. What if he found out I slept with his father? What if she found out? My nephew could be dragged into this. My brother, oh shit. "It was nice meeting you." I look at Murielle and grab Caleb's hand, walking toward the stairs we came up. He grabs his hockey bag, and I hold his slush.

"Do you want me to carry the bag for you?" I ask. He just shakes his head, and I lean down to kiss his head as we walk down the stairs.

A tear escapes, and I wipe it away as fast as I can. With my head down, I walk out of the arena, making sure to get him in the car as fast as I can. I pull out of the parking lot with my chest hammering and my hands sweaty. Should I tell Tim and Veronica? Should I tell them how I slept with a married man?

And not just any old married man. No, that would be too easy. No, I slept with one of Caleb's friend's father. Oh my god. I put my hand on my forehead as I make my way over to Tim and Veronica's.

I swallow down all my hurt I feel when I pull into their driveway. I get out of the car, opening the back door for Caleb, who jumps out. I grab his bag for him and walk to the front door that is now open with Veronica coming out.

"Thank you so much," she says after she kisses Caleb hello, and he runs into the house.

"Of course," I say, and she reaches for the hockey bag. "It was fun."

"Do you want to come in? We just ordered Chinese," she tells me, and I shake my head.

"I've had a long week," I say, not lying. "I'm going to go soak in my tub."

"That sounds divine," she says, and I nod at her and walk back to my car. "I'll see you tomorrow for lunch," I say, and she nods at me.

"Do you want to come to the hockey game with us?" she asks, and the burning in my stomach comes back.

"Maybe some other time. I have a couple of boxes left to unpack." I lie to her this time. Everything that I had was unpacked this week. I did it to keep my mind from thinking about Manning. She holds up her hand and waves at me as I drive away.

Only when I'm away from the house do the tears come. Instead of the memories from Saturday coming at me, it's the face of his son. It's the look of his wife smiling and being duped to who her husband really is.

"I've never had a one-night stand." I hear his voice in my head. *"I've never done this. Never wanted to,"* *he whispered to me while he slid into me over and over again. "Until you."* I close my eyes, and my stomach roils.

"Liar!" I shout in the car as I make my way home.

Walking in, I don't even bother turning on the lights. Instead, I walk to the fridge and open it, grabbing the white wine I keep in there. I take the cork out and just drink it straight from the bottle. I close my eyes as the cold liquid makes it down to my stomach.

"Holy shit," I say, taking another gulp. "Holy fucking shit." I take another swig, this time kicking off my shoes. Putting my hands on the counter, I drop my head. "Married." I shake my head, trying to erase him from my mind. I head back to my bedroom, walking straight to the bathroom and starting a bath.

Putting the wine bottle on the white marble counter, I light the candles around the bath. I undress and grab the bottle, then slip into the tub. Holding my legs to my chest, I finally let the tears come. I slept with a married man. The thought replays in my head as I drink the wine.

My whole life, I would hear stories about my friends' families going through divorce, and there was always the main theme. One cheated on the other. I couldn't wrap my head around it. Fuck, I was cheated on, so I know how it feels to be deceived. I know what it feels to be hurt, to be lied to, to be the one left in the dark.

I wipe away the tears, getting out of the tub when the water turns ice cold. I slip on the plush white robe and walk to the kitchen. Opening the fridge, I look to see what I can whip together.

My phone rings, and I look at the clock to see it's almost nine thirty. I walk to the front door, picking up my Gucci purse and opening it as the ringing stops.

I look and see that it was from an unknown number. I

wonder if it's one of the clients I met with today. Now is not the time to do this, but they need to know that I'll be there no matter what. So I call the number back as I walk back to the kitchen.

"Hello?" he says, and I stop walking. "Evelyn," he says my name, and I am in shock.

The only thing that comes out of my mouth is, "Who gave you this number?" I don't wait for him to answer because it doesn't fucking matter who gave him this number. What matters is that he used it. "Don't call me again," I say, hanging up, and my heart sinks in my stomach. I put the phone down and then hear it beep.

My heart hammering, I pick up the phone, not sure what to expect. Whatever it is, it's not what's there.

Unknown: We can do this the easy way or the hard way.

I laugh. He has some nerve, and then another text comes in.

Unknown: I have no problem calling your brother to ask to see you.

My mouth opens. What the hell is his problem? I'm pissed now, fucking pissed. I dial his number, and I can hear that he's in the car. "Evelyn," he says my name in a desperate plea. "Please let me explain."

"I don't really know what game you are playing," I tell him. "But—"

"I'm not playing any game. I just want five minutes of your time, and then I'll never bother you again."

"I won't say anything." My voice comes out. "It's not necessary to talk about it. We can forget it ever happened."

"Not a chance in hell," he says, and I have no idea what he means. "I can come to you."

My head is spinning. "I don't have to come inside. We can talk outside." His voice goes softer now. "I just need . . ."

"You aren't going to let this go?" I ask, and I close my eyes when he answers.

"No," he says.

I think about meeting him in person, and then I imagine if someone catches us, and the thought of that is too much for me to bear. "I'll send you my address," I tell him. "You get five minutes. After that, I never want to see you again."

"Text me your address," he says, and I hang up, sending him the address. I put the phone down and get a text now.

Unknown: There in fifteen.

THIRTEEN

MANNING

I TOSS THE phone on the seat next to me as I make my way over to Evelyn's house.

The last three hours are a blur.

I watched her pretend she didn't know me, and it killed me just a little inside. I watched her walk away, and the whole time, I wanted to run after her and get her phone number. I wanted to tell her everything. I watched her avoid looking in my direction, and the whole time, I hoped she would if only for a minute. I hoped she saw the truth in my eyes when she looked at me.

"What do you want to do for dinner?" I heard Murielle from beside me. My eyes were still on Evelyn as she walked down the steps with her nephew. I shook her arm off me while I watched Jaxon drink his slush. I side-eyed her because she's never fucking kissed me on my lips in front of people before.

I looked into her eyes while I wiped her lipstick off

my lips. "I'm taking Jaxon out for pizza," I told her. "Boys' night," I said, just so she wouldn't cause a scene. Of course she looked around to make sure no one had looked over at us.

"Don't keep him out too late," she said. "He has a game tomorrow afternoon."

"I'm aware of his schedule, Murielle," I said as I grabbed his bag and walked down the stairs with Jaxon. "Were you waiting long with Evelyn?" My stomach sunk each time I said her name. Now even more so.

"Nah," he said as we walked out of the arena, and I could swear I caught sight of her in a black BMW. When she stopped at the stop sign, I made her out, and I knew it was her for sure.

"She was going to give us money for arcade games," he said, "but you got here."

"That was very nice of her." I opened the door for him, and I wanted to ask him more questions. I wanted to know if he liked her. I wanted to know anything he had to tell me.

I tried to listen to him as he told me about his week, but all I could do was think about Evelyn. When we finally got home, I saw that the trainer's car was there, and I just shook my head.

We walked in, and Jaxon didn't even ask for his mother before he made his way to the shower. I sat down in the family room with the lights off and started doing my research on Evelyn now that I knew her full name.

I opened up Safari, and I googled her name.

The biography of her taking over for her father at the

firm comes up right away, and I quickly go and search my emails for an email that I got two weeks ago from Tim's firm.

There it was, in black and white, her name and cell phone number.

I closed the email when I heard the sound of footsteps coming up from downstairs. "Thanks for coming over to scratch the itch." I heard Murielle tell her trainer. "You always know just the right part to scratch."

"If you caught an itch," I said as I got up, both of their heads swinging around as they looked at me, "then I suggest you go get that checked out." I headed to the stairs and walked upstairs to tuck in Jaxon.

As soon as he went to bed, I walked out of the house, closing the door behind me.

I pull up to her house and see the porch lights on and the black BMW parked in the driveway. I park behind her, and I don't even know what the fuck I'm going to tell her, but I have to see her. I have to at least tell her something. She deserves that; to be honest, she deserves better than that. She deserves better than me. My phone rings, and my heart speeds up, thinking it's Evelyn telling me not to bother coming. But instead, I see it's Murielle.

"What?" I say, answering the phone.

"Where are you?" she asks, and I just shake my head.

"Is Jaxon okay?" I ask, and she huffs out.

"Okay, then bye." I can hear sheets rustling, and I don't bother saying anything else to her before I hang up. She calls me back again, and I know if I don't answer her, she is just going to call me over and over again.

"What is it, Murielle?"

"Don't what is it, Murielle me. I'm your wife," she says, and I laugh. "I have a right to know where you are."

"I have a right not to have your trainer fuck you in our home, too. I have a right to ask you for a divorce. We can't all get what we want," I say. "Now if Jaxon is fine and sleeping, we have nothing else to say."

"Are you fucking around on me?" she shrieks, and I laugh.

"I'm not that lucky," I say and hang up on her. When she calls back, I send it to voice mail. I wait to see if she calls again, but instead, she just sends a text.

Murielle: We need to talk.

I walk to the front door and ring the bell. I look down at the concrete walkway and then look up when I hear her unlocking the door. The door opens slowly, and I see her. She is wearing a sweater that hangs down to her knees and tights. Her red hair is piled on top of her head, and I can see she has been crying. The tip of her nose is red, and her eyes are swollen. It is a kick in the balls.

So many things are going through my mind, so many things I want to say, but the only thing that comes out of my mouth is her name. "Evelyn," I whisper, the pain in my chest a bit more than I can bear.

"You have five minutes," she says, and I know that I have to give her that.

"Do you want to do this out here or . . .?" I look around, asking her, and she opens the door to let me in. I walk in, and I can feel the hominess of her house. I look at the table with the black purse she was holding tonight.

On it is a vase of roses, and I wonder if she got them herself. I wonder if she likes roses and what her favorite flower is.

"Thank you." I look at her and wish I could kiss her. I put my hands in my pockets or else I'll grab her, and then she will likely kick me in the balls and kick me out. And I want every minute that she will give me.

"I figured it would be better to keep it quiet," she says, stepping away from me and crossing her arms over her chest. "Out of sight."

"Before I say anything," I say, "I just want you to know that I'm sorry."

As she laughs, I watch her, and something clicks into place, but I don't know what to do about it. This whole week has thrown my world off.

"Sorry for what, exactly?"

It's a loaded question. "For a lot of things but most of all for the way you found out like that." She rolls her eyes at me. "Okay, not the best thing to say."

"Why don't I do the talking?" she suggests. "Whatever happened between us on Saturday," she points at her and then me, "it's between us. It will not go anywhere." I take a step toward her, and she snaps. "You're married!" she yells. "Married!" She puts her hands to her stomach. "Do you know how that makes me feel?" Her eyes turn a bright green, and I want to hold her face in my hands and kiss her lips and tell her everything, tell her every single fucking thing. "You cheated on your wife, and I helped you." She shakes her head. "Married . . . you are married."

It's now or never. "I don't tell anyone my business," I say. "I'm the most private person you will ever meet. My name is Manning Stevenson, and I play hockey for the Dallas Oilers. I'm their captain."

"Oh my god." She puts her hand to her lips. "That's why the bartender called you captain."

"Yes," I say. "I'm not on social media. I keep to myself, and the only time I do interviews is after the game or when it has to do with the foundation or children. That night when I went to the restaurant . . . I want you to know that what we had, what we shared . . ." I try to find the words.

"Was all a lie," she tells me, and I see the tears in her eyes. "The whole week, I thought about you. The whole week, the only thing I regretted was not staying with you that morning." She swallows, and I can see the one tear got out. "But now I regret it all. You made me be the person I hate most in the world. You made me a home-wrecker." She puts her hands to her stomach.

"You are not a home-wrecker," I say. "I swear to you with everything that I have, you are not a home-wrecker. Murielle and I . . ." I run my hands through my hair, scared to tell her, scared to see the pity that might wash over her face. Most of all, I'm scared she won't believe me. But I have no choice because I will not let her beat herself down. "You are the opposite of a home-wrecker. There isn't even a home to wreck." I see the confusion on her face. "Are Murielle and I married?" The words are bitter in my mouth but not more bitter than the next word that comes out, "Yes. But . . ."

She shakes her head. "There are no buts," she tells me and walks past me to the door, opening it for me. "Goodbye, Manning."

FOURTEEN

EVELYN

"GOOD-BYE, MANNING," I tell him. My heart is not sure it can take much more of him being here. Standing here in front of me, knowing that he can never be mine. Knowing that he was never mine to begin with. Knowing that our night together was just another night for him.

I look at him, and he looks just as broken as I do, and I wonder why. Is it because he's scared I'll tell his wife? Is it because he's scared I'll tell my brother? "Everything that I told you last week was the truth," he says. His voice comes out strong, and his feet don't move toward the door. "Before Saturday, I was existing." I look at him, not sure what he means. "Last Saturday was the first time in a long time that I put myself before anyone else. It was the first time that I saw that I deserve it. I deserve to have something for me."

"I don't even know what that means," I tell him honestly. "If you are worried about me telling anyone about us"—I shake my head—"I won't tell anyone what happened between us." I look to see if maybe he does a sigh of relief, but he doesn't even flinch with this news. "Is that why you kept looking around on Saturday?" I ask as the pieces of the puzzle come together now.

"I kept looking around because one, I hate to be exploited, and two, I wanted to protect you and not have you plastered all over social media," he says. "Do you know how amazing it was that you liked me for me?" he asks, and I don't answer. "It just made everything." His voice trails off. "Everything that night was perfect."

"Do you know why I moved back home?" I ask, and he just looks at me. "Because I walked in on my boyfriend balls deep into his business partner while my best friend rode his face," I tell him. "I'm that person." I point at myself. "You made me that person. You." I point at him, and then at myself. "You made me just like her. You made me that person I hate," I tell him. "You made me a liar and a cheater!" I shout. "I'm just as bad as her."

"You are not as bad as her," he tells me, and I roll my eyes. "You could never be that person."

"But I am." I put my hands up and then down again. "It was a lie," I say softly, and that hits him more than what I said before.

"Nothing about that night was a lie." He gazes at me. "Being in that hotel room with you. That was me. It was the real me. It was a me that no one has ever bothered to get to know. I wasn't Manning, the captain of the Dallas Oilers. I wasn't Manning, the guy who poses for pictures. I wasn't Manning doing an interview. I was Manning, just the man." I can't say anything because of the huge lump forming in my throat. This was supposed to be me telling him to fuck off and calling him a cheater. This was supposed to be easy. I'm finally seeing that nothing is easy when it comes to him. "All week, I replayed that night over and over again. All week, it's the only thing I could think of. You." He points at me. "You were the only thing I could think of. Walking in and seeing you today was . . ." He runs his hands through his hair. "Fuck, it was like seeing a fucking angel. I thought my eyes were playing tricks on me."

"I looked for a ring," I say. "After the second time we bumped into each other, the first thing I did was look for a ring when I came to the bar."

"I never really wore a ring," he tells me. "But I especially wouldn't wear a ring now."

I throw my hands up in the air. "I don't even know what that means."

"Four years ago, I asked Murielle for a divorce, and she . . ." He starts to say. "She took off with Jaxon for two weeks. I couldn't find her, and I had no idea where she went. She took my son and just left." His voice cracks. Oh my god. I see when he takes his hand out of his back pocket now and uses his thumb to wipe away the tear.

"I have never felt so helpless in all my life. She agreed to come home only if I would never mention it again." He doesn't stop talking. "I would have promised her anything just to get Jaxon back.

"She came back, and I sat down with her. I poured out my heart to her, asking her why she loved me. Why she even wanted to be married to me." My hand falls off the handle. "She didn't even know the answer. She sat there, and I waited. I waited and waited, and the only thing she could say was how it would look."

He puts his head back. "Her main concern is how people would look at her. I asked her if she loved me, and she said she did, but then she couldn't tell me why. I was honest with her and told her that I didn't love her. I loved her for giving me Jaxon, but other than that, we were so opposite." My mind reels at all this information. I'm expecting him to stop talking, but he doesn't. "I begged her to let me go." He swallows now as his voice cracks again. "But she refused. I moved out of my bedroom that night. From that day forward and well, many months before, I stopped touching her. We were married for the sake of people. We were married for show. For fucking show. Me, the one person who keeps everything to myself. I am living a fucking lie." He looks at me. "I stay with her for one reason and only one reason, and that is for Jaxon." My heart breaks for him.

"I stay for my son. I stay so she doesn't drag my kid through shit. I stay to keep the peace. But in the end, pieces of me were dying." He shakes his head. "I didn't even know until I saw you." His voice trails off. "Until I touched you. I was happy to just go through life and give everyone else what they wanted. And then I saw you." He stares at me. "I saw you, and something in me jumped off the ledge." He steps to me, and I don't move or do anything. He stands in front of me, and the smell of him comes over me. "Something in me woke up." His voice trails off, and he looks at me. I don't know what to say. He just gave me his whole fucking heart on a platter, and I don't know what to tell him.

"Manning," I whisper, my heart breaking for him.

His hand comes up now as his thumb rubs my cheek. "You are not a home-wrecker. Don't you ever put yourself down like that," he tells me, my heart hammering in my chest. He stands so close to me that if I took one step forward, we would be chest to chest. "In fact, you saved me." He bends down now, and I stop breathing with his lips right next to mine. "You were the one who made me see," he says, his own breath hitching. "That I wasn't dead inside." He leans closer until there is no space between us, and his lips are on mine in the softest kiss he's ever given me. His hand cups my cheek as he pulls back. "You, Evelyn." My eyes flicker open, looking at him. "You are what dreams are made of." I just look at him, his eyes almost pleading with me. I can't say anything. Not a word comes out. The lump in my throat makes it almost impossible to say anything without a sob ripping from me, and his hand falls from my cheek. "I am over my five minutes," he says, his voice sounding so defeated. "Thank you, Evelyn," he says and walks out of the house.

I put my hand on my cheek as I watch him drive away. The tear rolls over my pinky all the way to the floor. My hand moves from my cheek to my lips as it still tingles with his kiss. I don't know how long I stand here before I quietly close the door. I don't even know why I was waiting for him to come back.

Something in me was hoping he would come back. I sit in the darkness and play his words over again in my head. "Four years," I say into the darkness as one hour turns into another. "Loveless." A shiver runs through me. "I was just me."

I lie down on the couch, closing my eyes, and I hear his voice as if he is right beside me. *You are what dreams are made of.* I close my eyes as sleep takes me.

FIFTEEN

MANNING

YOU MADE ME a liar and a cheater.

I hear her voice as if she is right next to me, and my eyes fly open. "I'm just as bad as her." I look at my bedroom wall now. Then I turn to look at the ceiling, the heaviness in my chest is even heavier than last night, if that is even possible.

Driving away from her was the hardest thing I ever had to do. Watching her in the rearview mirror as she stood there holding the door. Her kiss still lingering on my lips. My hand itching to hold her face. My body aching for her.

My eyes close again, and I try to fall back asleep, but all I can hear is her telling me how she was this awful person, and I couldn't stand it. I couldn't let her stand in front of me like that and say those things about herself. For the first time in my life, I opened up to someone. For the first time, I didn't hold back. For the first fucking time, I showed somebody that I wasn't perfect, that my life was not what it seemed, and that I hurt just as much as everybody else. I wanted her to know that those hours with her were not a lie. Nothing we did was a lie.

I hear footsteps coming to my door, and I look over as the door opens slowly. "Hey," I say to Jaxon as he comes running in the room and getting into bed with me. "Morning," I tell him as he cuddles up to me. I put my arm around him and kiss his head. "Did you sleep well?"

"Yeah," he says and leans over to get the remote to turn on the television. He puts Netflix on, and I get up to go to the bathroom. I wash my face and look in the mirror. The marks from last weekend are etched in my memory even though I can no longer see them. I raise my hand and touch the spot where she bit me. The memory rushes back so fast I can't stop it.

"Are you sure about this?" I asked her as I carried her to the bed. It was one thing to attack her at the door, but I wasn't going to fuck her again against the wall. Maybe the fifth time, I thought to myself. My mouth devoured hers as she shook her head.

"Condoms," she said, stopping me from moving another inch. "Purse."

I put her down on the bed. "I'll get them," I whispered to her, and I wanted the lights on. I wanted to see her face when I slid into her. I walked back over to the door where her purse was on the floor with the flap opened and the condoms sticking out. I bent over to pick them up, and when I went back into the room, she was completely naked. Her feet were on the bed with her legs tucked up to her chest and her ankles crossed. Her hair cascaded all around her shoulders. "You are beautiful," I said as I kicked off my shoes and slid down my pants.

I tore off the corner of the condom wrapper, my cock hard and ready for her. I rolled it down and then looked at her. She lay back with her head on the pillows behind her and her legs spread eagle. I put my knee on the bed and made my way over to her, bending and licking her one last time before rubbing my cock up and down her slit.

"Perfect," I told her as I watched myself slide into her. I took my time to savor every single second of it. Only when I was balls deep did I realize that I hadn't taken a breath. She fit me like a fucking glove. Like she was made for me. I put my arms down beside her head as I moved in and out of her. I did it as slowly as I could until she kissed under my chin and then I slammed into her. The minute I did that, she bit me.

"Dad." I hear Jaxon call me, bringing me back to the present. "Can you make me pancakes?" he asks.

"Yeah, buddy," I say, walking into my walk-in closet and getting a T-shirt. I won't go downstairs without my shirt. The last time I did that, Murielle rubbed her finger down my back and then put her palms on my chest. "Go brush your teeth," I tell him, and he tosses the covers off and walks out of the room.

I pick up my phone, and I don't know why I'm hoping to find a text from Evelyn, but I see nothing from her and delete the text I sent her last night. I also store her number under her father's name. Walking downstairs, I start my coffee. I take some sausage and some turkey bacon out and get those started, then start making some pancakes. Jaxon comes down ten minutes later dressed almost like me. "You want some orange juice?" I ask him, and he nods, walking over to the fridge and pouring his own glass. "Want blueberries in yours?"

He shakes his head. "Chocolate chips," he says, smiling.

"You play in three hours," I tell him, and he slaps his head. "So blueberries?"

"Yes, please," he says, getting on the stool in front of me, and we talk about the plays he's going to make. We are both sitting down, getting ready to eat when Murielle comes downstairs dressed in short shorts and a tank top.

"Morning," she says, walking over to the coffee machine. She makes her coffee and sits on the stool next to me. "What time did you come home?"

"Not late," I answer, eating and ignoring the fact that she is sitting so close to me. She reaches over me to grab a slice of turkey bacon, and I glare at her. She knows I won't tell her to fuck off in front of Jaxon.

She just smiles at me. "What time do you have to be gone today?"

"We leave here at ten," I say of Jaxon and me. "His game is at eleven."

"I wish I could come, but I have a foundation meeting. We are going to be doing a toy drive in December," she tells me. I will give her that—she is very involved with the foundation. I mean, she has to be since she's the captain's wife. "Sorry, buddy."

"That's okay," he says, getting up and placing his plate in the sink. "Can I play on the iPad a bit?" he asks, and I nod.

"We leave in forty-five minutes. So you get thirty minutes on the iPad. Is your bag packed?" I ask. He nods as he skips off to the couch, grabbing the iPad.

"Are you going out after the game?" she asks, and I look over at her. "I'm just wondering."

"I don't ask you where you go, so you don't ask me." I get up, putting my plate in the sink.

"You could ask me," she says, and I turn around and look at her leaning against the counter. "I'm an open book."

"Oh, you are open all right," I say under my breath. I watch as she drinks her coffee, and I don't know what comes over me. Maybe it's the fact that I had Evelyn. Maybe it's the fact that I was happy for two point three seconds. Maybe it's the fact that I finally admitted I deserve to be happy instead of miserable. I deserve to wake up every morning and not dread seeing the woman who shares my house. "Aren't you tired?" I ask, and she just looks at me, confused. "Of this?" I point at her and then at me. Her eyes show me that she is still not getting it. "Of living a lie? Of pretending? Don't you want to be open and free?"

Her eyes glare at me as she looks to the couch to make sure that Jaxon isn't listening. "I don't know about you," she says, her voice low, "but I sleep very good at night." She folds her arms under her chest. "Now if you want to change things and come back to our bed, I wouldn't say no.”

"Are you insane?" I say. "Murielle, it's over. It's past over. It's buried and dead." I look at her, and I ask her again.

"Do you love me?" She just looks at me.

"Yes," she says, and I laugh, shaking my head. "I do love you."

"Okay, what do you love about me besides my money and status?" I tilt my head to the side.

"We have a good life," she says. "A great life. We are both . . ."

I put up my hand. "Save it, Murielle."

"Why are you like this?" she asks. The doorbell rings, and I look over at the camera to see it's her fuck buddy.

"Your scratching post is here," I say, pushing away from the counter. I look back at her, stopping beside her. "If you change your mind, we can talk about it."

She glares at me. "There is nothing to talk about," she hisses at me, and the bell rings again. She pushes away from the counter and starts to walk out of the room.

"The minute my son figures out that his mother gets fucked in the basement, it's really over," I say.

"Our son," she repeats. "I would hate to have to take our son away."

I grip her hand in mine when she tries to walk away. "You caught me off guard the last time," I say, my voice as low as I will allow it. "This time, I'm ready for you." She snatches her arm out of my hand.

"Don't you dare threaten me," she hisses.

I shake my head and smile at her. "I wouldn't dare

think of threatening you," I say and walk away, going to the couch. "Let's go, buddy." I pick up Jaxon, and he laughs when I throw him over my shoulder.

"Dad!" He laughs, and I walk up the stairs at the same time that Murielle is opening the door. I make sure he doesn't see as I walk to my side of the house.

"Are you leaving again?" Jaxon asks when I take out my going away tote bag and place it on the bed while he plays on his iPad.

"Just for a couple of days. I leave tomorrow, and then I come back on Wednesday."

"Can you take me to practice when you get back?" he asks. I grab my phone, and my heart does a little flip, hoping there is a text, but then is let down. I check my schedule. "I think I can. So far, it looks good."

He gets up off the bed when the timer goes off on the iPad, letting him know he has to get dressed. "Thanks, Dad," he says, walking out of the room.

"Anything for you," I say to the empty doorway. "Anything for you."

SIXTEEN

EVELYN

"YOU LOOK TIRED," Veronica says to me when I get to the restaurant, and I laugh.

"That's a polite way to say you look like shit." I kiss her cheek and then bend to kiss my brother's. "Sorry I'm a bit late." I kiss my nephew, and I'm shocked when I see Jaxon there. My heart speeds up in my chest, and I look around nervously to see if he's here with his mother or his father. I spent the whole night thinking about him. Thinking about what he said. Thinking about the fact that I met him one week ago today, and it feels like I've known him forever. It's so stupid.

"Hello, you," I say to Caleb, kissing him on the head, and Jaxon looks up at me and smiles. "Hello, you, too." I ruffle his hair, and my face scrunches. "Why is your hair wet?" He laughs at me. "Is it hockey sweat or shower?" His laughter gets louder. "Please tell me shower." I try to keep my heart at bay as I look around without making it look so obvious.

"We took a shower," Jaxon says, laughing. I look over at Tim and Veronica and see two empty chairs, and my mouth gets super dry.

"Are we just us?" I ask, trying not to make a big deal out of it. They both nod their head, and I let out a sigh of relief. I sit next to Veronica, leaving the seat next to me empty. "So how was the big game?" I ask the boys.

"We lost by one," Caleb says. "Jaxon scored two goals." My mouth opens, and I put my hand up.

"High-five for the two goals." He reaches over and high-fives me. "Is that a trick?" I ask, looking at them as they laugh at me.

"Auntie Evie, I told you already," he groans out, putting his hand to his forehead. "That's three goals," Caleb says, shaking his head. "I told you this five times already."

I put up my hands, laughing. "I don't get hockey." I look back at Jaxon, who laughs with Caleb. "Well, I'm sure you can do it next time then," I tell him, and he just looks at me. Then Caleb and he both look down at their menus.

"You should come to the hockey game with us tonight," Tim says, and I just look at him. My stomach twists and turns at the thought of seeing Manning.

"I would rather sit on my couch and catch up on that Joe exotic guy," I tell him. "And then search how I could adopt a tiger." I shrug, knowing that I'll be on my couch curled up and spend the night trying not to think about Manning.

Veronica laughs. The waitress comes over, and the kids both order burgers with bacon and fries. Jaxon asks if he can have soup with that, and then Caleb asks him if he ate breakfast.

"I did," he says. "Dad made me blueberry pancakes with sausage and turkey bacon."

"Wow," Tim says. "Well, you played hard today so you can have whatever you want."

Lunch is chatty with both of them talking loudly to each other. I use one ear to listen to the stories he tells, wanting to hear about Manning. I wonder where the mother was while he made breakfast. Was she there?

I lean over and grab a fry from Caleb's plate and then grab one from Jaxon, also laughing with them. "Who is going to get dessert?" I ask them, leaning on my arm. "I want a bite of each."

"No." Caleb shakes his head. "Not some of mine."

"You can have a bite of mine," Jaxon says. "But I'm ordering chocolate."

"Oh," I sing-song, "I love chocolate."

"Me, too," he says, and his eyes go big. "Dad and I love it. Mom doesn't." I smile while swallowing around the lump at the mention of his mother and his father.

"Go wash your hands," Tim tells them, and they get up and go wash their hands.

"He's a nice boy," I say, watching them as they walk to the bathroom.

"He is," Veronica agrees, drinking the rest of the wine she had in her glass. "I hate his mother," Veronica says, and I just look at her.

"Don't start," Tim says to Veronica.

"Don't start, my ass. It's your sister. Who is she going to go tell?" Veronica looks at him, leaning forward on the table with her arms. "Tim says I have to be nice."

"I just said behave," he says, leaning to her, and she kisses his lips, and something in me makes my chest hurt.

"I do behave. We all behave." She rolls her eyes. "She's a class A bitch. In case you didn't know, her husband plays for the NHL." I pick up my glass of water and bring it to my lips. I hope they don't notice the glass shaking in my hand. "He's the captain, so if we need anything, she can get it for us. You know us little people are peasants."

"She is not that bad," Tim says, laughing.

"Last month, she came to see me to tell me that all snack and cupcakes have to be organic and all that shit." Veronica looks at him while she talks. "Then she asked me if I could afford it. Me. I'm a fucking doctor. She's . . ." She throws her hand in the air. "She's a stay-at-home mom with a nanny, a cleaning lady, and a chef." My heart sinks as I think about Manning and what he told me. "Don't even start with me, Timothy," she says his full name, and I open my mouth, looking at him.

Tim rubs her back. "Okay, okay, enough. It's not Jaxon's fault she's like that."

"Don't you think I know that?" she says. "It's a good thing he's nice like his father because . . ."

"Shh," I say, hushing them when I see the boys walking back. "Did you use soap?" I ask, and they both nod.

They get their dessert, and my heart literally is going

to burst in my chest when he asks the waitress for two spoons so he can share with me. I look at him with a smile. *He really is like his father.*

He hangs around with us until Tim gets up and drives him back home with Caleb. I hug Veronica and thank her for lunch, then make a stop at the florist before going home.

I kick off my shoes when I get home, and I spend the night watching some show on Netflix. Then I fall asleep, but this time, my dreams are of Manning and Jaxon. Sunday flies by with the bridesmaids fitting and then dinner. The whole time, I remember the last time I was with them, and when I get home that night, I'm exhausted from spending most of the day trying to block him from my mind.

By the end of Wednesday, I walk into the house, kicking off my heels at the door on the way to my bathroom. A soak in the tub is just what I need. Only when I get out, I order a burger instead of a salad as I walk back to the bedroom and put on my shorts and tank top. I grab the long cashmere sweater, putting it on as I walk to the fridge and take out the white wine.

So far this week, I've been in back-to-back meetings with everyone my father wants to switch over to me. I also had about fifty-five million questions about what I do and don't do. It's almost as if I'm interviewing for a job each time someone new walks into the room. The cool wine goes down smoothly as I turn on the television and it's on *SportsCenter*. Okay, fine, I was watching the hockey game last night. I caved, and just seeing him on the ice gave me butterflies. I lasted three minutes before the butterflies turned to dread, and I changed the channel.

The doorbell rings, and I put down the remote next to the glass of wine and make my way to the front door. I unlock the door and open it, expecting the delivery guy, but it's not.

"Manning," I whisper. He stands there in his suit with his hands in his pockets, and he looks even better than he did in the club. "What are you doing here?"

"I . . ." He starts to say, and he looks up at the sky. "I know I shouldn't be here. I know that."

I don't say anything to him. I can't because I'm still in shock. "I was trying to tell myself not to come and this was a bad idea. But my car started coming here, and I just," he says, "I couldn't not see you."

He walks toward me now, my heart beating in my chest. "Manning," I say his name.

It's the only thing I can actually say. His hands come up to my face. "Evelyn," he says, rubbing my cheeks with his thumbs. "You saw Jaxon?" he says, and I nod my head. "I have never been so jealous of my son before in my life." He smiles, and I can't stop the smile that fills my face. I couldn't if I tried. "I can't stay away from you." He bends his head, so our foreheads meet. "Your face," he says. "It haunts my dreams."

A tear escapes my eyes. "I watched you last night." I finally say the only words that come out. "I couldn't last for more than three minutes without my chest hurting."

"Evelyn," he whispers, and my heart speeds up, my stomach flips, and I know what he's waiting for. I know he won't go any further until I tell him it's okay. I know that no matter how much he wants me, no matter how much it kills him, he will not make the next move. It's up to me.

"Manning," I whisper. It's the only thing I say before I make a move. I move my head just a touch so my lips touch his, enough for him to know I'm okay with this. "Manning." It's the last thing I say before his mouth claims mine again, and I feel like I've been kissing him my whole life. I feel like this is where I was always supposed to be. But with his lips on mine, everything else disappears.

SEVENTEEN

Manning

"Evelyn," I SAY. My hands are tangled in her hair after she asked me to kiss her. I bend my head again and take her lips. This kiss is like nothing I remembered. Our tongues dance together softly, gently as we savor this fucking moment. I'm about to pick her up when I hear a car approaching. I turn to see a car parking in her driveway.

"Go inside," she tells me, and I suddenly wonder if she was expecting someone. My eyes watch the guy open the driver's door and then lean over to the passenger side. "It's my food. He might recognize you," she says, and I nod my head. I hate that I have to leave her out here by herself. Hate it. I walk into the house and go to the family room, and I look around. Her light gray couch is in the middle of the room with plush black pillows. An oversized gray table is in the middle of the room in front of the television hanging on the wall and is paused on some show. I see a glass of wine on the table. I look around, seeing family pictures placed on the side tables. She's been here for less than a month, and this house already feels like a home.

I didn't know what to expect when I rang the doorbell. I didn't even know if she would let me in. It didn't matter, though, because there was only one thing that mattered. I had to see her, even if it was six feet apart. Even if she slammed the door in my face, I knew that I had to see her.

"Sorry," she says, coming back, and I see that she has on shorts under her long robe. "I just didn't want the guy to see you and then make trouble for you." The feeling happens again in my heart—like a thud—but I'm not sure what it is.

"You were worried about me?" I ask, not sure I understand it.

"Well . . ." She puts the brown paper bag on the counter, then turns to me. "He might know who you are and wonder why you're here." I nod my head, hating another thing that comes with the territory that I'm in. "Did you eat?" she asks, and I nod as she walks to me. "I can't believe you're here," she says softly.

"Trust me, I know," I say. I want to take off my jacket and sit on the couch with her so we can talk. She walks to me, grabbing my hand and pulling me to the couch.

"Give me your jacket," she says. I shrug off my suit jacket, and she gently folds it, then lays it on the arm of the couch. "Come sit. We need to talk."

Nodding, I walk to the couch and sit down. She sits

down away from me, and I lean over and bring her closer to me. "I missed you," I say when she's under my arm. "It's fucking crazy, and I can't even explain it if I tried, but I just . . ."

"I know," she says. Her hand comes up to touch my face, tracing my lips with her index finger. "I missed you also, which is insane to say since I didn't even know you until last week," she says and looks down as if she is embarrassed by the declaration. I put my finger under her chin and raise it so I can see her eyes.

"Don't hide from me," I say, and she tilts her chin forward. I lean in and kiss her. Her mouth opens for my tongue, and the kiss turns needy. Both of us are needing to feel the other. She leans in now just a bit more, and I pull her to me. Her legs go over mine as she straddles my lap. Her pussy lands straight on my cock, who is ready to come out and play. "I didn't come here for that," I say, making sure she knows I really didn't come here for this. "I came to see you."

"I know," she says, leaning in and biting my bottom lip before I slip my tongue back into her mouth. My hands have a mind of their own when I cup her tits over her tank top. Her nipples are itching to be played with. While our tongues fight with each other and our heads move from side to side to deepen the kiss, I pull down her tank top, and my finger moves over her nipple lightly. She lets go of my lips to moan. I bend, taking the nipple into my mouth while she arches her back and her hips move. "Manning," she says, running her hand through my hair. I pull down the other side and bite the other nipple. "God," she hisses out.

"Manning," I say, smirking at her as I suck her nipple into my mouth.

"Bedroom," she says to me, and I stop and look at her face. Her cheeks are flushed pink, and her tits are out and perfect. "I want to be spread open for you. I don't want any restriction." I wrap an arm around her waist, standing, and she wraps her legs around my waist. I decide it's my favorite way to kiss her. "That way." She points at the door on the side of the family room. I walk into the dimly lit room, and I see her in this whole room. It is everything I thought it would be.

The walls are a light gray, the ceiling has wood all over it, and it's the same color as the walls. A bench is in front of her king-size bed. The lights on her side table are on low. I look at the frame above her bed.

You will forever be my always.

I stand here thinking about how that quote sums her up perfectly. I walk to the bed, stopping at the side. She unwraps her legs from my waist and gets on her knees on the bed. Her fingers come out and slowly unbutton my shirt. My stomach sinks in when she opens it and then kisses the middle of my chest. She reaches up, pushing the white shirt off my shoulder, and kisses the middle of my tattoo.

"Baby," I say, and she smiles, putting her head back. I lean down and kiss her lips softly. Her hands go to my hips, and I pull her sweater off her and then her tank top. "Lean back," I say, and she gets on her back, and I see the wet spot on her light gray shorts. I touch the wet spot, and her head rolls side to side as her eyes close. "I've thought about this moment ever since I woke up that Sunday alone."

"Me, too," she pants out. I pull the shorts off her hips, and I find her bare. All fucking bare. "Mine," I growl out and get on my knees. Pulling her to the edge of the bed, I bury my face, "I thought about doing this to you five times a day." I lick up, and her legs open more for me. She puts her leg on my shoulder, and I watch her face as I slide two fingers in her.

"Manning." She calls my name, and it's even better than in my dreams. "Please."

"What, baby?" I ask as my fingers fuck her a bit faster. Her hands are on her tits as she plays with her nipples. "Tell me what you want."

"I want to come on your tongue." She looks at me. "Or your fingers." I lean forward and take her clit into my mouth as I look at her. One hand reaches down to grab my hair. "But what I really want," she says, and her pussy gets tighter and tighter. I nibble on her clit. "What I really want," she repeats as she tries to focus on speaking while my fingers move faster and faster.

I let go of her clit long enough to ask her. "What do you want?" My tongue flicks her clit.

"Your cock." Her eyes close halfway as she moves her hips up and down. "I want your cock in my mouth." Her hand pulls my hair. "I want your cock to fuck my tits." She's the hottest thing I've ever seen in my life. "Then I want you to fuck me with your cock." It's me now who groans out. "Then I want to ride your cock until I can't stand anymore." She stops talking when she comes on my fingers. I finger fuck her until she stops moaning and then slip my fingers out of her. She watches me with her eyes half-closed. I stick my fingers into my mouth, licking her off me, and she closes her knees now and tries to move up and get friction.

"My turn," she says, sitting up. She kisses my lips and then tries to pick me up. "Stand up," she tells me when she can't move me. "I want your cock," she tells me, and I stand. She unbuttons the top button, licking her lips when she sees my cock. "My dreams," she says, licking the tip. "Fuck," she says, taking the tip into her mouth. Her hair falls in front of her face, and I push it to the side as I watch her try to swallow my whole cock with her hand grasping the base.

"So good," I say, moving my hips to fuck her face. I don't want to stop watching her, but my eyes close as I take in the heat of her mouth. The wetness of her tongue as she lets go of my cock and twirls her tongue around the head. Her hand moves up and down the whole time.

"Oh, baby." She trails her tongue all the way down the shaft and takes one of my balls into her mouth. I swear it's nothing like it was last week. And that was the best blow job of my life. She sucks my other ball and then sucks up my shaft until she gets to the tip.

"Your cock is so fucking beautiful," she says, moving from a sitting position to her hands and knees, her ass in the air moving side to side. She holds my cock, taking in the tip with her eyes on me the whole time. "Where do you want to come?" she asks me between licks and sucks. "My mouth." I see her hand slide to my balls as she arches her back and her ass wiggles. "My tits." My eyes look down at her tits that are swaying as she sucks my cock.

"Where do you want it?" I ask between clenched teeth as she slips one of her hands between her legs. I grip her hair in my hand and pull her off my cock.

"Your pussy is mine," I say. "If you want to play with it, you have to ask me." I move her head to my cock and allow her to suck it one time. "Ask me," I say, my cock not happy I have to play this game. He wants to come down her throat, and then he wants to fuck the shit out of her.

"Can I finger your pussy?" she asks, her ass moving side to side, and I have to hold her head tighter.

"That ass of yours is going to be punished," I say, and I swear her eyes light up. "You want that?"

She nods her head. "I want everything you have to give me."

"Fuck," I hiss out as she attacks my cock, the both of us teetering on the ledge. Her hand plays with her pussy as I fuck her face. "I'm going to come," I say when I feel my balls get tight.

"Me, too," she says between sucks, and when she doesn't move, and she groans on my cock, I know she's coming, and I let go, and she swallows all of me. She sucks my cock long after I finish, and it doesn't even have a chance to go to half-mast. I pull her hair back and swallow her mouth, the taste of both of us making my cock even harder.

"Manning," she says with her teeth clenched. She says the three words I've been telling her in my dreams for the past week. "I need you."

EIGHTEEN

EVELYN

"I NEED YOU," I beg. "I need to feel you," I tell him, and he kicks off his pants. I thought I remembered his body, but I was wrong. I was so fucking wrong. I sit on my knees as I watch him. His eyes turn a darker shade of blue. The tattoo on his shoulder seems bigger now, brighter, and I see it now, the letter J in the middle of the black, blue, and red. His abs are on point, and the two side abs scream to be bitten.

His chest seems bigger than I remember, and I suddenly miss seeing my mark on him.

"What are you thinking about?" he asks, coming to the bed with his cock in his hand.

"About how I miss seeing my mark on you," I tell him the truth. "Will you promise me something?" I ask, and my stomach flips when I see the worry wash over his face.

"Anything," he says softly, putting his knee on the

bed.

"That you won't lie to me," I tell him. "That if you have to say it, you just say it." My heart hammers in my chest.

"I promise you," he says, pushing my hair away from my face, "that I will always tell you the truth."

I nod my head, and he leans down. "I was sad on Sunday when I woke up and didn't see your mark on me," he says, and his finger goes exactly to where I remember biting him. "You know what that means."

"What?" I ask. He stops in front of me, taking my face in his hands. I lean my head back like I always do when I want him to kiss me.

"It means you have to give me another one." He smirks, and I smile as he kisses me. He pushes me back, and my legs open for him. Our kisses are soft at first, and then they get more frantic.

He lets go of my lips to kiss my neck, and my nipples are tight, and I raise my hand to pinch them. "Manning, you need to fuck me." I don't even care if I sound like a hussy at this point. All I know is that I need him. "Condom," I say, and he looks at me, his eyes going wide. "You did bring condoms."

"Um, no," he says, not moving, and I swear I can hear my pussy weeping. "I didn't think that we would . . ."

I look at him, not fucking sure what to say. Do I tell him to get his ass out the door to go buy them? Then it dawns on me. "Oh my god," I say, leaning over to the side table to take out the box of condoms Veronica bought me as a joke. "Oh my god." I show him the box of Magnums. "Veronica bought me this as a housewarming gag gift." I open the box and take the condoms out. "Joke's on her." I toss him a condom.

"I'm not even going to think of another woman when I'm in bed with you, but I could hug her right now," he says, taking the condom and tearing it open. "I swear I think my cock cried when you asked for a condom." I laugh at him now as he sheaths himself. "Now, where were we?"

"I believe you were going to fuck me harder than you did last week," I tell him, opening my legs for him. "And if we're taking notes, you fucked me so hard I felt you three days later."

"Challenge accepted," he says, coming over to me on his knees and rubbing his cock up and down my slit. He pushes my knees back, lifting my hips just a bit off the bed as he slowly slips inside me. I swear I feel every single fucking vein as he buries himself balls deep in me. When his balls hit my ass, we both moan. "Fuck," he hisses out as he pulls and pushes my legs back, and he slams into me again. "I was wrong," he says, taking his cock out slowly and then slamming into me, my eyes rolling in the back of my head. Everything about last week is gone because nothing could compare to the feeling right now. Nothing is as good as it is right now.

"All week," I tell him as he picks up his pace. "All fucking week, I dreamed of you fucking me. In my dreams, I swear if I closed my eyes hard enough, I could feel it." He puts one of my legs over his shoulder, and my hips tilt back. He slams into me over and over again, getting so deep I can't even talk. I have nothing to say; I can only watch his cock pounding into me. I watch as my pussy takes him. "I'm." I start to say, pinching my nipples now. He takes my other leg and places it on the other side, and when he slams into me, I see fucking stars as I come on his cock over and over again.

One leads into another, my legs now falling to the sides of his arms, and he leans down now. My legs wrap around his hips as he puts his hand beside me. His lips come down to mine as his thrusts are just as hard. His nose touches mine as we look in each other's eyes. One hand goes to the back of his head, and I move it up to hold his head in my hand as he kisses me. His tongue mixes with mine as it goes around and around in a circle. The softness of his kiss pushes me over the edge again, and I cry out his name, but it's swallowed with his mouth. He waits until my pussy stops gripping his cock before he throws his head back and cries out my name.

He collapses on me and rolls me. My legs wrap around him and now so do my arms around his neck. Our chests are stuck rising and falling at the same time. "That," he says, "was better than my dreams." I smile and bury my face into his neck. "It was better than I thought." I don't tell him that he's the best I've ever had. I don't have to because I'm sure he can feel it.

He picks me up, and we shower together, but our hands tease us, and by the time I step out of the shower, he bends me over and fucks me so hard from behind, I will definitely be feeling him tomorrow. We collapse on the bed, and I fall asleep in his arms, and it's my alarm the next day that wakes us. I groan as my hand comes out to shut it off. "What time is it?" he asks from beside me, and I feel his cock right between my ass cheeks.

"Time for you to open another condom and fuck me awake," I mumble out, and three seconds later, he is sliding into me softly. He fucks me delicately now. He fucks me, taking his time. He fucks me until I beg him to fuck me harder. He fucks me until I'm so strung up I'm ready to pull out his hair.

He slaps my ass when we both come, me three times more than him. "I'll start the coffee," he says, and I try to raise my hand, but I can't.

"I think you are going to have to roll me out of bed," I say, my head still on the pillow.

"Or you can call in sick, and we can do that all day long," he says, walking out of my room. I wait until I smell the coffee before I roll myself out of bed. I can still feel him in me. He was not lying with the whole challenge accepted. I grab a robe and walk into the kitchen, seeing him making two cups of coffee.

"What do you eat for breakfast?" he asks, and I shake my head.

"I usually grab something on the way to work," I tell him, sitting on the stool and wincing. He hands me his cup, and the sinking feeling comes over me. He must sense it as he looks at me.

"What did you just think right now?" he asks, and I shake my head and bring the cup to my lips. "Evelyn," he says my name, and I look at him. "We said no lying."

I glare at him. "You can't use that on me right now."

"I'm waiting," he says, looking at me.

"You're married," I say, and I want to vomit. I put my hand to my stomach. "Like you are going to leave here and go home to your wife."

"My wife fucks her trainer in my house," he tells me, and I look at him, shocked. "In the basement, actually." He looks at me. "So I am going to go home to my son."

"I don't know if I can do this," I tell him the truth, my voice going soft. "I don't know if I can be with someone who is married regardless." He walks around now and turns me on the stool. "This sucks."

"You have no idea how much this sucks," he says. "I've never been happy to come home." I look up at him. "For the past four years, I looked forward to leaving and going on the road so I would be away from her. I would miss my son, but I would be free."

"And now?" I ask.

"Now, I fucking hate it because you're here, and I'm not here with you." His voice goes low. "I don't know how this is going to go. I don't know anything at this point."

"You aren't the only one," I tell him. "In my heart, I know that you aren't going home to her, but in reality, you still are. You have breakfast with her and then make plans for dinner. You live with her." The thought makes the coffee in my stomach roil.

"That's where you're wrong. I have breakfast with Jaxon, and I have dinner either with him or by myself," he says, and my heart hurts for him, living in a house like you're a stranger.

"I don't know what the right answer is," I tell him, and he bends to kiss my lips, and I have to live in the moment.

"I don't know either," he says, pushing my hair behind my ears. "But I do know one thing for sure."

"What's that?" I ask, drowning in his blue eyes. His lips are still wet from my kiss. I lift my hand to touch him. To make sure he's real. To make sure it's not just another dream. My finger touches his lips, and he kisses it, and then he bends down to kiss me softly again. I wonder if he feels the same. I wonder if he needs to touch me just to make sure that this isn't his dream, either.

I don't know what he's going to say, but I do know that when he says them, it leaves me speechless and breathless, and it just makes everything a bit more complicated because just like him, I feel the same emotions. Just like him, I'm torn; just like him, I don't have the answers. "I can't let you go."

NINETEEN

MANNING

I SLAM THE door behind me when I walk into the house two hours later. "Well, look at who decided to show up." I hear and look up the winding staircase to see Murielle standing there in her workout clothes. Ignoring her, I walk up the stairs and go to my bedroom. "Manning." She calls out for me, and I want to vomit.

"What?" I say, looking over my shoulder.

"I was talking to you," she says, walking toward me. I don't want her to get too close in case I smell like Evelyn, and she picks up on it. Not that I give a shit. But I don't want to bring this shit to Evelyn, not when I just got her back.

"What do you want, Murielle?" I ask. She stops, and I breathe out a sigh of relief.

"Where did you sleep last night?" she asks. "I know that you guys got back last night."

"What do you need from me?" I ask.

"I need you to answer me." She glares at me.

"I'll be home by five to take care of Jaxon." I ignore the question. "So you can go get that itch checked out." I turn to walk away. "If it helps, one of the rookies caught it last year, and all he had to do was take four pills."

"You are such an asshole," she tells me, and I nod.

"Yet you refuse to let me fucking go!" I shout, and she looks around to make sure the cleaning lady isn't buzzing around. "You're kidding, right? You fuck your trainer in the basement, and you think she doesn't know?"

"Well, she signed an NDA." She folds her arms over her chest. "So the joke's on her if she tries to sell the story."

"I won't sue her." I walk now to my room. "I might actually help her win her case. Bye, Murielle," I say, shutting the door behind me and locking it.

I undress, throwing my shit in the wash and then take a shower. Grabbing my track pants and jacket, I make my way over to the rink to work out. I walk in and see that most of the rookies are coming off the ice. Today was an optional skate, so the "old" guys usually just work out in the gym.

When I toss my keys and wallet on my shelf in the locker room, I grab my phone when it beeps. I see it's from Peter, my financial advisor, and only when I open it do I remember that I put Evelyn's number under there. I smile when I read what she wrote.

Peter: Remember that challenge you accepted? Well, I just had to pretend that I went hard at the gym last night.

I laugh at her, smiling as I answer.

Me: If you want, I can massage you tonight.

Peter: If it's the massage I'm thinking of, that isn't going to help anything. I literally groaned when I got up.

The smile on my face is permanent, and when I walk into the gym, I'm not surprised to see Ralph and Miller both on the bikes. They look over at me, and Miller stops pedaling right away. He looks around, and when he sees it's just the three of us, he points at me.

"You had sex." He looks at Ralph, who stops pedaling to take a drink of water. "And he did it all night long."

"What?" I ask, shocked, and I walk to the door of the gym and lock it in case someone tries to come in while we are talking. "I don't know what you're talking about." I don't make eye contact with him as my phone buzzes in my hand, and I look down, seeing it's Evelyn.

"I'm talking about the circles under your eyes." Miller points at me. "It means you didn't sleep."

"This could be true," Ralph agrees with him, and I roll my eyes.

"And you didn't come in dragging your ass, so . . ." He shrugs. "That means you're happy you stayed up all night."

"That is definitely true. Remember last week when Ariella kept us up all night teething? I was not a nice person the next day. I definitely didn't smile." Ralph looks over at Miller, who nods his head. "Coach sent me home five minutes into practice."

"He did," I agree with them, and then I look down,

and I look up. "I was with Evelyn last night." They both look at each other and then back at me. "The redhead."

"The hot chick from the club," Miller says, and I'm about to throat punch him when Ralph puts up his hand to stop me.

"What did we talk about?" He looks at Miller. "How do you feel when someone says they love Layla's ass?" Miller, in turn, glares at him. "Exactly," he tells him, then turns to look at me. "How the fuck did you find her?"

"Um." I think about how to word this. "I found her last week. She was with Jaxon."

"Your son?" Miller asks, and then Ralph gasps, and Miller's eyes go wide. "Oh my fucking god, you banged a hockey mom." He doesn't even give me a chance to answer before he gets off his bike. "Dude, a fucking hockey mom?" His voice goes high, and Ralph shushes him. "A hockey mom?" he whispers. "How big is the father?" he asks with his hands on his hips. "I mean, you're a monster, so I think you can probably take him unless the guy is like a sumo wrestler or a cop." He puts his hands to his mouth. "I saw a *Dateline* episode with Layla the other day. The cop killed the ex-wife's lover, and they didn't know for twenty-seven years."

"Does he come with an off button when he gets like this?" Ralph looks at me and asks, and I shrug. "Miller, can you fucking relax and let him talk?"

"Thank you," I say to both of them. "She's the aunt of Jaxon's best friend."

"Oh my god," Ralph now says, laughing. "What are the fucking odds?"

"Slim to none," Miller says.

"Yeah, well, it went from amazing to see her to miserable when Murielle showed up and was all over me," I tell them, and Ralph's and Miller's face both show disgust.

"That's why you were dragging your ass last week," Ralph says, and I nod.

"Jesus, I thought someone killed your dog," Miller says, and I laugh.

"I don't have a dog," I tell him. "Anyway, she sent me away, and yesterday when we got back home, I just went to her."

"Nice." Miller smiles and folds his arms over his chest. "Went to get your woman."

"Yeah, whatever," I say. "But I'm married, guys."

"I mean, on paper," Ralph says.

"What would you do if the roles were reversed?" Miller says, looking at Ralph. "If Candace was married to an asshole and went home to him every night."

"Yeah, I don't know about that," Ralph agrees. "Did you talk to her?"

"I did a bit this morning, and then she had to go, so I'm going to talk to her tonight." I look down and then look up. "I've never felt this connection before. I've never wanted to even take that step with anyone. It was Jaxon and me, and in two years, I was going to force Murielle to divorce me. I had a plan, but . . ."

"Sometimes plans change," Ralph says. "Look at me. I had Ari, and my main goal was to be her dad." He smiles so big. "And then Candace fell into my lap."

"Same," Miller says, and I laugh at him now.

"Dude, Layla fought you for four years. She hated your guts." I point at him. The two of them, well actually, it was just her that hated him. He was in love with her, and he wasn't quiet about it.

"Hate is a strong word," he says, and now he smiles the same smile as Ralph did. I have to wonder if I will ever get to smile like that. "But in the end, I wore her down."

"I have never felt this way before," I tell them. "This fucking pull toward one person." I shake my head. "I just never had it before, so it's foreign to me. I know I love my son. There is no mistaking that. I would die for him. But with Evelyn, I want to make her happy. I want her to smile at me all the time. I just can't explain it."

"Falling in love," Ralph says. "It's the best fucking feeling in the world."

"Waking up next to her," I say, and I can't even hide my smile. "I had this fucking feeling as though I've been doing it my whole life. Like this is where I'm supposed to be. All that was missing was Jaxon."

"Listen, man," Miller says. "There is nothing more I want for you than for you to be happy." I look at him. "But fucking over Murielle is going to make your fucking life hell. Like what is under hell."

"Burning hell," Ralph says. "I agree with Miller, and I can't believe I'm saying this, but if this is how you feel, then I say go for it, but you have to tell Evelyn what she is up against."

"I told her," I tell them, and now they look at me

shocked. "Everything."

"Everything?" They both repeat at the same time.

"Everything, right down to the trainer fucking Murielle in my basement."

"She's it," Ralph says. "She is it for you."

I don't tell him he's right because I'm afraid to admit that. "I don't know," I say, playing it off, and now I look at Miller.

"How many times do the puck bunnies throw themselves at you?" he asks, and I don't answer. He knows because he sees it. It's about twenty each time we land in a new city. They find our hotel, and they wait for us and attack once we get back. "How many times were you tempted to take one up on their offer?" I glare at him. "But one look at Evelyn."

"She deserves more than I have to give her." I admit my biggest fear to them. "She deserves someone who will take her out and wine and dine her, not someone who will keep her a fucking dirty secret."

"I think you need to leave that up to her," Ralph says. "Don't throw her away because of your fears. Lay it out for her and let her make the decision."

I nod. Someone knocks on the door, and I get up to unlock it. "Sorry about that. It got stuck." I pretend, and the rookie nods his head at me.

Miller and Ralph slap me on the shoulder and walk out of the gym, leaving me alone with my thoughts. I get on the bike and ride for two hours, my mind going nuts. A plan comes to me, and I text the only person I know who can help me with this.

Becca: Need your help. Call me.

I get home at the same time that Jaxon gets off the bus. He runs to me, and I swing him in my arms. "Hey there, buddy," I say, kissing his neck. "I missed you." I do his homework with him after we eat, and then I tuck him into bed, and when I walk out of his room, Murielle walks through the front door.

I grab my phone and keys. "He just went down. Call me if he needs me."

"Where are you going?" she asks.

"Meeting with Becca," I say, and she just nods as I walk out.

TWENTY

EVELYN

"Hey, IF YOU don't need anything else, I'm going to head out," my personal assistant, Chantal, says. I look up at her from the paper that I'm reading. She has been working with my father for the past year, and he handed her off to me, and I have to say I don't know how I would do it without her. "Do you have big plans this weekend?"

I smile at her. "Not that I know of. I have a lot of files to catch up on," I say, and it's not exactly a lie.

"Well, all work and no play makes Jack a dull boy," she says, laughing. "My grandmother always tells me that."

I laugh now. "I have never heard that. But I will keep that in mind. Have a great weekend, Chantal."

She nods at me and takes off. My computer beeps with an email alert, and I see it's from Dex. I roll my eyes and open the email.

From: Dex Lennon

To: Evelyn

Subject: Checking in.

Wondering how you are. Thought I'd reach out. Give me a call.

Dex

I delete the message without thinking twice, and then my phone beeps, and I look down, seeing a text message from Manning.

Manning: I miss you.

Three words. Three words and my face lights up like a Christmas tree. Three words and my stomach gets little butterflies. I'm looking down at the message, and my phone rings in my hand, and I see it's Dex. I think about sending it to voice mail or even blocking his number, but something else gets me.

"Hello," I say, putting the phone to my ear and turning in my chair.

"Evelyn." He says my name, and it does nothing to me. I don't want to smile; I don't want to sigh. It does nothing to me. "I didn't think you would answer."

"Is that why you called?" I ask, putting my head back.

"No," he says, and his voice goes low. "I'm just surprised. I've been calling you for the last two weeks."

"I've been busy," I say curtly. "What do you want?"

"I . . . I miss you," he says, and unlike the feelings I felt when Manning just texted me those three words, with him, I don't feel anything. I've known Manning less than a month, and I already feel more for him than I think I ever felt for Dex.

"What do you miss?" I ask, wondering if maybe he's

going to say something to make me remember why I fell for him.

"I miss us," he says. "I miss going home and having you there."

"Do you miss me before or after you fuck Ally and Joshua?" I ask, my voice going low.

"I can explain," he says, and I roll my eyes.

"There is really not anything that you can say that will explain that, Dex," I tell him. "It's not like you wake up one day and decide to become a vegetarian. You're bisexual, but instead of having a conversation with me—"

"You were never supposed to find out," he says. "We should have been more careful."

"Well, I think you guys were as careful as thieves in the night since I only found out now." I wait to see if the hurt is going to come, and I'm shocked when it doesn't. I feel nothing for him. I don't even feel hurt because he did it. My mind flies to Manning. When I walked away from him, it hurt me harder and deeper than it did with Dex.

At this moment, I know that Dex was never the one. "Dex," I say, "I'm going to be honest with you. I think we were together because it was the right thing to do. We were just there for each other, and it just made sense, but if we are honest, we didn't fall head over heels in love with each other. Fuck, I think the only reason you miss me right now is that you hate change. You hate going home by yourself."

"But I love you," he says, and I shake my head.

"You think you love me. But if you loved me, you

would never think about touching another person. I have to go, Dex. I hope you find that person."

I hang up, and my eyes stare at the phone in my hand.

Tim comes in. "Hey, I'm out." I turn now, seeing his head peeking in the room.

"What are you wearing?" I ask, and I see the Dallas jersey.

"I'm wearing the Dallas jersey," he says, pointing at his chest. He turns, and I see that it has Manning's last name on it. "It's Jaxon's dad's jersey." I try not to smile when I think of him.

He left my bed this morning before the sun came up. Ever since he showed up at my house two days ago, I've fallen asleep in his arms. It still bothers me that he's technically married, but I try not to harp too much on it. It's always there in the back of my head, though, like the devil sitting on your shoulder, letting you know how fucked up it is. "Nico, the owner of the team, is my client, and he gave me tickets to his box tonight."

"That is a good thing?" I ask, not sure, and he just looks at me with his mouth open.

"Nico, the owner of the team. He's huge. I mean, not huge, but he's getting there. He is the youngest owner of a team there has ever been. He's even younger than you." He points at me and winks when I flip him the bird. "Anyway, watch the game. You might see me on television."

"Or," I say, putting my elbows on my desk and leaning forward on them. "You can let me know if I missed you." He laughs and walks out of my office at the exact time my phone rings. I look down, seeing the man who has me in knots. Also, the man who has made me look like I went hardcore at the gym. When I came to work yesterday, I swear I felt like he was still in me. It took me time to set to a standing position and even a sitting one. I blamed it on leg day, but if only they knew. "Well, hello there, you," I say, smiling.

"Hey, baby," he says, his voice soft and all the doubts I've had before are out the window. Just the sound of his voice and my chest fills with so many emotions. "Are you free to talk?"

"I am," I say, leaning back in my chair, and I hear a horn honk. "Are you in the car?"

"Yeah, I'm on the way to the arena," he says. "We play Carolina tonight."

"I know," I tell him. "My brother just left here wearing your jersey. He is going to be in a box somewhere."

"You should have come with him," he tells me, laughing.

"I'm going to just say it right now. I don't really get hockey. I know of it. I lived in Chicago where they won the cup a couple of times," I tell him.

"A couple of times." He laughs. "They won three cups in ten years."

"I'm assuming that's good?" I joke with him. "How was your day?"

"Good. I had practice this morning, then went home, napped, and now I'm on my way to the rink. We leave Monday for four days," he tells me. "Back Friday." I try not to think about how this is all going to work. It's the first time I've dated someone since before Dex and I don't know the do's and don't's right now. "Just got to work. I'll call you after."

"Good luck. Score a hat trick," I tell him, and he laughs. "I mean, if you can."

"I'll try, Evelyn," he says and disconnects. I get up now, closing everything down and heading home.

I slip out of my jeans and take a quick shower, then order Chinese food. I'm watching *Unsolved Mysteries* when I hear a soft knock on the door. Looking at my phone, I see it's almost eleven.

Unlocking the door, I'm surprised to see Manning standing there, dressed in a blue suit this time, holding on to a brown takeout bag. "How do you just open the door without asking who it is?" He asks, walking in the door and wrapping his arm around my waist and bending down to kiss me. He smells like he just got out of the shower. "I could have been anyone."

"What are you doing here?" I ask him, my heart suddenly speeding up. He picks me up to walk into the house and close the door behind him with his foot. "I didn't think I would see you." "There is nowhere else I want to be," he says softly, and I wrap my arms around his neck now. "I missed you."

"I missed you, too," I tell him the truth. He puts me down now, and I walk, holding his hand to the kitchen. "Did you bring food?" I ask him, and he nods his head. "Sit down," I tell him, taking the bag. "I'll prepare it for you." I grab the bag from him and put it on the counter, going over to the plates. "What are you doing?" I ask him when he just stands there. "Sit," I tell him, and he shrugs off his jacket, and he looks at me weird. "What is going on with you?"

"It's just." He starts to say, sitting down on one of the stools and looks at me. "I usually do everything myself."

I look at him and open the bags, not sure I can say anything right now. "Did you get your hat trick?" I ask, taking out the black container and seeing a prepared meal.

"I did not," he says, laughing, and I open the fridge and get him a bottle of water, bringing it to him, thinking he must be thirsty. I hand it to him, and he grabs my hand and pulls me to him. "Hi," he whispers, his hand wrapping around my waist. I look up at him, and he bends down to close the distance, and our lips meet. "Best thing after a game," he says to me, and his phone starts ringing. I kiss him on his lips one more time before walking back over to do a plate for him.

"Did you win?" I ask, handing him his plate and going to get cutlery.

"We did," he says, and I clap my hands together, making him laugh, and I hand him a fork and knife.

"I brought you one, too," he says, pointing at the bag that still has the meal in it. "Thought we could eat together."

"I had Chinese food," I tell him. "I didn't even know you were coming if you told me." I get up, getting my own bottle of water, and then going to sit next to him. "Tell me." I look at him, seeing the back of his hair still wet. My hand comes out automatically, and I touch it.

"What do you do after a game usually?"

"It's a bit nuts," he says. "Everyone usually does it differently. The rookies usually hit up a restaurant together. The 'old ones' usually just go home. Me," he says, cutting a piece of chicken. "I usually eat and then watch television until about two. Let the adrenaline leave my body."

"Well, I'm glad you came," I say, and then he looks at me.

"Let's play twenty-one questions," he says to me, and I just look at him, "until I finish eating and then we are going to go on the couch and make out."

I laugh now. "Is that so?"

"Bed or couch? Either way, one of us is getting naked soon." He chews. "So how did you end up in Chicago?"

I lean back on the stool and watch him eat. "I went to school, and then I just fell in love with it." I take a sip of water. "How did you end up in Dallas?"

"They were the ones that paid me the most," he says, laughing. "Are you happy you are back home?"

I nod my head. "I am. I didn't know how it would be coming back and taking over for my father. It worked out a lot better than I thought it would. But it isn't that bad." He looks at me.

"I'm sure he's happy you are here," he says, and I look at him. "I heard about you." My head goes to the side. "Your father takes care of my finances," he tells me, and I look at him with my mouth hanging down. "That's how I got your number. It was in the email."

"Tim has to take you as a client," I tell him. "I don't

even know how I'm going to tell them. I might have to bring my mother in or Veronica. Are you close to your parents?"

He nods. "I am but not as close as I would like to be. But I'm working on it." He chews a piece of chicken. "Murielle doesn't really like when they come down, so they don't." I swallow down the lump in my throat. "It was a rough time for a bit there. I didn't know how to tell them that she didn't like having people in her house. I felt like I was choosing her over them, and it killed me."

"Did you talk to her about it?" I ask, not knowing what to say. I don't know how I would feel if Dex had told me that my parents were not allowed over. "It put you in a very difficult position."

"It did. I was kind of left out of certain things and family functions because they didn't know if I would go or not, and then they didn't want to put additional pressure on me." He looks down. "My only regret is Jaxon not knowing them as well as he should. But we are working that out now. I bring him to see them when I can, and we FaceTime my mother once a week."

"She must love it." I smile at him when he puts his fork and knife on the plate.

"She does. He tells her all about his week." He brings the water to his mouth. "How long were you with your ex for?"

"We met while I was in college. The four of us always hung around with each other. He was roommates with Joshua." I swallow now. "Close to ten years. He called me today," I say, and I'm shocked that I'm sharing it with him. "It was weird talking with him, but I think it was a good time because it made me see that we weren't the ones for each other." I look at him. "I think in the end we stayed because it was easy. What about you?" I ask, and unlike with Dex, I get a burning sensation in my stomach when I ask him this question. I mean, it's stupid because they have a child together.

"About the same," he says. "It would be less if she would just give me the divorce." I look down.

"Where does she think you are?" I ask, and he shrugs.

"I don't know, don't care. I'll be home when Jaxon wakes up, and that is all that she needs to know."

"But," I start to say, and he pushes away from the table. "She doesn't come into this," he says to me. "This." He points at him and then at me. "It's mine. It's the only thing I have that is mine and mine alone." I look down, and he puts his finger under my chin, raising it so I see him. "It's you. It's only you." He bends his head, and he kisses me. I swallow back down the dread that I have there. That I'm sinking deeper and deeper with him, and I'm not sure if I'm going to be able to survive this.

TWENTY-ONE

Manning

"I HATE LEAVING you," I tell Evelyn while she walks me to the door. I spent the night with her in my arms. She stood with me until I was ready to go to bed. She tilts her head back, and I push her hair away from her face as she stands there in her robe naked underneath it. "I'll call you later."

"Okay," she says, giving me one last kiss.

"Lock up," I say and walk out, and she stands there looking at me as I drive away right when the sun comes up. I fucking hate this. I hate that I had to leave her.

I take my phone out and send Becca a text.

Me: Did you hire him?

I don't know if she is going to answer me right away, so I put my phone down. It rings right away. "Yes," she says, and I hear her panting. Becca has been one of the best people to have in my corner. She came to me about five years ago, and if it weren't for her, I wouldn't be as successful. She guided me in the right direction, and I would do anything for her.

"Why are you panting?" I ask and see that it's almost five a.m.

"I work out from four thirty to six, seven days a week," she says, and I shake my head. "This is what I have to do in order to eat cake, chocolate, and carbs. The question is, what are you doing up?"

"I'm on my way home," I say. Two days ago, I went to her house and told her about Evelyn. She didn't like it. Only because she didn't want Murielle to hold it over my head. So she set a plan in motion, and hopefully, I'll be free in the next month.

"Where does Cruella think you are?" she asks. She gave Murielle that nickname three years ago when she tried to get Becca fired.

"No idea. I didn't see her at the game. I'm going home now. I'll be there for Jaxon, and then I have no idea."

"Well, I'll see you tonight," she tells me, and I don't say anything. "You forgot, didn't you?"

"What are you talking about?" I say.

"There is an ugly sweater party tonight. They do it every year before Thanksgiving. Nico invited me," she says, and I suddenly remember. "He knows I am going to have the up-and-coming rookie sign with me, so he's wooing me," she pants out. "Anyway, I'll see you to-night."

She hangs up, and I get out of the car when I get home and walk in, carrying my jacket. I walk to my bedroom and slip into the shower. I slip on shorts and a T-shirt and get into bed, falling asleep until Jaxon wakes up at eight thirty.

He slips into bed with me, and I cuddle him while he watches television. He lets me sleep an extra hour before he complains he's hungry. I get up, walking down to the kitchen to start the coffee and make him breakfast. I'm cleaning up the mess when Murielle walks into the kitchen, kissing Jaxon on the head.

"Look who decided to come home," she says, and I look over to see if Jaxon heard her. He is oblivious as he plays a game on the iPad that I told him he could play. "You're going out often these days." She brings the cup of coffee to her mouth, and I don't even bother answering her. "What time should I be ready?"

"For?" I dry my hands and shut the dishwasher.

"The ugly sweater thing. I have yours upstairs in my room," she tells me.

"Can't you take your car?" I ask, and she just looks at me.

"It's a team function, so the press might be there. What is it going to look like if we don't show up together?" I roll my eyes at her. "Jaxon, do you want me to get Elizabeth to come and watch you tonight?" He looks up and nods.

"Dad, are we still having a guys' day tomorrow?" he asks, and I nod. I grab a bottle of water and walk to the living room, turning on the television. I'm itching to call Evelyn, but I wonder if she's up already. I wonder what she's going to do today. I grab my phone and check the highlights of last night's game. When I hear Jaxon walk up the stairs, I follow him to my room. Locking the door behind me, I call Evelyn.

"Hey," she answers, and she sounds like she is out shopping.

"Are you out?" I ask her.

"I'm out with my mom. She wanted to go have lunch, and then we decided to get manis and pedis. How are you?"

"I'm good. Tired but good. We have Jaxon's game at one," I say. "I have a team function tonight."

"Okay," she says, her voice getting soft, and I wish she was coming with me. I wish that I was walking into the party with her. "Talk to you later," she says and hangs up. I get up when I hear a knock on the door and see it's Murielle, and she hands me the sweater.

"What the fuck is this?" I say, looking down at what looks like a moose head.

"It's a moose head." She points at it. "You put the head in the front and the ass in the back." She turns and walks away. "I have the glam squad coming at one."

"It's a small get-together," I say. "Just the team's members."

"There are going to be pictures taken, and I need to look my best," she says, walking away.

"Then I suggest you get a bag and put it on your head," I mumble and close the door.

Jaxon's hockey game is uneventful, and he runs into the house to take a shower. I do the same, and I'm slipping on my shirt when I hear Murielle yell my name. I grab the moose head and walk out, stopping when I see her. "What the fuck are you wearing?" I ask, and she turns around as though I said that in a good way; she wears black nylons and thigh-high boots. "You don't think a leather skirt is extreme?"

"I think I look good," she says, and I shake my head, walking down the stairs. I kiss Jaxon after he helps me put the head and ass on.

"I want to take the Porsche," Murielle says of the two-seater car I don't really take anywhere.

"Get in the BMW," I say, "unless you want to drive yourself." I smile at her. She glares at me but gets into the car, and her smell makes me ill. I pull out and make my way to Nico's house. The whole time, she is on her phone.

"Why didn't you park in the driveway?" she huffs when we have to walk far. "These boots are not for walk-ing."

"Your mouth should not be for talking," I say, and then the front door opens.

"Welcome," someone tells us. "Please come in. The party is right down there."

She grabs my hand as we walk in, and I shake it loose as soon as I see Nico to hold it out and shake his. He is wearing a green sweater with Christmas trees and snow-flakes all over it with stay cool written in white. "There he is, the captain." I smirk at him as he takes my hand. He is the youngest owner in the whole league, and he isn't just an owner. He is hands-on. He is there when trades are decided, he is there when we lose, and he is there when we win. If anyone deserves the cup to come to him, it's Nico. "Is that a moose?" he asks of my sweater, and I nod. "There she is, the woman behind the man," he says, and Murielle's whole face lights up. I have to refrain from rolling my eyes. "You look fantastic. Have you been working out?" She nods at him.

"Oh, her trainer rides her hard," I say, chuckling at my inside joke. I grab a water bottle from the passing waiter.

"Hello, everyone," I say, looking over and seeing Becca walk in. She is wearing black jeans and a shirt that has lights all lit up on it.

"Who invited her?" I hear Murielle from beside me, and I see Nico side-eye her and then look at me.

"I did," he says. "Becca," he says, taking her hand. "So glad you could make it."

"I have to say, Nico," she says, grabbing a glass of wine from a passing waiter, "there is nothing quite like when you want something from me." She takes a sip of her wine. "It is legit the best feeling in the world." She smiles and looks around. "Well, that and when I make you pay through the ass. It's right up there."

Nico throws his head back, and he laughs at her. "If I ever get married," he says, "I'm going to want you to negotiate the contract."

"Deal," she says to him, smiling. "Hey, Manning," she says to me, and I just nod.

"Excuse me," Nico says. "I see some of the guys arriving."

"I'm here also," Murielle says when Nico walks away.

"I'm fully aware," Becca says to her. "I must have missed the memo. I thought it was an ugly sweater costume and not an 80s drag party.”

"You're such a fucking bitch, Becca," Murielle says and looks at me. "I'm going to the bar." She comes close to me for a kiss, and I bring the water bottle to my mouth. She looks around to make sure that no one saw before she walks off.

"Please tell me he has something," I ask Becca, and she looks at me.

"He's working on it," she says. "I told you it would be done. It's been two days."

I look at her, drinking my water as Miller gets there with Layla, both of them wearing beer pong sweaters with glasses pinned on them. Ralph gets there with Candace by his side. She wears a sweater with an elf, and he wears a sweater as Santa.

"We should get a picture," Candace says, and I shake my head. "Do it for the Gram, Manning."

"No," I say, and she looks at me. "Fine, but one picture."

She claps her hands, and I stand in the middle with the guys beside me. I see Murielle coming our way with Nico behind her. "That is a nice one," she says, and then Nico looks at us.

"Couples," he says, and Murielle is the only one happy about it. "Okay, let's get the captain first."

"Why don't we take a group shot?" I tell him and look at the guys who just stare at me.

"Yeah, that sounds like a good idea," Miller says. "We should get all the guys over here and take it." He looks at Ralph. "Let's go round up the guys."

Murielle comes to me and wraps her arms around my waist, and I'm about to tell her to get off me when her foot twists in some sort of way, and I wrap an arm around her to stop her from falling on me. "That looks great," Nico says and takes the picture.

188

TWENTY-TWO

Evelyn

"THIS IS LOVELY," my mother says from in front of me as we have dinner together. "Spending the whole day with you and now dinner and a movie."

I smile at her. For the whole day, we walked around the shopping mall, got manicures and pedicures, then decided to see the new romantic comedy and then get dinner. "I will admit," I say, "that this is one of the things I missed about being home." I grab my glass of wine as she laughs.

"One of the things?" She tilts her head, just looking at me. "Well, as much as I hate why you had to come home." My mother was the one who flew out and helped me pack up and move. She didn't say anything mean or that she knew it was coming. She just did what was best for me. "I'm happy you are here."

I look down at my phone that hasn't buzzed since I spoke to him, and it concerns me how much I'm bothered by it. "So tell me what's on your mind." I look up at her. "Something is going on. You've been quiet of sorts."

I think about how to answer this question because the last thing I want is for my mother or anyone in my family to be disappointed in me. "I met someone," I say, my heart beating in my chest at the same time as my stomach falls.

Her eyes go wide, and the smile fills her face. "I had a feeling it had to do with a man. Is it the one who called you before?"

I look at her, and my mouth opens. "You eavesdropped." I tried really hard to lower my voice as much as I could, and I thought with the jets of the water and the vibration of the chair, she wouldn't be able to hear me well.

"You were right next to me." She pushes her hair over her shoulder. "How was I not supposed to hear?" She rolls her eyes, and I laugh. "Now tell me all about him. Where did you meet him?"

"I met him at the bachelorette party," I say, and I leave out the fact that I had a one-night stand. "Then I saw him again." I stop talking. "I ran into him at a restaurant."

She puts her hands together. "Do you like him?"

I swallow and have to take a sip of my water before I answer this. "I do," I say, my palms getting sweaty. "A lot. More than I should."

"Oh, don't say that." She swats her hand in the air. "I knew five minutes after meeting your father that he was the one for me. From the minute I met him at that house party from across the room, I knew I had to meet him."

"We had a connection, that is for sure," I say, "but it's a bit complicated on his end." That's all I will say about it because I get a sick feeling in my stomach when I think about it.

"What does that mean? Complicated on his end?" she asks, and I know she would have.

"He is just going through things with . . ." I stop talking, trying to come up with the words. "I like him, Mom," I say, my voice going low. "Like he comes over, and I wait for him. I am anxiously waiting for him. I want to talk to him all the time."

"That is usually a good thing," she tells me.

"I feel like I've known him forever," I finally say. "And it's so dumb because I haven't. But I don't know how to explain it."

"He settles you," she tells me, and I tilt my head. "Like pieces to a puzzle, Evelyn. You keep searching for that piece of the puzzle that is missing. The piece that makes it complete." I take the last sip of my wine. "Why does it sound like you're fighting this?" I want to tell her it's because I know deep down I can't accept the fact he's married. Deep down, it kills me that he goes home to her. Even if he tells me that she doesn't come between us, it's always in the back of my mind.

"I'm just scared," I say, and she smiles now, looking at me.

"Love is scary, Evelyn. It's easy when it comes, but it's scary when you fight for it." She takes the last sip of her water, and the waiter comes over and brings us the dessert menu.

My mother doesn't bring it up again. She knows me and knows that I have to play it out in my head. When I drop her off at home, she begs me to come over tomorrow for lunch and will not take no for an answer.

I walk into my house after nine with my hands full of bags. Things I really don't need but bought anyway. I take my phone with me when I unload everything, and when I slip into the bath, I'm on edge, and I have no idea why. None whatsoever.

I slip on my robe and walk to the couch, turning on the television. Grabbing the throw blanket, I lie down. I put the phone on the table in front of me, and I don't know when I drift off to sleep, but I wake up and see it's after three in the morning. I get up, seeing that he texted me.

Manning: Hey, something came up. I won't be able to make it tonight. I'll call you in the morning.

I don't bother answering it. Instead, I walk to my bed and slip into it and fall asleep. I get up angry, and I hate it. I walk to the coffee maker and start it, turning on the television while I do it. The movie from last night is still playing.

Grabbing my phone, I sit on the couch and open my Facebook. Using my thumb to scroll through my news-feed, I see nothing good. I open Instagram, and the picture hits me right away. I see it's from the Dallas Oilers. I started following them two days ago.

My hand shakes when I see Manning in some ridiculous sweater with a moose and his wife next to him. My stomach sinks, the sting of tears come now. His wife is wearing a leather skirt, and I use my fingers to zoom in just a bit. Her arms are around his waist as she smiles and his arm around her. The caption is what pushes it over the edge.

The captain and his wife at the team's ugly sweater party last night. A great time had by all.

I unfollow the team and then close the app. I get up and walk to my bedroom. I slip on my blue jeans with a white long-sleeve shirt. After grabbing a thick knitted gray sweater and my purse, I leave my house.

I look at the time and see that it's just after eight o'clock in the morning. I also know that I rushed out of my house in case he just showed up this morning because I am not ready to face him. I'm not ready to see him. So I go to the bakery that I have been eyeing for the past two weeks. I pick up two boxes of sweets, and I head over to my parents' house. I call my mother on the way there to make sure she is up.

"Hello," she says, and I'm thankful she sounds awake.

"Hey there. I'm on my way over to help with lunch," I lie to her. "I got some goodies."

"Wow, you are up early," she says, laughing. "See you soon." I disconnect, and a ping shows me that I have a text. I pick it up and see it's from Manning.

Manning: Morning. I'm so sorry about last night. I missed waking with you in my arms.

I throw the phone on the seat next to me, not bothering to answer. I know that I'm going to have to face the music, but I'm going to do it when I'm ready and not when he's ready.

I walk into my parents' house and see my mother already dressed as she stirs her pasta sauce. "It smells amazing in here," I say, and she looks over at me.

I put the two boxes of pastries that I bought on the island. "How much stuff did you buy?" She comes over to me to hug me and kisses my cheek.

"You know what you always used to tell me." I walk to get a cup and make a coffee. "Never shop when you're hungry." I walk over to the fridge, grabbing the milk. "You were right."

She throws her head back and laughs. "I told you."

I roll my eyes. "You also used to tell us not to go swimming after eating, or we would get a cramp and die."

She gasps out. "I never said you would die. I said you would get cramps." I laugh, and my father walks into the kitchen.

"I thought I heard your voice," he says, coming over to me and kissing me on the cheeks. "Now this is what I want to see."

"Me in your kitchen at nine a.m. on a Sunday?" I shake my head, and my phone rings from my purse. I walk over to it, taking it out and see that it's Manning. I decline the call as my father turns on the television in the family room adjoined to the kitchen.

I hear the announcer. "The Dallas Oilers had an off night last night," he says and then laughs. "But from the pictures all around social media, it was a fun night." He throws up a picture with the whole team in sweaters. I see Manning in the back of the picture, his face filled with a smile as he stands with his guys. The next picture is of three couples, and there he is in the middle with his wife on his side. Okay, fine, he isn't touching her, and she's standing in front of him. The other two couples have their arms around each other. But the last one is the one that I stumbled upon this morning. "Our captain looks like he is having a great time, don't you think?"

I look down now, blinking away the tears threatening to come out. I walk out of the room, going to the bathroom and closing the door. The phone is ringing in my hand. I shake my head and look down at it.

Manning calling. I press the red decline button and just sit on the toilet. I refuse to look at myself in the mirror, not sure I can even stomach myself right now. I wash my hands, and with my hands wet, I pat my cheeks and then dab them dry.

I'm walking out of the bathroom when my phone pings.

Manning: Hey, just tried to call you a couple of times. Wanted to hear your voice.

I delete the text and walk back into the kitchen, slapping my hands together. "Okay, what can I do to help?" I ask my mother, and she looks at me, not sure what to say. She sees my eyes red and just smiles at me when I shake my head.

"Well, how about we make the meatballs?" She walks over to the fridge, and I take off my sweater and ignore the ping of my phone again from my back pocket. I take it out and put it on vibrate, but the last thing I see is the text that is across the screen.

Manning: I miss you.

TWENTY-THREE

MANNING

ME: I MISS you.

I delete the text and put the phone in the pocket of my shorts while I flip the pancake for Jaxon. Last night was a clusterfuck of clusterfucks, and I am still pissed about it. "Get the syrup." I look over at Jaxon while Murielle walks into the kitchen.

Her hair is piled on her head, and her "glam makeup" is still on. She is still wearing last night's clothes on top of that. Her eyes look like raccoons. "I need coffee." She walks and stops beside me, reeking of alcohol.

"You need a shower, too," I say, shaking my head.

"I can't believe you left me in your car," she hisses. "I had to crawl up the stairs."

"You're lucky I even drove you home," I say. I should have known that something was up when she took the picture with me and then stumbled on her heels. Little did I know, she was doing shots with two other wives all night long.

When her voice started getting louder and she starting getting touchy-feely, I knew it was too late. "Why are you being such a prude? So what if I drank a bit."

"You drank a bit." I scoff, laughing, placing the plate in front of Jaxon, who is watching us. "Eat up, and then you can go play your Xbox," I tell him, not willing to talk more in front of him.

Murielle lays her head on the island, closing her eyes. "Why is the room still spinning?" Jaxon finishes as fast as he can to get away from her.

He walks over and puts his plate in the dishwasher. "I'm going to go play the game, and we can watch a movie after."

"Sounds good, big man," I tell him and wait for him to leave before I talk to her.

"That is the last time that is going to happen," I say, cutting a piece of egg and then looking at her.

"Oh, please," she says, not moving her head. "It's not that big of a deal. Angela was drunk, too."

"Angela is always drunk," I say. "I'm talking about you hanging all over me."

Her eyes open now. "Is your memory foggy?" I say. "You were hanging onto my neck."

"It's not that big of a deal. You're my husband, after all," she says. "Yet you left me passed out in the BMW."

"I told you we were home," I say. "You groaned, so I figured you were okay."

"I woke up and didn't even know where I was!" she yells.

"That sounds like a you problem and not a me problem," I say, and I get up now, going over to the dishwasher. Pissed that she was drunk, I knew I couldn't just leave Jaxon alone.

I fell asleep on the couch, waiting for her to come in, and when I finally woke up, it was after five in the morning.

"Goddammit, Manning. It was freezing outside." She slaps the counter.

"It's November in Texas." I laugh at her. "There is no freezing."

"Why the fuck are you such an asshole?" she asks, folding her arms over her chest.

"Why are you still a bitch?" I ask, but I don't wait for her to answer me. "Why the fuck won't you just give me a divorce, and we can be amicable?"

She glares at me. "I will never fucking give you a divorce."

"Never say never." I push away from the counter. "I have to go and spend time with my son," I say.

"Fuck you," she mumbles.

"Right back at you," I say. Walking up the steps, I take my phone out and see that Evelyn still hasn't texted me back. I pick up the phone to call her again as I walk into my room and sit on my bed.

"You've reached Evelyn. I can't take your call right now. Leave a message, and I'll get back to you as soon as I can." I smile as I listen to her voice.

I wait for the beep and then speak. "Hey, it's me. Just wanted to hear your voice. Talk to you soon." I hang up and send her another text.

Me: Are you okay?

I get up, going into the cinema room, and sit down to play a couple of games with Jaxon. The whole time, I'm watching my phone, waiting for her to text me. Murielle doesn't come in at all, and when we walk down for lunch, I see that she isn't there.

I pick up my phone and send Evelyn another text.

Me: Getting a bit worried. Hope you are okay.

An uneasy feeling comes over me and the rest of the day goes by at a snail's pace. I feed Jaxon dinner, and only when he's going to bed does Murielle finally come out of her room.

"I have a meeting with Becca," I lie to her. "I'm leaving after I put Jaxon to sleep."

She looks over at me. "You've been having a lot of meetings with Becca lately." I ignore her question and tuck Jaxon into bed. I change into jeans and a shirt.

I call her one more time before I show up, and it still goes to voice mail. My stomach is in my throat, thinking that something happened to her, and I wasn't there for her. I see her car in her driveway, and I breathe out a sigh of relief.

I jog up to her door and ring the bell. My heart speeds up even more when I hear the locks. The smile on my face can't help but come over me when I see her there. "Hey," I say, walking in. I wrap my arm around her waist, and I notice a change in her right away.

"Hi," she says, her hands staying on my arms and not going around my neck. She usually puts her head back so

I can kiss her, but this time she doesn't.

"I've been calling and texting you all day," I say, releasing her.

"Yeah, I saw. I was with my parents at a family lunch," she says, stepping back. And I'm suddenly jealous that she had family time.

"That sounds nice," I say, and the whole room is filled with tension, and I hate it. "What is going on right now?"

"I think we need to talk," she says, and I see her cross her hands together.

"What is going on right here?" I ask, my heart hammering in my chest.

"I can't do this," she tells me, and I see the tears come out of her eyes. "No matter how much I try to think I can, deep down inside me, I can't."

"What are you talking about?" I ask, and I want to hug her. I want to sit down and hold her in my arms.

"You said you had a function. What you didn't tell me was that your picture with your wife would be splashed all around social media today," she says, and I'm so confused.

"What?" I ask her, and the blood drains from my body when she shows me the picture of Murielle and me. The only picture I took with her. I look back up at her, and my heart hurts. "It's not what it looks like," I say, my voice going low.

"That is the whole thing," she tells me. "I hate feeling this way. I hate that I feel this way. I hate that I ignored you all day because I had to process this. I hate that I doubt myself. I hate that I doubt you," she says, using the back of her hand to wipe away another tear. "I just . . ."

"I was making sure she didn't fall," I say. She has to know that at least. "Nothing happened. Nothing. I left her sleeping in the car."

"But it's not just last night," she says. "It's about you going home to her. It's about you sharing a life with her." She looks at me. "Put yourself in my shoes. How would you feel knowing I was going home to someone else? Knowing I share a life with this person and sleep under the same roof as him." My stomach hurts, thinking about it. My stomach sinks just thinking about kissing her good-bye and knowing she would go home to someone else. "Bottom line. You're not divorced. You are still married."

"Evelyn." I say her name in almost a plea, praying she just gives me a little bit more time. I just need more time.

"I won't be the one who makes you chose. I will not be that person." She shakes her head. "I won't ever let you choose between your son and me because the only answer should be your son. Always. So I am going to walk away." My heart literally breaks, the pain coming so fast I have to put my hand to my chest. "Maybe it was never meant to be." I want to yell at her and tell her no, it's meant to be. That this thing between us is strong for a reason. "All day, I kept thinking that there was a reason, but then I couldn't think of one."

"Evelyn." It's the only thing I can say. "Please."

"If you care about me, even just a touch, you will let me be." Her voice goes low. I see her bottom lip tremble, and I can't bear the thought of her hurting. I can't bear the thought that she felt this hurt all day, and she had no one to turn to. She felt this way all day, and I am the one who caused it.

This woman who has done nothing but accept the little that I have to offer and refuses to let me pick a side. She is giving me up so I don't have to fucking choose. "I'm sorry." It's the only thing I can tell her. "I'm sorry that you hurt. That I hurt you even for one second in all this."

I walk to her now, not willing to leave without giving her one last kiss. She doesn't move back, so I put one hand on her cheek. "Evelyn." She shakes her head.

"This sucks," she says. "You're amazing." She looks in my eyes. "Jaxon should know how amazing you are."

The fact that she cares about my son more than herself makes her even more perfect. "This sucks more than you know," I say, and I look into her eyes when I say the next words. "You're perfect, Evelyn." I bend down and kiss her lips softly for the last time. My hands fall from her face, and I walk over to the door, grabbing the handle. My whole heart feels like it's shattered in my chest, like I've been stabbed. I take one more look at her. "This time with you, the little time we did have was everything." I turn and walk out of the house, closing the door behind me. The sound of the door closing echoes in my ears even when I get in my SUV and drive away.

Getting home, I walk in, hearing the television playing from the family room. I don't bother stopping and go straight to my room. The silence doesn't make it easy. My eyes close, and all I can see is Evelyn's face. All I can do is feel her pain. I lie here and say good-bye to the only woman who wanted me for me.

TWENTY-FOUR

Evelyn

FIVE DAYS. IT'S been five days since I've last seen him—one hundred and twenty hours—yet at night, he comes in my dreams so vividly that when I wake, I want to go back to bed. "You are starting to look better," Tim says, coming into my office.

"Yeah," I say. "I'm feeling a bit better." When I came into work on Monday, I was pale as a ghost, so my father sent me home to work. I pretended I had a fever, and I only came back to work on Wednesday because I refused to be stuck in bed. They said I was only allowed back at work when the fever resolved, so Wednesday, I walked in with coffee and doughnuts for everyone, and I went to my office.

"Don't forget you promised Caleb you would be at his game tomorrow," Tim says. I want to crawl into a hole and die. I promised him last Sunday at lunch when I was put on the spot. "It's tomorrow at noon. I have to be there at eleven, but you can come from ten to twelve, so he can see you there."

"Yeah," I say, swallowing down the lump in my throat. It's one thing waking every day and going through the motions, but I'm not sure I'm going to be okay seeing Manning again. Especially now. I want to ask Tim if Dallas is in town playing. Maybe he's on the road, and I'm freaking out for nothing. "I can't wait. Should I buy flowers and stuff like if he scores a goal?"

Tim shakes his head, laughing. "Flowers?"

I throw my hand up in the air. "I don't know. What does one do if they score?"

"You can buy him a slush," he says, and I laugh.

"We can take him out to Chuck E. Cheese," I say, excited now for the first time in the past week.

"Why don't we play it by ear?" he says, shaking his head and walking out.

I spend the whole night on the couch yet again. I'm waiting for my couch to tell me to get my fat ass off it and go do something.

I toss and turn all fucking night long. The looming thoughts of seeing him are in the back of my head where I pushed them. It's where I put everything that has to do with Manning. It's the only thing I can do, or I'd text him and ask him if he's okay. I would text him to tell him I'm sorry for not having more faith in him. I would text him to tell him I made a horrible, horrible mistake and that I want to have anything that I can have of him. But deep down in my heart of hearts, I can't do it. I can't. I kept thinking about how Christmas would be, knowing he's spending Christmas morning with her exchanging gifts. It was just too much, and frankly, it would make me into a person I'm not and don't want to be.

I take a shower and dry my hair. "It's better this way." I give myself a pep talk as I slide my blue jeans on. "It'll be fine. What's the worst that will happen?" I button my jeans, and they fit me just a touch looser than the last time and then slide on the long-sleeved black shirt. "The worst that can happen is that I see him and tell him that I miss him." I slip on my black boots and then grab my green army jacket and matching scarf. "I mean, would it be so bad to see him." I grab a black purse and walk out of the house. "Yes," I say to myself. "Yes, it would."

I park in the parking lot, and I take out my phone, texting my brother that I'm here.

Tim: Upstairs sitting at a table.

It's twenty minutes until he starts playing, so I walk in the same arena that I saw Manning again, and my heart speeds up so fast that I feel like it's going to come out of my chest. I walk to the back stairs and take a quick look around to see if I see him. I walk up the stairs and see tables everywhere. When I spot my brother, I start walking, and then I see who he is sitting with, and I swear I almost fall on my face. *Why?* I think to myself. *Why the fuck is this happening?*

My brother spots me and raises his hand with a smile. Manning turns around and sees me, and I see something flicker in his eyes. I walk over to them. "Hi," I say to Tim.

"Why are you dressed like you're a biker?" he jokes,

looking down at my boots, and I roll my eyes. "Did you come here on a bike?"

"Yeah," I say, joking. "I'm an old lady now, and my man is parking the Harley." I smile and look over at Manning.

"Manning," Tim says. "This smart-ass is my sister, Evelyn. This is Jaxon's dad," Tim says, and I don't know what to do. Manning leans over and holds out his hand, and I just look at it for a second, not sure I should shake his hand. I don't want to touch him, but my head has other ideas. My hand slips into his, and I can feel myself shiver.

"It's nice to meet you," Manning says softly, and I blink away the tears that come with the sound of his voice. "I've heard all about you."

"If Tim said it, I wouldn't believe it too much," I joke with him and slowly let his hand go. I know he doesn't want to let my hand go. He looks so good, but he has circles under his eyes, and I wonder if he's having trouble sleeping, too. I wonder if this week has been easy for him. "Where is Veronica?"

"She might come later," Tim says, and I look around. "Sit down." He points at the chair between him and Manning. I look at the chair. It's too close to Manning, and I don't know how good I'll be at not leaning over or toward him.

"I'm going to get myself a coffee," I say to him. "Then I'm going to grab a seat." I point at the rinks. "Which one is he going to be playing on?"

"That one," Tim says, pointing at the door. "I'll meet

you in there.”

I smile at Manning. “It was nice meeting you,” I say, and I walk away, hoping not to fall flat on my face. I order a coffee and then walk into the arena, grabbing a seat. I watch as the Zamboni cleans the ice, and then I hear my name being called. I look down to see Caleb and his team lining up by the glass.

“Hi.” I wave to him, and then I see Jaxon beside him. “Hi there.”

“Hi, Evelyn,” Jaxon says, and then they both turn around.

I see Tim approaching, and he sits next to me. “Where is Manning?”

I ask, and he points down toward the door. He sits by himself. “Why is he sitting by himself?” I ask him. “Is it ’cause I’m here?”

“No,” he says. “He always sits by himself. He tried to sit with the parents once, and they introduced all of their family to him, and it was just too much. So he sits by himself now.”

My heart is literally all over the fucking place. “He’s not a circus monkey,” I say, my tone pissed. “God, what is wrong with people?”

“Calm down,” Tim says, laughing. “Besides, he doesn’t want to take away the spotlight from Jaxon, so it’s just easier this way.”

I look over at him, and he looks my way, giving me a small smile. I wish I could sit with him. I wish this whole fucking thing came with an instruction manual. I also wish I hadn’t fucking fell for a married fucking man. Goddammit.

The game starts, and I see Jaxon and Caleb skate together. "They are really good," I tell Tim, and he nods his head. "Are you one of those hockey parents who yells?" I ask, laughing. My laughter fills the arena, and I have a couple of people look at me.

The game starts, and I have to admit I am into it more than I thought. "Hey!" I shout when I see a kid hit Jaxon and then hit Caleb. "That is not nice," I tell Tim, and he laughs. I try to keep my eyes away from Manning. I try so hard, but by the end of the second period, I have to pee so bad. I get up and pass the seat that Manning was sitting in, and I see that it's empty, and I wonder if he had to leave for work. I look around for the signs to the bathroom. I walk to the end, my head down as I turn the corner of the brick wall and smack straight into someone. I don't have to look up to know who it is. I would know his touch anywhere. I would know his smell with my eyes closed. My body wakes up as soon as I look at his hands that are holding my arms. "I'm sorry," I say, looking up at him.

A smile fills his face. "This reminds me of the first time we met," he says, his voice low as we stand here.

"I really need to watch where I'm going," I say to him as neither of us makes a move to walk away.

"Never a third without a second," he says to me, repeating the words he told me, and my heart pitter-patters in my chest.

"So I've been told." I laugh nervously, and I look up at him. His eyes are a clear blue as he smiles down at me. It's the look he always gives me. It's a look I've had etched in my memory since we first met.

"You're beautiful," he says as his hand moves from my arm to my cheek, and I want to turn my face and kiss his hand. "I miss you," he says. The same words I'm thinking and want to say to him. "I think about you all the time."

"I know." Those are the only two words that come out. "It's been hard." I tell him the truth. "I faked sick for two days."

"I know," he says, his hand falling from my face. "I was away for three days, so it made it a little easier. But then seeing you walk in here."

He swallows, and I swear I feel like it's just the two of us. I hear cheering coming from somewhere, but right now, right here, it's just him and me. "You walked in, and I felt settled if that even makes sense. For this whole week, I've felt like I had all these balls in the air." I listen to him as he tries to get out what he has to say as fast as he can before someone comes our way. "But the minute I turned around, it was just peace. It was just you."

"Manning." I whisper his name, and I'm about to say something else when I hear the sound of heels coming our way, getting louder and louder.

I take a step away from him, but he doesn't move. "Well, well, well." I hear and look up to see his wife. "What do we have here?" she says, looking at me and then at Manning.

TWENTY-FIVE

MANNING

"WELL, WELL, WELL." I hear and look up to see Murielle. "What do we have here?" she says, looking at me and then at Evelyn. She crosses her arms over her chest. "Is this a secret meeting I don't know about?" She smiles, but there is nothing friendly in her smile. There is nothing friendly when it comes to Murielle.

"Murielle, you remember Tim's sister."

"Right," she says, coming to stand next to me. "Evangeline, isn't it?"

"Actually, it's Evelyn," she says, now giving us her own fake smile. "It's nice to meet you again. I was just telling Manning what a special boy you have."

"He really is," she agrees and nods her head. She tries to grab my hand, but I put it in my pocket, so then she wraps her arm around my waist. "Just like his father."

Evelyn looks like she wants the floor to swallow her. "Well, it was nice seeing you again, Evelyn," I say and then walk around her.

"Yes, it was nice to see you again," Murielle says, and I hear her shoes clicking on the floor. She joins me, and I look over my shoulder to see that Evelyn didn't follow. I want to go back and make sure she is okay.

"You have got to be kidding me," Murielle says between clenched teeth. I don't have time to ask her what she is talking about because I open the arena door and make my way over to the seat where I was sitting before.

I'm expecting Murielle to walk to the other parents like she usually does when she shows up for a game. Nothing like basking in the glory of your son. She gets it at the hockey games with me, and then she gets it here, too. It strokes her ego more than anyone knows.

"Why are you sitting here?" I ask, and she just stares ahead. "I thought you had such a busy day that you couldn't come."

"I'm sure you would have liked that." She glares at me now, her voice low. I stare at the game, and then I see movement from the side, and I look down the ice and see that Evelyn is back sitting next to Tim.

I try to get her attention a couple of times, but she never looks down this way. Her eyes never leave the ice, and when the game finishes, she is the first one out of her seat. She doesn't move from beside Tim.

"I have to go," I say, getting up. "I want to get a nap in before the game tonight."

"I'm bringing Jaxon tonight," she says from her seat, getting up at the same time I get up. "When do you leave?"

"Monday morning," I say. "Back on Wednesday afternoon. Are you going to wait for Jaxon?"

"He is my son," she snaps, and I just look at her.

"At least you remember sometimes," I say and don't wait for her to answer before walking out of the arena. I sit in my car for longer than I need to, checking to see if she walks out. I know that I'm chancing it by sitting here, but something in me won't leave.

It takes twenty minutes, but I see her walk out with Tim as she holds Caleb's hand, who smiles at her. She is so fucking beautiful. I can't breathe when I look at her. I spot Jaxon coming out next, no smile on his face as Murielle walks beside him, letting him carry his own bag.

Pulling out of the arena, I call Becca. "Manning," she says my name as she answers. "My favorite client."

I laugh at her. "You mean the one who makes you a lot of money."

"That means the same thing." She laughs now. "To what do I owe the pleasure?"

"Becca, I'm losing my mind." I start to say. "You have to tell your guy to speed shit up."

"Manning, how do you want him to speed things up exactly?" she asks me.

"I can't take it much longer," I admit. "I can't."

"You've lasted four years," she reminds me, and I want to tell her I lasted four years because I wasn't living. I want to tell her that the only reason I lasted that long was because I didn't know what I was missing. I knew nothing. "You can last a couple of more weeks."

"A couple of weeks?" I shout. "Fuck, no."

"Let me call him and see what he has for me," she says, and she hangs up. I get home and walk up to my bedroom, and my nap is nonexistent.

When the alarm rings, my eyes are already open. Getting up, I shout down the stairs for Jaxon, and he runs up to my room. He sits in the middle of my bed as I get ready. "So how do you think you played?"

"Good," he says. "The other team was bigger."

"And?" I look at him. "What excuse is that? You're faster than them." I slip on my pants while I talk to him. "They get in your head. You have to think that you are ten feet tall. That is what I do."

"But you're huge," he says, and I laugh.

"I wasn't always huge. Where is your mom?" I ask.

"She went out when she dropped me off," he says, and I stop dressing.

"What do you mean?" I ask him, my heart beating fast. Yes, I was home, but my door was closed. Had I known, I would have left my door open.

"She had an appointment to do her glam," he says, and then the front door opens and closes.

"Hello!" she shouts up the stairs. "Jaxon. Manning."

"I'm in Dad's room!" he yells, getting off the bed and going out of the room to the railing. "I'm here."

"Do you want a snack before I go and get ready?" she asks, and I slip on my shoes as Jaxon walks down the stairs to the kitchen. I slip on my cuff links and my Rolex watch. Running my hands through my hair, I walk down the stairs. I stop in the family room, first seeing him sitting there eating a snack while he watches some cartoons.

I walk into the kitchen, grabbing a water bottle, and I see Murielle sitting at the island. I look at her and see that there is no fucking glam done to her face; she looks like she did the last time I saw her. Her hair isn't even done differently. "I thought you went to get 'glam'?" I ask her, closing the fridge, turning to look at her.

"Now you care where I go." She shakes her head. "You have some fucking nerve."

"Oh," I say, opening the water bottle and drinking a sip of the cold water. "I don't give a shit if you went to join the circus and never came back. I give a shit that you left our son home alone." I put the water bottle down on the counter, then lean back on it. "That is what I care about."

"You were here," she points out, "which means he wasn't alone. He was with a parent." She cocks her head to the side, and I see that her hair is a bit messed up. I wonder if she went to meet her trainer. Not that I give a shit. She could fuck him at center ice during overtime, and I would not even blink an eye or care. "This isn't about Jaxon, and you know it," she hisses, then laughs bitterly. "So tell me, Mr. Fucking Perfect," her words dripping with hatred, "is she the reason you've been fucking moping around all this fucking week?"

My mouth gets dry, but I refuse to let her see any of my emotions. I stare at her, our eyes locked on each other as she tries to get under my skin, but I won't let her have any of that. She doesn't get a piece of that. She doesn't get to touch what I have with Evelyn. Not now and not fucking ever. "I have no idea what you're talking about."

I don't know if that is the right thing to say to her, but with the way her eyes stare daggers at me, I know it's not. "That fucking bitch you were giving goo-goo eyes to at the arena. In front of fucking everyone." She slaps her hand on the counter, and her voice starts to go higher.

"You better lower your voice, Murielle." My tone comes out tight as my neck starts to get hot.

"You are insane." She looks at me. "To fuck someone who knows our kid. The backlash from that would be huge. Not to mention how disrespectful it is to me."

"Disrespectful?" My hands clench into fists while she talks. "You fuck your trainer in my fucking house that I pay for. You fuck him in the gym that my hard work built. You want to talk about disrespect, Murielle? You are barking up the wrong tree."

"Do you know how it would look if someone caught you two?" she asks, and I look at her. "What do you think they would have said?"

"I don't know what you think you saw." I put one hand on the counter and act like she saw nothing. But in reality, I want to kick myself for letting her see that Evelyn has a hold on me. "But nothing was going on. She was talking to me about Jaxon." I brush it off as nothing.

"Don't fucking lie to me!" she yells, and I glare at her. "For this whole fucking week, you've looked like someone stole your dog. You went to work, came home, ate, and then sat on the couch with Jaxon, and then you went upstairs." I look at her. "Then I see you with that bitch, and all of a sudden, it clicks into place. So what's the story? She break up with you? Kicked your ass to the curb when she realized how fucking boring you were?"

I have to choose my words wisely right now to make sure she stops looking at Evelyn. "Did it ever occur to you that I was miserable this week because I'm stuck here in this fucking house with you?" She folds her arms over her chest and rolls her eyes. "Did it ever fucking occur to you that staying here with you is killing me?"

"You are so fucking dramatic," she hisses. "And don't think I don't know that you are changing the subject. The next time I see her, don't think I won't have words with her."

My heart beats so fast in my chest, and my hands itch to throw the water bottle against the wall. "Do it," I tell her, pretending I don't care. "I beg you to do it." I chuckle. "I want you to do it so everyone can see what I get to see every single day. That you're unhinged and crazy." I use my finger to do a circle near the temple of my head. "It might just be what I need to get you the fuck out of my life." I open the water bottle again and smile at her before taking a sip of water.

If looks could kill me, I would die in that room. "Fuck you, Manning," she hisses, and I smile as big as I can.

"No, Murielle, fuck you," I say, pushing off the counter and walking out to my SUV. Only when I'm in the privacy of my own vehicle do I let out the breath I've been holding this whole time. Only when I'm alone do I let my head hang with defeat.

TWENTY-SIX

Evelyn

"Good morning," I say to Chantal, putting a Starbucks cup on her desk, and she smiles at me.

"You spoil me," she says, picking up her coffee and following me into my office.

"It is pouring rain out there," I say, taking off my beige Burberry rain jacket.

"One of these days, I'm going to beg to come over to your house and go through your closet," she says, looking at my outfit. I am wearing a high waisted gray pencil skirt that hugs me tight to my knees. The black cotton short-sleeved cross-over shirt is tied at the side. "Especially your shoe closet," she says of my gray stilettos with a thin metal heel.

"I will share anything you want," I tell her, pulling my chair out. "Except for my YSL shoes." I try not to remember the last time I wore those shoes, but the memory comes back before I can stop it. All I see is Manning in my head. I sit down, opening my laptop. "So how does my day look?"

"You have three conference calls and a meeting this afternoon with Kavanaugh," she says, and I lean my head back and groan.

"Jesus, that man," I say of the man who has been pushing me to my limits in order to prove to him that I'm just as good as my father. He had me building his whole portfolio again and again. "I swear I don't even know if I want him at this point."

She laughs at me. "I will order you lunch," she says, getting up and walking out. "Besides, you love the rush of coming up with new ideas."

"I don't know if I have any other ideas when it comes to him," I tell her. "Can you tell me when my father comes in, please?"

"I will," she says, and she walks over to her desk. I click on the local news, and Manning's face is there front and center. He is looking at something off camera, his face all sweaty as he chews his mouth guard, and all I can do is look at him. I read the bold headline.

Someone lit a fire under the captain's stick. Dallas takes the game against Buffalo.

I look at him, and I wait for the butterflies to disappear. But they come each fucking time. I swear if I close my eyes hard enough, I still feel his touch on me.

I read the article, not understanding all of the hockey lingo, and if I'm honest, the only thing I think about is the last time I saw him. The last time his wife was there. I stepped away from him right before she turned the corner. I knew it wasn't smart to be alone with him, and I knew that I wouldn't be able not to be close to him. I knew all of that, and still, the pull to him was so strong. I ignored her staring at me when Caleb came out of the room, and I even ignored the snippy way she grabbed Jaxon when he asked if he could join us for lunch.

"Your father has arrived." Chantal's voice comes through the phone, bringing me out of my daydream.

I get up and walk toward my father's office, knocking on the doorjamb, and he looks up, smiling when he sees me. He is sitting behind his desk, his jacket hanging on the back of his chair. His white button-down shirt is rolled up to his elbows as he reads his newspaper in front of him. "Knock, knock, knock," I say, and he takes his glasses off.

"Come in, sweetheart," he says, leaning back in his chair.

"Are you still reading the paper every single morning?" I ask, knowing that it gets delivered to his house, and he brings it with him to the office.

"Seven days a week," he says.

"Dad, you do know they are going to stop printing those papers one day, and it's going to be all digital." I stand here in the middle of his office.

"Bite your tongue, young lady," he says, and I shake my head, laughing.

"Dad, I don't think I can handle Kavanaugh," I tell him. "He is coming over today to talk about his portfolio, and I'm going to hand him over to Tim."

My father leans back in his chair. "Oh, come on," he

says. "You thrive when it challenges you."

"I used to but not with him. I'm annoyed to the tenth degree," I say, and he shakes his head, putting his glasses on and picking the paper back up.

"You'll be fine," he says. "You'll be even better than me." He picks up his cup of coffee and winks at me. I turn my head and walk out of his office.

I'm almost at my office when I hear her voice. "I think she'll take the time to speak with me." I'd know that voice anywhere, and I turn around to see her walking toward the back. She is dressed in black leather pants with a black turtleneck and her brown hair is done perfectly, even with the rain outside. Her face is perfectly made up, and she looks like she walked off a runway. "There she is." Her voice gets just a touch louder, making people look up from their desks. I see Chantal get up from her desk.

I don't know why I stand here, but I don't move. "Evelyn," she says my name and stops in front of me.

"Murielle," I say her name, and my stomach feels like I'm going to vomit. "Is there something that I can help you with?"

She laughs loudly, and I see my father stick his head out of his office. "Actually, there is something you can help me with," she says. "You can stay the fuck away from my husband." I open my mouth to say something, anything, but she just continues her tirade. "What's the matter? You have nothing to say to me. You can stop pretending," she hisses. "He told me everything." When she tells me those four words, I know she's lying. I know in my heart she is lying.

"First off, I will have you lower your voice in my workspace," I tell her. "If you want to have a conversation about what you think you know, then I will have that with you. But I'm not causing a spectacle in the middle of my office."

She throws her head back and laughs. "You have some nerve coming into my house and having an affair with my husband." Tim comes out of his office now, and he stands there listening. "You are nothing but a fucking home-wrecker." The moment she says that, I feel like she slapped me across the face as the blood rushes out of my body.

"Um." Tim starts to say. "Murielle, I have no idea what is going on right now."

"Fuck off, Tim," she hisses at him.

"I'm going to give you thirty seconds before I have someone call security."

"Call your security!" she shouts. "Call whoever you have to call. Look around, people," she says, spinning in a circle with her hands outstretched. "Little Miss Perfect coming back home to take over the family business. She decided she wanted to take over my family, but I'm not going to fucking let you."

"That's enough!" I shout. "I don't know what you heard or think is going on," I say, stepping up to her, "but know this, there are only two people who can ruin your marriage. That's you and your husband." I fold my arms over my chest. "So the big question is who ruined it first?" She swallows now. "Now you came here to cause a scene. Consider it done." I step closer one more time, showing her I'm not going to back down. "Now get the fuck out of my office." I motion with my chin. "Take you and your bullshit stories somewhere else."

"Stay the fuck away from my husband!" she shouts.

"Stay the fuck away from me," I counter. "Next time you think of ambushing, remember who has the most to lose." She turns around and storms out.

I look around, and everyone quickly averts their eyes. My father stands there with questions on his face. I know I'm going to have to tell him something, but I'm not ready.

I turn and see Chantal looking at me. "I'll get you some water," she says, and I just look at her and nod. "And I'll cancel your day."

"Thank you," I say, my voice low now as the lump forms in my throat. I walk with my hands shaking and my head held high. Well, as high as I can when the world is weighing down on me.

My chest is heaving as if I just ran a fucking marathon, my heart beating so fast in my chest. My legs are weak at the knees, and I use my hand to hold on to the desk beside me. The tears sting my eyes as I hear her voice over and over in my head. *Home-wrecker.*

"She doesn't come in here." I hear Manning's voice in my head. "This is between you and me, and no one else."

I swallow down the lump in my throat, and I turn and walk back into my office, feeling every single eye on me. Every person sitting there is judging me, wondering how much of what she said was the truth.

Walking to my chair, I almost collapse in it as the thing I feared the most just happened to me. In front of my co-workers, in front of my brother, in front of my father, the biggest secret that I had was laid bare. My hands shake in front of me as I look up and see my brother standing there. "Evelyn," he says my name. "What the fuck is going on?"

TWENTY-SEVEN

MANNING

"THREE HOURS AND we'll be home," I say, walking up the stairs to the plane. I sit down and take off my jacket for the three-hour flight home. "My body feels like I got into a fight with five fucking guys," I say, stretching my arms.

"You did," Miller says, sitting down next to me. "You took four of them. Ralph tried to take one."

"Fuck you," Ralph says when he sits down in front of me, turning to look at me between the seats. "You and that fucking chip you have on your shoulder these past couple of weeks is going to get us in trouble."

"I don't know what got you into this frame of mind," Miller says to me. "But seriously." I don't tell him that my life is literally falling apart piece after piece. The only thing I can control right now is what happens on the ice, and I refuse to let go of that last piece. "You need to chill out there. It's not you against the world."

He looks at Ralph. "You know we'll have your back no matter what."

"That depends," Ralph says from the front, and I laugh at him. There is nothing like having your team stand behind you.

I chuckle. "Hey, we won. Didn't we?"

Ever since Murielle confronted me in the kitchen, she's been trying to get me to slip up. She waited for me after the hockey game on Saturday, pretending she found out things when I knew that there was no way she knew anything. I also knew I would not even give her one ounce of information. What is between Evelyn and me was ours. Just ours. Always ours. Only ours. It was the one little thing that gives me the strength to go on, and she isn't going to take it from me.

"You think I don't know that is where you went the whole time!" she shouted the minute I closed the door behind me. "You look down your nose at me for fucking Thomas when you had your own whore all along." I walked away from her, not giving her anything.

"Are you okay?" Miller asks from beside me when the plane takes off. "You've been on edge."

"Shit is happening," I tell him. "Things that I can't talk about right now." I look out the window at the white clouds. "But I'm really fucking hoping this roller-coaster ride I'm on finally stops, and I can get off."

"You know I'm here for you," he says. "No matter what it is, I'm on your side."

"Me, too," Ralph says. "Whatever you need."

I nod my head at them, not ready for the storm that

is brewing. Nothing could have prepared me for the shit that is waiting for me once the wheels touch down.

I turn my phone on and wait to get my signal. The circle spins around and around for so long that I end up just tucking the phone in my back jeans pocket and get up to disembark. "I'll see you guys tomorrow," I say, walking to my SUV. I check and see that it's just after lunch, so I make my way home.

Parking my SUV, I see that Murielle is home, which is weird since she is always so busy during the day. I get out, slamming my door, then opening the back door to grab my carry-on bag.

Walking into the house, I smell food cooking. I drop my bag off at the door and make my way to the kitchen. We usually have a chef come in, but he comes on Monday and Friday, never on a Wednesday.

I step into the kitchen and see Murielle in front of the stove. "What is going on?" I ask. She turns around, and I see her face fully done with her hair tied. She is wearing leather pants, and I think about how ridiculous she looks.

"Oh, good, you're home," she says, turning off the stove. "Right on time." Something about her tone makes the hair on the back of my neck stand up. "I made your favorite," she says, draining the pasta. "I called your mother." She walks to the sink and tosses the pasta in the colander, the hot steam rising in front of her. "She didn't answer, of course, so I kind of improvised." I watch as she prepares two plates.

"It smells amazing, doesn't it?" She ignores the shock on my face. "I forgot how much I like to cook. I really should just do it." She walks toward the island and places the plates down in front of the stools, and then turns to get forks. "I came back home, and I had so much energy in me." She stops and looks at me. "So much energy." She puts down the forks. "Aren't you going to ask me where I went?"

"I'm not sure I want to know," I say, almost afraid. The phone in my pocket pings four times. I'm about to get it from my pocket when she says the words that make ice run through my veins and puts the nail in her coffin. "I went to see your whore." My head snaps up, and my hand tightens on my phone. "Good, that got your attention."

"What did you do?" I ask, my teeth clenched, my heart beating so fast I don't know if I can even listen to her without hearing the beats in my ears as it echoes.

"Well, you left me no choice," she says. "I had to tell her that she is not going to come into my home and just take what's mine. I had to lay down my claim."

"Lay down your claim?" I repeat the words, not sure if I heard her right.

"She was surprised." She unties the apron she's wearing. "I'll give her that. She thought I was going to do it quietly. Oh, no." She shakes her head. My phone rings in my hand now, and I see Tim's name.

"Oh my god," I say.

"Oh my god is fucking right!" she shouts. "She is lucky that I have class, and I didn't knock her fucking teeth out."

I walk to her now. Stopping right in front of her, I

make sure she looks into my eyes. "You fucked with me for the last time," I tell her. She tries to push me, and I grab her wrists in my hands. "You wanted a fucking war." I get closer to her face. "You have one."

I let go of her wrists. "Don't you threaten me, Manning."

I don't bother saying another word to her. Instead, I turn and practically run out of my house. The first place I call is the school.

"Hi there, this is Mr. Stevenson," I tell the secretary. "I'm going to be coming to pick up Jaxon in ten minutes. I forgot he had an appointment."

"No problem," she says, and I see that I have Becca calling on the other line as I race to the school.

"Hello." I switch the calls, my heart beating in my chest.

"We got it," she says, and if I didn't have to rush to Jaxon, I would pull the car over. I would stop the car and ask her what she means by that, but I don't have time. "Manning," she says, "we fucking got it. I sent everything to your private email."

"I need a favor," I tell her. "I'll be at your office in thirty minutes. I will have Jaxon, and I need you to watch him for a couple of hours," I say, honking my horn while I pass a yellow light, and she hears my voice.

"Manning, I need you to tell me what is going on," she says, and I hear the urgency in her voice.

"I'm done," I tell her. "Done playing the game. Done waiting for shit to happen. It's time for me to make shit happen. Can you watch him?"

"Of course," she tells me. "I'm going to rent a room."

"That sounds like a good idea," I tell her. "I don't know how she is going to react."

"Oh, I can tell you right now how she's going to react," Becca says. "Bitch is going to fly on her fucking broomstick. I hope you're ready."

"Almost," I tell her. "Is everything ready on your end?"

"It is," she says. "The papers are ready."

"Good. I'll see you soon." I hang up on her, and I call Tim back. My heart beats so fast in my chest that I have no idea how I'm driving right now.

"Manning," he whispers. "Did you not get my fucking texts?"

"I didn't," I tell him. "Or maybe I did. I just landed." I don't know if he knows anything, and I'm afraid to say anything. "What's wrong?"

"What's wrong?" he says. "What's wrong? I'll tell you what's wrong. If your wife steps one fucking foot in this company again, I'm putting a fucking restraining order against her. I will knock her the fuck out if she thinks she's going to come in here and spew her shit."

I stop at a red light, my blood pressure going higher and higher. "What did she do?"

"She came here to attack my sister about sleeping with you," Tim says, and now if I wasn't done before, I'm done now. "In front of her whole staff. In front of everyone who works here and our father."

"Tim," I say, my voice soft. "I am so sorry. I had no idea."

"No shit," he says. "I don't know what's going on."

"Where is she?" I ask, hoping he tells me, but knowing that even if he doesn't tell me, I'm going to fucking find her.

"Murielle?" he asks. "Fuck if I know. Hopefully, a fucking house fell on her, and someone is wearing red fucking slippers."

"Evelyn," I say her name, my heart breaking for her. "Where is Evelyn?"

"She went home," he says. "From your tone, I'm guessing some of what Murielle said is true," he groans. "Fuck me."

I pull up to the school. "Listen, Tim, I can't explain right now," I tell him, getting out of the car and rushing into the school, "but the second I can I will."

"You need to keep my number in case shit goes down." His voice goes low. "My sister does not need this shit."

"I'll agree with you there," I say and open the door, disconnecting. I walk into the school and hear Jaxon yelling my name. His backpack is on his back, and he's carrying his lunch box in his hand.

"Daddy." He runs to me. I grab him in my arms and kiss his neck. "I missed you," he says to me, and I look over at the secretary, who smiles at us.

"I signed him out for you." I nod at her and walk out of the school. My phone rings again, and this time, it's Murielle. I send her straight to voice mail, and then a text comes in.

Murielle: Don't make me fucking find you, Manning.

"What appointment do I have?" Jaxon asks when I buckle him in the car in record speed and kiss his cheek. I run around the SUV and get in, taking off before anyone can stop me.

"Actually, I'm taking you to visit Aunt Becca," I say to him, and his eyes light up. "She wanted to spend some time with you."

"Cool," he says, looking out the window. "She always has the cool toys at her house."

"Actually," I tell him. "You guys are going to go to a hotel."

His eyes open wide, and so does his mouth. He loves going to hotels and ordering room service while he watches all the movies his heart can handle. "Yeah, knowing her, she probably has a whole suite ready for you."

"Yes," he says. "Is Mom going to come?"

"No," I say, looking out and checking my rearview mirror to make sure I'm not being followed. "Actually, she went away on vacation."

He doesn't ask me anymore questions once we pull up to Becca's house. Becca is outside waiting for us. "Well, if it isn't my favorite eight-year-old," she says, opening the door and grabbing him out of my SUV. "Go get into my car. I have a whole night planned for us." She closes the door and then looks at me.

"Everything is set up," she tells me. "I just need you to call me, and I'll send it out. Candace is also ready for whatever is going to come. I haven't spoken to Nico." I rub my hands over my face. "If you ask me, you should be the one to tell him."

"I'll call him after I see Evelyn," I tell her, and she looks at me. "Did you call my mother?"

She nods her head. "She was ready when I called. Good thing you gave her warning."

"I have to go," I tell her.

"Manning." She calls my name before I get into the car. "It's not too late to turn back."

"She went after Evelyn," I tell her. "She went after her, and the only thing Evelyn is guilty of is letting me into her life." I shake my head. "This ends, and it ends now." She nods her head at me. I get back into my SUV and make my way over to her house in record time. I see her car in the driveway, and I get out, running over and ringing the doorbell.

I wait a couple of seconds, but it feels like hours. I ring it again and nothing, then I start knocking on the door. I hear the door being unlocked, and the sight that greets me cuts me off at the knees. If I wasn't holding on to the door frame, I would fall.

Her face is streaked with tears, her eyes red, and she sobs out my name. "Manning."

TWENTY-EIGHT

Evelyn

I THOUGHT IT would be Tim at the door or my mother. I thought it would be anyone but him. But seeing him in front of me looking like he had run seven marathons was just what I needed. "Manning." The sob rips through me, and I can't stop it.

"Baby," he says, rushing in and putting his arms around me. "Oh my god, I'm so sorry." He closes the door with his foot as he carries me through the house, only holding on to my waist with one hand. He places me down and moves the hair away from my face to see me. "Do you want water?" he asks, and I just shake my head, not sure I can say anything without making a fucking fool of myself.

My hands are on his chest, and I feel his heart beating under my hand. "Your heart," I tell him. "It mimics mine right now."

I don't know what I'm expecting, but he takes one of

his hands and brings it up to my chest, laying it flat over my heart. "I'm so sorry," he says, and I look up from his hand to his eyes and see tears in them. "I never wanted you to be . . ."

I step out of his touch, and I see his hand fall. "You will not fucking take the blame for this. You will fucking not," I say, swearing twice and getting angry. "You don't get to take her shit and make it your own. She is a grown-ass woman," I tell him. "A mentally unstable woman, I might add."

"I know that." He runs his hands through his hair. "I know that, but . . ." He looks at me, and his hand cups my face just like he did at the arena. But this time, I turn my face in his hand and kiss his palm. "What happened?"

"I'm not going to lie to you," I say, and he nods. "I will never lie to you." I need him to know this. "Ever." He nods again. "She came into the office and was pushy with the receptionist, pretending we were friends." He scoffs and shakes his head. "Then she came down and saw me, and in the middle of my office, she let them know that I was a home-wrecker." I try not to shed any tears, but they come anyway.

"Oh my god," he whispers and brushes away my tears. "I know this is hard, but I need you to tell me everything."

"There really isn't much more to say. She said you told her about us," I whisper, "but I didn't believe her."

"I would never." He steps closer to me. "I would never tell her anything about us. That is ours and only ours. It's yours, and it's mine, and I will never ever tell anyone about it."

"I know," I say, looking at him and putting my hand on his hand. "I knew she was lying." I swallow now. "I didn't show her how much it hurt me, and I was really proud of that." I smile with the tears coming again. "I walked back to my office with my head high." I shrug now. "My knees were shaking so much I thought that I would fall and my hands . . ." I look down and then back up again. "I couldn't get my hands to stop shaking."

"I wish I could make it go away," he says as he bends his head and puts his forehead on mine. "I wish I could make it all go away."

"I know it's not true," I say. "Tim came to my office after, and I didn't tell him anything. He asked if I was okay, and when I just shook my head, he didn't say anything else. He went back to the office floor and clapped his hands, telling everyone to get back to work. Everyone has signed an NDA, so if anything gets leaked, he is going to sue. My father also made sure to remind everyone of that little fact. I'm not a home-wrecker."

"You're not," he says to me.

"How did you know?" I ask, and he lets go of me now and walks to the couch to sit down.

"I got home, and she was cooking for me." He tells me what happened. "She said she spoke to you, and you told her everything. I knew she was lying. I can't get into details right now," he says. "But there is shit happening. It's going to hit the roof, and I don't know how the outcome will be, to be honest, and I'm both petrified and anxious about it."

He looks as if he's going to war. His eyes are wide, and his leg is shaking. I walk over to him and sit next to him, taking his hand in mine. "Are you going to be okay?" I ask him, my stomach burning with the thought that he gets hurt in any of this. "Is Jaxon okay?"

"I'm going to be okay," he says. "We are going to be okay. I have to believe that. I need you to know that I'm going to make this better."

"You don't have to worry about me," I tell him. The last thing he needs is the added pressure of me on his plate. "I'm fine. I'll be fine."

"I'm going to fix this for you," he says softly and then looks down. When he looks up again, he has the biggest tears in his eyes, and one of them escapes before he can blink it away. "I know that I don't have the right to ask this."

"Manning." My heart beats for him at the same time as it breaks for him.

"I have no right to even think of asking you this, but I'm not as noble as I thought I would be." His voice goes down so low for the next part. "Will you wait for me?" He doesn't stop. "I want to be the man who deserves you. I want you to be the one holding my hand at the end of this." He puts his head back. "I'm such a selfish bastard, and I know that, but when it comes to you . . ."

"Yes," I say softly, making him finally stop talking. Shrugging, I smile. "Besides, who is going to want to be with a home-wrecker anyway?" I try to joke with him.

His phone rings, and he looks at it. "I wish I could stay," he says. "There is just so much happening right now." I want him to tell me everything, but something inside me knows I'm not ready for it.

"Will you tell me?" I ask. "Not now," I tell him as his phone goes off again, and this time he gets up to answer it.

"Hello?" I hear him say, and he looks at me. "I'll be there in twenty." He hangs up, and I get up to walk him to the door.

"I want you to know something." He starts to say, and I look at him. This man who I met walking into a restaurant. The man who I spent the night flirting with, the man who I left the next morning thinking I would never see him again. The man who has snuck into my heart without even me knowing.

"I didn't just start this." He swallows now, and I see his finger tapping the back of his phone. "When you told me that you couldn't be with me, I walked out of here, and I've never felt hurt like that before. My chest felt like an elephant was stepping on it." I listen to him, shocked that he went through the same pain as me. "I left here and put my plan in motion. Then when I saw you again, I pushed for it to go faster." His phone rings again.

"Go." He looks down at his phone and then looks up again at me. "You need to go, and it's okay. I'll be here."

"I don't know if I'm okay with you being by yourself," he says, and I look at him.

"I dare her to come here," I tell him. "She blindsided me at work, but she isn't going to come into here and taint this house."

"I want to kiss you," he says to me, unsure if he can

or should.

"Well, then, get your ass over here and kiss me," I say, and he smiles as he charges to me. One of his hands wraps around my waist, lifting me off my feet while his other hand cups one of my cheeks, and his lips crash down on mine. I wrap my legs around his waist, and I kiss him like it's the first time. His tongue comes out and twirls with mine.

His phone rings again, and I let go of his lips. "You have to go."

"I do," he says. "I don't want to."

"I don't want you to leave either," I say, slipping my feet off his hips as he holds my waist until my feet are on the floor. "Can you just send me a text later to tell me you're okay?"

"I will," he says. "As soon as I can, I'll call you." I nod at him, and I hold his hand in mine as I walk him to the door.

He kisses me one more time, and I watch him jog to his car. He stops and looks over at me. "Don't open your door!" he shouts. "If she shows up here, you call the cops, and then you call me."

"I'll be fine," I say, and he puts his hands on his hips. "Don't you think me calling you and you showing up is going to add fuel to the fire?"

"Evelyn," he says my name, and I roll my eyes.

"Fine," I tell him. "Now go," I say when his phone rings again. He gets into the SUV, and I watch him drive away. I close the door and lock it and then walk back into the house. I turn the lights off, then grab the throw blanket and snuggle up on the couch.

I'm watching television, but my head is just thinking

about Manning, wondering if he's okay. I want to text him to ask if he is okay. No, actually, I want to be with him and support him. Hold his hand or even stand back in a corner as long as he knows I'm there for him.

My phone rings, and I jump up, seeing it's Veronica. "Hello." I answer her right away.

"Oh my god," she says, her voice coming out in a rush. "Where are you?" I turn off the television and sit up, my heart sinking. "I just sent you a link. Jesus, Evelyn."

My hands shake; they shake so fucking much it takes me three tries to click on the link.

Pictures start to load, and I gasp out in shock. There is a picture of Murielle in a back seat of a truck, and she is sitting on a man, her head thrown back in the middle of what looks to be an orgasm. The next shot is of the man kissing her and then one of him with his face buried in her tits.

But the one that kills me is the one of her getting out of the car, trying to make sure she is covered. She buttons up her top, and the guy comes out of the back seat. His hand is on her hip, and her head is turned to him as he devours her lips. Then she walks away from him and smiles and then turns back to blow him a kiss.

I scroll back up and see the headlines:

Dallas Captain is hot on the ice, but apparently not hot enough to keep his wife satisfied. The captain's wife is seen here getting hot and heavy with an unnamed man in what looks to be someone's car. From the looks of it, she left him looking mighty happy.

TWENTY-NINE

MANNING

GETTING IN THE car, I watch her as I drive away from her, and then I call Becca. She answers right away. "Hey."

"Hi, it's me. Everything okay?" I ask, and I hear Jaxon laughing in the background.

"Seems your mother was already in town," she says, and I know that she did this. She knew it was coming and made sure that I had backup.

"Where are you?" I ask. I hear her walking now.

"Don't freak out," she says, and she knows I'm about to freak out. "I got you a house."

"What?" I ask her. "What do you mean?"

"I mean that I knew this would be coming down, so I rented you a house."

I close my eyes. "Thank you," I tell her. "Okay, I'm on my way over to Nico's." I look at the clock. "I have an hour and a half."

"Yeah, you do," she says. "Let me know if he's playing hardball, and I'll call him."

I hang up the phone and then dial Nico. My heart speeds up just a touch. "Manning," he says, answering after two rings, and I can hear that he's out of breath. "What can I do for you?"

"Are you home?" I ask as I make my way over to his house. "Can I drop by?"

"Yeah," he says. "I'm here."

"I'll be there in twenty minutes." I hang up the phone with him and make my way over to his house. The rain finally stopped, almost as if the sun is shining for me today. I park my car in his driveway, and he's waiting at the door for me. He's wearing his basketball shorts with running shoes and a towel slung over his shoulders.

"Hey," he says, taking a look at me. "Is everything okay?"

I put my hands on my hips. "No," I say.

"Are you in trouble?" he asks. "Did you get arrested? Do you need a lawyer?" He looks at me.

"I'm good," I say, knowing he is probably thinking the worst. "I'm leaving Murielle."

"Okay," he says, not sure what to say.

"I tried to leave her four years ago," I tell him, and he stands there listening. "She took Jaxon and ran away with him. Refused to come back until I told her I would not bring it up again."

"I had no idea," he says, and I can see in his eyes he's shocked. "We would have done whatever was necessary to make sure you got your son back."

"I know," I tell him. "But it's changed. I'm done. I can't live like that anymore."

"I have the best attorney you can find," he offers.

"I have it all taken care of. Well, Becca took care of it."

"That woman has a brass set of balls," he says, smirking.

"I went to her three weeks ago. We hired a private investigator to follow Murielle and catch her cheating on me."

"No way," he says, shocked now.

"I knew she was cheating, caught her spread eagle on my weight bench being plowed by her trainer." I look down, embarrassed, but it only lasts a minute. "I didn't care. I don't care. But now I just want out."

"Is she worth it?" he asks, and I look at him. "The girl who put the spark back in your eyes."

"I don't know what you mean," I say.

"I didn't know you were having problems with Murielle, but I did notice your eyes lighter and brighter the past couple of weeks. I didn't know what it was, but now . . ." I smile and look down, thinking of Evelyn. "I won't ask you about it, that is for another time, but I hope you know that if she finds out . . ."

"I'm leaking a story at three thirty," I say. He looks at me, and I hand him my phone, bringing up the pictures. "I just wanted you to know that I'm going to be putting my life out there for the first time, and it's not going to be pretty." He shakes his head as he looks at the pictures.

"Whatever you need. The organization and I stand behind you," he says. "Now, I have to call Becca so we can go over a statement."

I nod at him. Another thing I can scratch off the list that came together so fast I didn't think I would be able to work it out.

"I have to go," I say, "but I wanted you to hear it from me."

He slaps me on the shoulder and squeezes. "Whatever you need, brother, I'm there for you."

"Thank you," I say, a weight lifted off my shoulders.

I make my way to the house, knowing she must have left to get Jaxon at school. I also know that I only have a few more minutes before it's showtime.

I'm sitting in the formal living room, the room with just the light coming in from outside. I look at my clock and see it's three thirty. The last three hours have been a fucking blur.

My phone lights up, showing me that it's Murielle. "Hello," I answer, my voice as calm as a cucumber. Meanwhile, I'm burning inside.

"Where the fuck is Jaxon?" she hisses. "I came to get him at school, and they said you picked him up."

"I did," I say, picking up the glass of scotch that I had poured myself. "I am allowed. I'm his father."

"Don't fucking play games with me, Manning," she hisses, and I laugh. This time, I'm in charge, and I'm the one calling the shots.

"I'm home right now. I don't know what games you think I'm playing," I say, setting the scotch down. I'm not lying. I am home.

"I'll be there in fifteen minutes," she says and hangs up the phone.

I pick up my phone and call Candace, who answers after one ring. "Do it," I say. When her voice goes low, my head starts to spin, and I know I don't have time for this. Not now.

"Are you sure?" she asks again. She's been asking me this every five minutes since I called her this afternoon.

"Candace," I say, and she groans.

"Okay, fine, I just . . . I just want to make sure you're okay."

"I'll be fine," I tell her. "In the end, we will all be fine."

"Can you please call me when you leave there?" she says, and I tell her I will, then hang up the phone. I sit down and wait with my heart beating so fast in my chest. I want to get up and pace the room, but she can't see me frazzled.

I refuse to let her see me frazzled. She doesn't get that from me. The front door opens at the same time that my phone pings again and again. I look down quickly and see it's from Candace.

Candace: Sent and it's live already.

Then there is one from Nico.

Nico: Just hit my phone. Call me after. I'm here for you.

I swallow, knowing that all the pieces have been set for this one moment. I didn't want to do it this way, but she left me no choice.

"Manning!" she yells. "Where the fuck are you?" I

see her walk by the room toward the family room. The sound of her heels are clicking on the floor. "Manning!" She yells my name, and I hear her running up the steps before I talk.

"I'm in here!" I shout, and I hear her heels click on the floor. The sound gets louder and louder once she comes into the room.

"What the fuck? Why are you sitting in the dark like a freak?" she says, walking over to the light switch and turning it on. Her eyes go from me to the two black bags sitting on the floor in front of the doorway.

"Hello, Murielle," I say to her and see her eyes move from the bags to me.

"What the fuck is this?" She puts her hands on her hips, and my phone pings again. "You're leaving me," she says in horror, and then she laughs. "Try it."

"I have something you should see," I tell her, leaning forward to put my phone on the table.

"What is that?" she says, coming into the room now, the carpet swallowing the sound of her heels. She reaches for the phone, and the color drains from her face. "I told you not to fuck with me." I lean back on the sofa, picking up the scotch in my hand and taking another sip. "I warned you." I put the glass down, and she looks back down at the phone, looking at the headline.

"All of this for that fucking whore," she says.

"I'd tread carefully right now, Murielle," I tell her, and she throws her head back and laughs.

"You want to leave me. For a fucking whore." She yells the last word, and I want to choke her but me staying calm is the key to this. "Do it. Leave me." She folds her arms over her chest, thinking she has the highest card in the deck, but little does she know I'm going to call her bluff. "You'll never see Jaxon again." Her phone starts ringing, and she ignores it. "Where is he?" She runs out of the room now and yells for Jaxon. She comes back into the room, her ponytail swinging back and forth. "Where the fuck is he? Where is he?"

I get up now as she stands there, grabbing the manila envelope that I had beside me. "I'm not the one leaving," I tell her, and I know she is going to fight this part. "You are." I hold out the envelope for her, and she snatches it out of my hands.

"What the fuck is this?" She opens the envelope, and her house of cards comes crashing down.

"Those are divorce papers," I tell her as she reads it. "You've been served by the way."

She flips the pages over and over again, bending the envelope, and now pictures fall out, and I look down. "What the fuck? You spied on me." She bends down and picks up the nude photos of herself.

"We could have done this the easy way," I tell her. "We could have done it privately and amicable. But"—I shake my head—"you couldn't just do it. You stayed with me just to be at the top of the food chain. Now look at you. A cheater for the whole world to see."

"So what," she says of the photos, pretending it's not eating her up, but I know her image is everything to her. I know that this is killing her inside, and I know that I did it to her. "So they know I cheated on you. Obviously, you didn't satisfy me, so I had to go elsewhere. This makes you look much worse than I do."

"Here it is," I tell her, putting my arms out. "I don't give a fuck if they caught you gang banging a whole circus of men," I say. "This is my out." I laugh now. "Don't you see? Don't you get it? You can't hold anything over me anymore. Nothing." I take a big breath. "Not even Jaxon. I'm not going to be low like you and use him as a pawn. I won't hold your son from you. Ever. I'll never stop you from seeing him. But until we decide on a couple of things, you can only see him when I'm there. I'm not going to lose him again."

"You want to ruin it all," she says. "You are going to ruin it all for her. Everything we built."

"No," I say, shaking my head. "That is where you're wrong. You ruined it all. You ruined it. This, Murielle, is all you." I've had enough of her, and it's done. I make my way to the doorway past the bags that I packed for her. "Oh, and also . . ." I turn around and look at her as she stands there with the divorce papers in one hand, gripped so tight her knuckles are white. "If you think for one second of going to Evelyn again . . ." I walk to her, my voice going low, and I look into her eyes when I say the next words. "You better fucking think twice." My voice goes even lower. "I have lots more pictures of you. Next time, don't fuck your trainer in my house. Next time, it'll be a home movie."

"I fucking hate you," she says the words with clenched teeth.

"Actually, I'm feeling generous. You can have the

fucking house." I look around. "I always hated it anyway. It was like my jail," I tell her, walking right out the front door and slamming it behind me.

THIRTY

Evelyn

I CAN'T STOP pacing. I sit down for a second, but then my leg starts to twitch, and I get up again. I have read the article so many times that I almost know it by heart.

I search the web on my computer, on my iPad, on my phone. I search his name, then his wife's name. I wonder how he's doing. I wonder how Jaxon is. There is so much going on that my head is spinning.

The soft knock comes, and I run to the door. I open it before looking outside and see him standing there. "Oh my god." I literally throw myself into his arms. "Are you okay?"

"You didn't even check to see who it was," he says, and I lean my head back to look at him or, better yet, glare.

"Your life is literally falling apart, and you're worried about me answering my door?" He pushes me in and closes the door behind him. Reaching for me, he pulls me to him, bending his head, and takes my lips in a kiss. My lips are half open in shock, and he takes that opportunity to slip his tongue into my mouth. My hands go to his arms, and I move them up to his neck. His kiss is soft as we take our time.

"Fuck," he says when he lets go of my lips, and my eyes slowly flutter open. "I missed that."

"Me, too," I say softly.

"I can't stay long," he says. I nod and grab his hand as we walk into the house.

"Do you want something to drink? Water, beer, tequila?" I ask, and he laughs, shaking his head.

"I'm good," he says, and I just look at him. "I'm guessing you saw the article?"

"I did," I tell him. "Manning, I'm so, so sorry." My heart breaks for him knowing that he's the most private person I've ever met. "You must be beside yourself."

"It was me," he says, and I just look at him, not sure I heard him. I must spend too much time blinking because he continues. "It was all me."

"I don't." I start to say. "I don't understand."

"I told you before that I started this plan before today," he says. I walk to him, and I put my hand on his chest. He puts his hand on mine. I tilt my head back, and he bends to kiss me. "Let's sit down." He walks over to the couch and sits, and I sit next to him. "When I left here after we broke up . . ." The way he says it hurts my heart. "I knew that I lost my shot at happiness." He looks at me shyly and then looks back down. "I called Becca, my agent, and I asked her to hire a PI."

"But you knew she was cheating?" I say, and he nods.

"I did, and I had video and pictures, but I didn't want to use those. I needed to have neutral pictures so no one would know it was me."

My mouth opens and then closes again with no words coming out. "When she came after you, I knew it was now. It was going to be today. I didn't care what pictures I used or if they knew it was me. End of the story, it was happening."

"Your reputation is on the line," I say. "Why would you do that?" I get up now. "For me." I shake my head. "I could handle her. I mean, now that I know she knows, I can handle her."

"But it's not about that," he says, leaning forward and putting his elbows on his knees. "It's about me being free of her. It's about me starting my life. It's about Jaxon living in a normal household without a mother and father who hate each other." I just look at him. "She did not take it well." He tells me about the showdown at the house. "I don't know what the future holds," he says, his eyes suddenly looking tired. "I know she is going to fight me every single second." His head hangs down now, and I walk to him.

I get down on my knees in front of him, touching his cheek with my hand. "Manning," I say, leaning in and rubbing my nose on his cheek.

"It's not going to be easy. I already filed for divorce with an emergency order that she not leave the state with him, and she has twenty days to respond. It might be the longest twenty fucking days of my life, but the first step is done." I lean in and kiss his lips softly. "I was going to kick her out of the house, but then I thought about it. I hate that fucking house. It was my jail cell. I felt trapped and after spending time here"—he looks around—"this is a home. I want to give Jaxon a home."

This man sacrificed everything he has for his son. "Becca rented a house, and I didn't even know. I had no other thoughts except getting away from her."

"What about Jaxon?" I ask, and he looks at me.

"He's with my mother," he says, his voice cracking. "Becca called her, knowing I would need help."

"I wish I could help you," I tell him. "I wish she didn't know about us, and I could help you and be by your side."

"I don't know what the future holds, Evelyn." He takes his hand and puts it on my face, moving his thumb up and down. "I know it's not going to be easy, but what I can tell you." He moves his hand to trace my lips with his thumb. "That it's going to be worth it."

"I will be here with whatever you need," I tell him, my heart hammering in my chest. "You just tell me what you need."

"You," he says softly. "All I want is you." He puts his forehead on mine. "Knowing that." My hand touches his face. "Knowing you'll be there is . . ."

"It's us," I tell him. "In here," I say. "In here, it's just the two of us."

"I don't know what I did," he says as his other hand cups my face. "But I'm so fucking happy that I went to that dinner." I smile now. "I'm so happy that . . ."

"That you flirted with me shamelessly," I joke with him. "You know this is the second time today you've come to see me." I smile.

"Never a third without a second," he says, and I kiss him. "I have to get to Jaxon. I know he's being taken care of, but I have to talk to him."

"Of course," I say, getting up from in front of him. I walk with him to the front door, sad he's leaving me again and sadder that I can't be there with him as he goes through this.

"I'll call you later," he says, and I just nod.

"Okay," I say. "Let me know if I can do anything."

"I hate this," he says right before he walks out the door. "I hate leaving. I hate that you can't come with me. I hate that."

"Hey," I say, putting my arms around his waist. "There will be time for all of that."

"That is what I'm counting on," he says, kissing me softly. "Lock the door, and for the love of god—"

I start to groan, and I push him out. "Go," I tell him. "Take care of Jaxon."

He starts walking away. "Evelyn." He calls my name and turns to walk backward. "I know I'm married and all, but will you be my girlfriend?" I shake my head, laughing. "I mean, after my divorce and all that."

"I think we went backward on that train, Manning," I tell him, and he laughs.

"Best night ever," he says, and I just take a deep breath and watch him leave, knowing that he is taking a piece of my heart with him.

I close the door and walk back inside. My phone rings, and I see it's him. "I want to tell my mother about us."

"What?" I say, shocked. "Don't you think you should wait?"

"No," he says. "Actually, I want to tell Jaxon and my mother so they know I'm going to be okay." He stops talking. "Is that okay with you?"

"Then I guess I should tell my parents, too," I say, sitting down and feeling like I just woke up on Christmas morning and all the gifts I asked for are under the tree waiting for me. "I mean, my father was there when the showdown happened, and although he didn't ask me anything, I'm sure he has a lot of questions."

"Okay, so I'll tell my mother and Jaxon, and you tell your parents," he says. "I'll call you after I talk to them."

"Oh my god, you're doing this tonight?" I shriek. "Don't you think that's going to be a big thing? I'm leaving Murielle, and I have a girlfriend."

"I figured like a Band-Aid, I'd just rip it off," he says. "I also have to call your brother."

"Wait, what?" I sit up now.

"I have to tell him what is going on. He needs to know in case."

"In case?" I say, my hands getting clammy.

"Baby," he says my name softly. "I don't know what Murielle is going to do. She can go quietly, or she can go like a bat out of hell."

"I think she's going to go with plan B," I tell him.

"Me, too, which means that I don't want you to get caught by yourself," he says, "so we have to make a plan."

"Shouldn't I be a part of this meeting?" I ask, and he laughs.

"I'll fill you in. I just got to the house," he tells me. "I'll call you later."

"Good luck," I say, taking a deep breath.

"With you on my side, who needs luck?" he says, disconnecting.

THIRTY-ONE

Manning

I WALK UP the pathway toward a house I have never seen before. The front door is unlocked, and as soon as I step inside, I smell cooking right away—my mother's cooking.

I also hear laughing, something I've never heard before when I walked into my house. It was always dead ass quiet. "Hello?" I shout as I pass the staircase and walk into a huge family room adjoined to a kitchen.

My mother stands at the island with Jaxon as he helps her cook. Her eyes come up, and when she sees me, she immediately gets teary-eyed. She grabs a hand towel to wipe her hands and then comes to me. "Dad, Nana came."

"I see that," I tell him.

"My boy," she says, and I have to bend to hug her. "You and me, we are going to have a talk," she says as she holds my face. "A nice long overdue talk." I laugh now, and then I look over to see Becca walking into the room. "I think your attention needs to be someplace else right now." She motions with her head and then walks back to the counter to stand beside Jaxon. "Now leave my grandson and me by ourselves while we cook dinner."

"Dad, I'm cooking," he says, smiling and then turns to my mother. "Can I pour it in now?" he asks her, and she nods her head.

I walk over to Becca, who just looks at me. "Well, you seem to be intact," she says, looking me up and down. "No bullet holes. I guess that's a good sign." I shake my head, laughing, and then I hear a knock on the door. "That should be Nico and Candace," she says, walking to the door and opening it.

Nico walks in wearing jeans, a white T-shirt, and a leather jacket. "Hey," he says to me and then looks at Becca. "Good to see you."

She just nods at him as the bell rings again. He moves over to me. "You okay?" I shrug my shoulder when I see Candace come in. Her eyes go soft when she sees me.

"Manning." She comes over to me and hugs me. "I'm so sorry."

"Okay, I set up in the dining room," Becca says, walking toward a door that I didn't even see when I got in. I step in and see Becca's computer out and her legal pad next to it with writing all over it.

I slip off my jacket and sit down, grabbing a water bottle from the middle of the table. "What a day," I say, chuckling.

Nico sits next to me. Candace sits next to Becca and takes out her own legal pad. "So what happened?"

I shake my head. "I gave her the divorce papers, and I'm hoping to fuck she doesn't fight me on it."

"She put out a statement," Candace says, and I look over at her in shock. "She did it herself."

"What did she say?" I ask, and my leg starts to move up and down. "I didn't see anything."

"Well," Becca says, laughing now. "She did call me two seconds after you left her and told me that I better make sure that I take care of this shit, or you'll regret it."

"What did you tell her?" I ask.

"I told her to eat my dick," Becca says, and Nico laughs. "Then I hung up on her."

"And then she called me," Candace says, looking down. "I didn't tell her what Becca said, but I did tell her that she was not my client. She then told me to eat a dick and hung up. The minute she hung up, I put out the press release that we wrote up." I nod, knowing she took care of it. "It contradicts what she says, though."

"That's her problem," I say, then look over at Nico. "Any news on your side?"

"You know me, Manning," he says. "People don't come to me with this shit because I'm not going to fucking answer it. They know better. I had Becca send out a press release on behalf of the organization asking that they respect your privacy as well as your son's," he says.

"How are you going to handle the press?" Nico asks. "You have a game tomorrow night. Luckily for us, we are home for eight days, but . . ."

"It's no surprise. I don't talk about my private life, and I'm not going to do it now." I look over at Becca and Candace. "Unless she comes out spewing shit and talks about Evelyn, I have nothing to say on the matter. I'm not the first man to get divorced, and I won't be the last one."

"Dad." I hear Jaxon calling me. "I'm making cupcakes." I laugh now and look at the three people who I know will be in my corner no matter what. "I'm sorry, guys." I put my hands together. "I didn't want it to come out the way it did. I didn't want this huge media circus. But she crossed the line with Evelyn. She broke it off with me because I was married even after I told her what was happening with Murielle. It killed her that she was the other woman and to be attacked at her work. I wasn't going to let it slide."

"Hopefully, this will be over very soon, and we can pop champagne for another reason," Nico says, getting up. "Becca, why don't I take you to dinner?"

Becca looks over at him and tilts her head to the side. "Depends. What are you thinking?"

"Whatever you want," he tells her, and she gets up, closing her laptop.

"I'm thinking pizza," she says. "In Italy."

"If we leave now, we can get there for lunch," he says, and they both leave.

"Ralph and Miller are going nuts," Candace says when I walk her to the door. "I didn't tell him anything, and he's being a big fat baby about it and pouting."

"I'll give them a call later," I tell her. "Thank you," I

say, "for everything."

"Out of all my clients," she says, opening the door, "you were the quiet one. I'd expect this from Miller." She shakes her head, laughing as she walks to her car. I lock the door and walk back to the kitchen.

Slapping my hands together, I ask, "So what are we eating?" My mother looks over at me. "I'm starving."

My mother takes over the whole conversation during dinner, talking about all the chores she does at home, and when I get up to walk Jaxon upstairs, I look over at her. "I'm going to have a talk with him."

She smiles and nods her head. "I'll be here when you're done."

I wait for him to slip on brand new pjs that we found in one of the bedrooms. Becca really did think of everything. "How was your day?" I ask, and he smiles.

"I had fun with Nana," he says and then jumps on the king-size bed in the room.

"I wanted to talk to you a bit," I tell him as he slides into the bed. "About your mom and me." I start, and he looks at me.

"Are you guys getting divorced?" he asks, and I'm shocked. "Katie's mom and dad are divorced," he tells me, "but she says it's okay."

I nod my head. "We are getting divorced," I tell him, wondering what else I can say. "But that doesn't change how we feel about you," I say. "Plus, now you get to have two rooms, and you can do sleepovers whenever you want."

"Sleepovers," he says. "Is it like the sleepovers that

Mommy has with Thomas when you go to play hockey?" My heart sinks, and my chest aches. She had him sleep over when I wasn't there. My hands shake with rage that she did that.

"Yeah, like that," I say, pretending that what she did was right. "But for the next couple of days, you are going to stay home with grandma." His eyes open wider.

"I'm going to ask her to make my favorite cupcakes," he says, and I shake my head.

"I think she'll do whatever you want," I say, and he sinks down into the bed. "Good night, son," I tell him, kissing his cheek and walking out.

I walk downstairs, my head still spinning about Murielle having Thomas stay over. I send Becca a message.

Me: She had Thomas sleeping over in my house when I went on the road.

I put my phone in my pocket and walk into the kitchen. My mother has cleaned up everything, and she is making herself some tea. "Hey," I say, and when she turns around, I see that she has been crying. I pull out a stool and sit down. "Stop crying," I tell her, and she just looks at me.

"Why didn't you tell us?" she asks. "We could have . . ."

"What could you have done, Mom?" I tell her. "I made my bed, so I was lying in it."

"You weren't the only one," she says. "I always hated that bitch."

I laugh now. "I met someone," I tell her, and she looks up at me with shock on her face. "By accident," I tell her. "We met one night and . . ." I look down. "Something shifted." I try to explain it. "She had no idea who I was, and I didn't tell her. One week later, I see her at the hockey arena with Jaxon. She was the aunt to one of his best friends."

"Oh my god, talk about the universe taking things into their own hands," she says. I tell her all about Evelyn, and my face ends with a smile.

"You love her then," she says, and I look at her. "When you came in before, I thought you would have this empty look in your eyes. The same empty look that you've had in your eyes for the past five years." I open my mouth to say something, anything, but she holds up her hands. "Don't even try to pretend." She shakes her head, walking over to the kettle and pouring herself some hot water. "I saw it. Your father saw it. We tried to pretend we didn't, but we couldn't. Then you got even more distant."

"I'm sorry about that," I tell her. "It was wrong, and I should have put my foot down."

"I know," she says. "Your father wasn't too happy about it, but we understood."

"When I found out Murielle was having an affair, it didn't even hurt me. I didn't even flinch."

"You didn't love her," she says. "You love that she gave you Jaxon, but you didn't love her."

"I guess I didn't." I agree with her, my finger tapping the counter.

"Go," she says, and I look up at her. "Go. I'll call you if Jaxon wakes up."

"How did you . . .?" I ask her.

"You've been antsy since you walked in. You checked your phone every second during dinner. Then you took it with you upstairs. You've never done that."

I get up. "Are you sure?" I ask, and she laughs. "I think I can handle it."

"Thanks, Mom." I walk over to her, and I kiss her cheek and hug her. I start to walk out of the room when she calls my name.

"Thank her," she tells me, and I just look at her, "for giving me back my son." I smile at her and nod.

I make it over to her house in record time and ring the bell. "Manning." I hear her say my name as she opens the door. "What are you doing here?"

I walk to her, grabbing her around her waist and shutting the door with my foot. "Never a third without a second."

THIRTY-TWO

EVELYN

THE DOORBELL RINGS, and I literally jump out of bed. My stomach starts to speed up, my palms sweat, and I take my phone with me as I walk to the door. I wrap my cashmere sweater around myself and walk quietly. I look out the peephole, and I see him. "Manning?" I say, opening the door. "What are you doing here?"

He doesn't answer me. Instead, he walks in and grabs me around my waist, causing my stomach to flutter for a whole different reason. He closes the door with his foot, and right before his lips crash down on mine, he says, "Never a third without a second."

My arms wrap around his neck, and my legs go around his waist as he walks into my house, going to my bedroom with his mouth on mine. I move my hands from his neck to his hair, and I swear I could kiss him every single day for the rest of my life, and it'll be like a first-time kiss. I let go of his lips. "Hi," I say softly, touching his face, the beard itchy on my hand. "I can't believe you came back."

"I couldn't stay away," he says, turning to sit on my bed. My legs stay around his waist, and I straddle him now. He pushes my hair behind my shoulder.

"Is everything okay?" I ask him, then lean in to kiss him softly.

"She released a statement saying it's a private matter and that we are working through it as a family," he says, and I just swallow, wondering if he will regret doing all of this. I look down now, not sure I can look in his eyes without him seeing that. The last thing he needs is more stress.

"I put out a statement saying that this is a private matter, and we are working on things separately. Tomorrow, Candace is going to drop that we are getting divorced."

"Are you sure?" I ask him softly. "It's okay if you changed your mind."

"I think I'm in love with you," he says, and I stop breathing. My heart stops beating in my chest. "I know it sounds stupid. I know we barely know each other, but . . ." He looks down at my chest rising and falling.

"I knew I was falling in love with you when I let you go, and I couldn't breathe," I tell him. "When the sadness seeped down to my bones. My whole body felt like I was run over by a truck, which was crazy. I broke up with Dex, and I went to work the next day. I think I cried for an hour."

"I hate that I made you cry," he says, touching my cheek with his thumb. Both of my hands are on his face, and I lean in to kiss him softly. "I hate that you went through that alone." His voice is almost a whisper.

My hands move down from his face to his shoulders and then to his chest. I open his jacket and slip it off his shoulders, then I lean in and kiss his neck. "I would wonder if you were thinking about me," I say, moving my hands under his shirt and pushing it up over his head. "Wonder if you were dreaming of me." I kiss under his chin. "I used to go to bed at night and pray you would be in my dreams."

"Every single night since the day I met you," he says, taking off my cashmere sweater and leaving me in a tank top and panties. "Every single dream is of you." He pulls down one spaghetti strap, almost snapping it. "I would wake up with your name on my lips," he says, taking a nipple into his mouth, and my head falls back. "Every night, I would fall asleep to your smiling face." He pulls down the other side. "You laughing." He bites the other nipple and then sucks it in. "You moaning my name."

"I missed this." I tell him the truth. "Us." I get up now off him. Pulling my tank over my head, I then slip my panties off. His eyes go darker blue now. I step between his legs, and he kisses my stomach as his hands rub up my legs to my ass. "I would think about all the things I wanted you to do to me."

"Tell me," he says, and I shake my head.

"Better if I show you," I say softly and kiss his lips. "Will you make love to me?" I ask, and he has me in the air and on my back in the blink of an eye. He strips himself of his pants, and I watch him.

"I want to kiss every single inch of you," he says, getting on the bed with his cock in his hand as I spread my legs for him. "I want you to come on my tongue and then my fingers." He talks so softly I get shivers all over me. "But my cock," he says, and he rubs his cock up and down my slit. "My cock needs you first."

I don't say a word to him, afraid that if I talk, he'll stop, and I can't have him stop. We both look down at his cock as he slowly slides into me. The minute his balls hit my ass, I lift my legs and wrap them around his waist. He props himself over me on his elbows. "Manning," I finally say when his mouth hovers over mine. I stick out my tongue to slide it into his mouth, and he sucks it in as he slowly begins to move his hips. He lets go of my tongue as he fucks me slow and steady. The whole time, we look in each other's eyes, and he rests his forehead on mine. I tilt my hips up, trying to get him deeper. "Harder," I tell him, and he picks up his pace, slamming into me. Both of us moan as my pussy tightens around him. The sound of our skin slapping together fills the room.

"Baby." He says my nickname, and I lick his lips as his tongue comes out to kiss me back. "I'm going to . . ." I nod, feeling the pull in my stomach that I'm going to come. "Your pussy," he says. "So tight." I close my eyes, coming all over him, squeezing him even tighter. He pounds into me now, and then he finally plants himself balls deep as he comes in me.

"I don't want to leave," he moans as he pulls out of me after round three or maybe four. Who knows at this point. "But it's almost six."

"You need to go," I tell him, watching him get up and hating it. "I don't think we've actually spent a whole night together."

"We did," I say, getting up and grabbing my cashmere robe. "On the first night."

"What are you going to do today?" he asks me, slipping on his shirt. I stop in front of him, grabbing his hips.

"My parents are coming over at ten," I tell him, and he just looks at me. "I figured I should tell them the story before they read it in the tabloids."

"Good idea," he says, kissing me when I put my head back. I walk him to the front door. "I'll call you later."

"Okay," I say. I'm about to go out with him, and he stops me.

"I don't want you out there," he tells me. "I don't know if she is crazy enough to tell the press about you. They could be outside and take your picture, and well"— he smirks—"you look like you spent the night rolling around in bed."

"I did." I smirk at him.

"Well, I don't want anyone seeing that," he says. "It's for my eyes only."

I shake my head. "Get going," I tell him. I close the door behind him, and I know that I'm not going to sleep even if I tried. Walking to the shower, I turn it on as my mind thinks of him the whole time.

I slip on my blue jeans and a white cashmere sweater, letting my hair loose. I don't check the news. Instead, I call Chantal and tell her that I'm working from home today. She tells me that she will send me all the things

I need and will drop off anything that comes in for me.

I sit at the island trying to work, but the whole time, I'm looking at the clock. My palms get sweaty when I hear the doorbell at nine forty-five. I get up and walk to the front door, and I open it, seeing both my parents. My mother tries to pretend she is okay and happy to see me, but I know that it's been killing her not to call me. My father puts both hands on my arms and kisses both my cheeks. "Honey."

"We brought you some cake," she says, and I see the box in her hand. "I figured we could eat away the emotions." I smile, and they walk in with me as I put the box on the counter.

"I'll make coffee," I say, turning to walk to the coffee machine when I hear the front door open and then close. I look at them, and they look back at me. "Is Tim coming?" I ask. I look now toward the entrance, and my mouth hangs open when I see it's Manning.

"Hi there," he says, going to my father and putting out his hand to shake Dad's. "Sorry, I'm late." He looks at my mother. "I'm Manning." She looks at him, taking his hand and her mouth literally hangs open. He walks around the counter, and he smiles at me. "Sorry I'm late," he says, kissing my lips.

"Oh, my," my mother says finally, and I just blink.

"What are you doing here?" I ask him as quietly as I can.

"I wasn't going to let you talk to your parents about us and not be here," he says, making my mother come out with another "Oh, my."

"Shall we sit?" my father says, and I just nod at him and watch them walk to my couch while Manning slips his hand into mine.

"You didn't have to do this," I tell him, wiping away the tear that is about to escape. He takes our hands and kisses my fingers. I walk over to the couch, and we sit side by side.

"Before we start," Manning says. "I would like to apologize to you both first." I look at him, and my mother has these goo-goo eyes for him. "I'm sorry about the scene that happened."

"It's not your fault," my father says. "Not even a bit."

"But it was," he says, and he looks at me. "I saw your daughter and the earth shifted." He puts an arm around my shoulders and pulls me to him. "I should have walked away, but I couldn't." He smiles shyly now. "I couldn't do it. It was wrong, and I know it was, and I will be forever sorry that I put her in that position. But I can't be sorry that we met. I won't be."

"You were married?" my father now says. "You are married."

"In name only," he says. "Four years ago, I asked her for a divorce, and she took my son away. I would have promised her anything to get him back. I was waiting until he was old enough to have a voice and choose. But sometimes things happen, and you have to jump."

"This woman attacked my daughter in front of her colleagues," my father says, and now I'm the one who speaks.

"She didn't attack me. She confronted me, and she

caught me off guard. I'm not going to justify our relationship. By no means should it have happened, but it did." I wipe the tear away. "I sent him away and told him I couldn't see him," I tell my parents.

"When you thought I was sick, that was me with a broken heart because the man I was falling in love with was married, and I knew it was wrong. I know it's wrong. But," I say, my shoulders going straight, "there is a huge but. Some things went on that you aren't privy to. They are private, and I'm not going to be the one to tell the story. But that woman does not deserve him. I don't even know if I deserve him. I do know I'm going to hope like fuck I can prove I deserve him."

"What if the press finds out?" my mother asks now.

"I don't care," I say, throwing up my hands. "So they find out we are seeing each other. We were seeing each other." I look at my parents. "It's us." I look at Manning now. "It's us, and we will get through this."

THIRTY-THREE

Manning

I GET TO the arena, and I know there is going to be press there. For the past two days, they've been trying to get in touch with me, and I have ignored them. Candace released one statement, and that is all I'm going to say.

When I step out of my car, I don't know why I'm shocked to see Miller and Ralph standing there waiting for me. "What are you doing?"

"Walking in with you," Ralph says, and I smile.

"I just want to be pictured next to you and get more press," Miller says, laughing.

"How're you doing?" Ralph says, ignoring Miller.

"As good as can be, I guess," I tell them. "Murielle calls no less than fifty times."

"A day?" Miller asks, shocked.

"An hour," I tell him, and his mouth hangs open.

"What does she want?"

"To tell me what a mistake I'm making. To tell me

that she is going to do a tell-all."

Miller laughs. "A tell-all of what, how you became a monk?"

"How is Evelyn?" Ralph asks, and I shrug my shoulders.

"She's pretending she is fine, but I know that this whole thing bothers her. I met her mother yesterday, and it was rough."

"It was rough?" Ralph asks. "Have you met my brother-in-law, Evan Richards? The Evan Richards who is in town with his team. The one who tried to put my daughter in his jersey. The same one who hid my wife from me." He mentions his brother-in-law, who plays for New York and who is here tonight.

"To be fair, she wasn't your wife at the time." Miller points out, and we start to walk into the arena. I stand in the middle of the two of them. I see the five cameras aimed toward us as we walk.

"Manning," one of them shouts, "can we get a statement?" I put my head down and walk into the hallway. When the door closes behind me, I let out a huge sigh of relief.

I'm walking to the changing room when I see Nico in the hall. He looks at me and motions with his head to the side. "I'll see you guys in there," I tell Ralph and Miller as they walk into the changing room.

"Hey," I say. He looks around and sees a closed door. He knocks on the door and then sticks his head in. He walks in and then calls me in.

I close the door behind me and look at him. "How are

you doing?" he asks, and I shrug. "I need to give you a heads-up," he says as he puts his hands in his pockets. "Murielle has been asked to step down from the foundation."

"Oh, shit," I say, putting my hand on my neck.

"Did she not tell you?" he asks, and I look down.

"I spoke with her this morning," I tell him. "I thought maybe she wanted to know how Jaxon was. She didn't." I shake my head. "So I told her I would speak with my lawyer. We have a meeting tomorrow afternoon with the mediator."

"What do I do if she tries to show up tonight?" he asks, and I look at him.

"Whatever you think you need to do, you do it. It's not my problem anymore," I say, and he looks at me.

"I have to go. I have a meeting with Matthew Grant in ten minutes." He walks to the door.

"Is there a reason you're meeting with Matthew Grant?" I ask him of the General Manager for the New York Stingers.

"You know me," he says, opening the door. "Just being respectful." He smirks, and I know Nico enough to know he doesn't need to be respectful, so he must want something. I shake my head and walk into the room just in time to see Evan Richards walk out with Justin Stone, both of them laughing.

"Hey," Evan says, stopping and extending his hand to me. "You okay?"

"Yeah," I say to him. Say what you want about the other team, but sometimes there are just some genuine people out there. "Did you come in here to ruffle his feathers?" I motion with my chin toward Ralph, who just glares at him.

"It's all fun and games," Ralph says. "You aren't allowed to talk to Ari when we get on the ice," he says of his daughter.

"You can't tell me that I can't talk to my niece!" he shouts back and then walks away with Justin, who just slaps my arm.

"We really have to fucking win tonight," he says to me, and I nod. He isn't the only one who wants to win tonight. I just want to show the press that this isn't getting to me. That this shit I'm going through doesn't matter.

The first period is rough, and New York gets ahead by two. We come into the locker room, and the whole room is pissed. It was just what we needed because at the drop of the puck in the second period, Ralph gets set up right in front, and he tips it in. He kicks up his foot and celebrates right next to Evan, who glares at him. Four minutes later, I'm taking the puck down the ice and skating into the neutral zone, looking around. I get over the blue line and wait for everyone to set up their position. I pass it to my defensive partner, Denis, and he passes it to Miller on the outside of the net, but then Ralph is blocked in the center, so he sends it back to Denis, and he passes it to me, and I wind my stick up, slapping it right back to the goalie, tying the game at two.

The third period is a mess with both teams trying to get the winning goal, and it happens with ten seconds to go. Evan goes to pass it to Justin, who skates just a bit too much ahead of it, and Miller intercepts it. He skates as fast as he can and slips it through the goalie's five-hole.

We go back to the locker room, and Nico is there slapping us on the back when we enter. Coach comes in and doesn't chew our asses, and then he looks at me. "Reporters are itching."

"Tell them to fuck off," Denis says. "No one needs to know your business."

"It's all good," I say, and the doors open, and the reports come in. I stand as ten of them surround me.

"Guys, just so we are clear," I say, "I'm not answering any personal questions." I look at all of them. "You want to talk about the game, fine, but it stops there." I see a couple of them roll their eyes, and I laugh. "Since when did I talk about my personal life before now?"

The reporters only ask me questions about the game, and one tries to slip in if there is anyone in the stands tonight who I would see later. I look straight at him and say, "Thanks for the questions, boys," then walk away and go into the shower area where I know they can't follow me. I shower and leave in record time, pulling up to Evelyn's house.

She answers the door, and I can tell she was sleeping. "Hey," I say, walking in and kissing her neck. "Were you sleeping?"

"Yeah, I took a nap so I can stay up with you when you get here," she says, and I stop looking at her. "I know that you're usually wired after the game, and I want to sit with you."

"I love you," I say, and her eyes light up. We've skated around the "I love you" talk for a while now, but I couldn't not tell her.

"I love you, too," she says to me, and I suddenly want to get her naked. I pick her up, and she wraps me up like she always does. "That was a nice goal today," she says. "We should celebrate."

"We should," I say, walking to her room. "Should we talk about the fact that we haven't used condoms? I got tested six months ago."

"I got tested when I got to town," she tells me. "And I'm on the pill."

She doesn't have to say anything else. The rest of the night I spend inside her until I have to leave to go home.

I hang out with Jaxon and then make my way over to my lawyer's office. I walk in, the receptionist taking me into my lawyer's office.

"Manning," she says, getting up.

"Hi, Yolanda," I say, putting out my hand for her to shake it. "Good to see you."

"Sit down," she says. "Would you like something to drink?"

"No, I'm fine," I say, sitting down and waiting for her to sit down.

She opens her file and takes out the papers she drafted up. "Okay, so she wants the family home."

"She can have it," I tell her. "I hate that house anyway." She nods her head, writing down something. "I want my clothes."

"I will arrange a time for you to go and get them without her there." I nod.

"She wants alimony," Yolanda says. "But thankfully, you had a prenup."

I look at Yolanda. "What does she want?"

"Well, according to her lawyer, she wants Jaxon full time since you travel."

"Never going to happen," I tell her, and she holds up her hands.

"I've already told him that we will do fifty-fifty with regard to your schedule, and he sounded like it was going to be okay." She looks down. "She wants you to put out a statement that you were separated before the video was taken."

I think about it. "I'll only do it if she signs the papers in twenty days. If she signs off on everything, I will put out a statement saying we separated four months ago. She has to stop communicating with the press, and I want an NDA." I don't want her to say anything about Evelyn to anyone, ever. Not now and not ten years from now.

"Are you sure about this?" she asks.

"I want to get on with my life," I tell her. "So if she agrees to that, we have a deal." Yolanda looks at me.

I get up and walk out of the office, and for the first time since this started, I see the end of the tunnel.

THIRTY-FOUR

EVELYN

"WHAT TIME WILL you be over?" Manning asks, and I look up and see it's almost three o'clock.

"I finish at five, and then I have to rush home and change." I tap my finger on the desk. It's been two weeks since the pictures have been leaked. Two weeks of me waiting for the other shoe to drop, yet nothing has come out.

"I just got home," he says to me. "And I was gone four days."

"I'm aware." I laugh. He's been over every single night that he's been in town. He stays home for supper and then sneaks out to come over here and then sneaks back in before Jaxon wakes up. But tonight, he wants us to have dinner together and for me to meet his mother.

"Murielle is getting Jaxon tomorrow morning for the weekend," he says softly. "Which means I get to sleep over and wake up with you."

"I might be busy." I roll my lips when he groans. "I will be over by five thirty," I tell him. "Can I bring anything?"

"Yeah, your ass," he says, and I shake my head, laughing. "See you later, baby." I hang up the phone, and my whole head is now thinking of Manning. I pack up my stuff at four thirty, and I'm in the car when he calls again.

"Where are you?" he asks, and I laugh.

"Did you plant a chip in me?" I ask, pulling out of the parking lot. "I just left the office."

"Change of plans. Murielle is going to get Jaxon at seven," he says, exhaling a deep breath. "Can you come over now so we can eat at five thirty? I really want to have a family dinner."

The way he says it, I would give him anything. "I can be there in thirty," I say. I don't tell him that I'm stopping at the flower shop to get his mother flowers.

"Okay, perfect," he says. "Guess the sleepover is going to happen tonight and tomorrow," he says, and I just hang up the phone. Luckily, I ordered the bouquet this morning, and it's ready when I walk in. It's right next to a bakery, so I swing in quickly and pick up a chocolate cake.

When I pull up to the house, my stomach starts to flip and flop, making me feel like I'm going to vomit. I'm about to open the door when it's swung open, and I look up to see Manning. He bends down, coming into the car. "Hi," he says, and his head comes closer to me. "I figured you wouldn't let me kiss you in front of my mother." He kisses my lips.

"You would be right," I say, giving him one more kiss. He moves out of the way, and I step out of the car and open the back door, grabbing the massive bouquet of wildflowers. "That box is a chocolate cake," I tell him, and he leans in and grabs it along with my purse.

"Are you ready?" He looks at me, and I shake my head. "Good, let's go."

He slips his hand into mine, and I walk up the pathway. "This house is nice," I tell him as he opens the door, and I step in, smelling the home cooking right away. "Mom." He shouts for his mother, and I exhale a big breath, and then she comes into the room.

"Well, hello there," she says. She looks a lot like Manning. They have the same eyes. "I'm Rachel."

"I'm Evelyn," I tell her. "I didn't know what flowers you liked, so I decided you can't go wrong with colorful," I say, handing her the bouquet and her whole face lights up.

"That is the sweetest," she says, bringing it to her nose. "Manning, take her jacket and bring her in." She turns and walks out of the room. I turn to shrug my jacket off, and once it's off, he wraps an arm around me.

"I missed you," he says, and I don't move in his arms. "A lot." He bends to place a soft kiss on my lips.

"Manning." His mother says his name as she walks back into the room, and I want the earth to open up and swallow me. "Would you let the woman be." She shakes her head.

"Nope," Manning says, moving his hand from around my waist up to my shoulder and then kissing my head. "I didn't see her for four days."

"Oh my god." His mother puts her hand on her chest. "I don't know how you survived," she mocks him. "I haven't seen Dad in two weeks. I survived. Him not so much."

I laugh. "It smells wonderful," I say as we walk from the front door to the kitchen.

"I'm making my famous pot roast." My eyes light up.

"That's one of my favorites," I say, and Jaxon looks up from the couch.

"Hi, Evelyn," he says, getting off the couch. "Nana has been cooking all day for you," he says.

"Hey there," I say, not sure what else to say. What does one say when meeting your boyfriend's child? "How are you doing?"

"Good," he says. That is the end of that conversation because he turns around and watches the television.

"Do you want a glass of wine?" Rachel asks me, and I nod.

"Not too much, though, because I have to drive home," I say, walking to the kitchen as she takes out a wine glass and pours a bit in the glass, and then she takes out a second one, pouring her own.

She hands me a glass and then holds hers up. "To new beginnings." I smile, clicking my glass with hers and then looking to my side, feeling his hand on my hip.

"What can I do to help?" I ask. She gives me some plates, and I set up the dining room table. We sit down to eat, and the talk is light. Manning talks about being in Philly and seeing the snow.

"How is school?" I ask Jaxon, and he shrugs.

"Good. Today, Caleb and I heard Macy fart, and she said it wasn't her, but we know it was." I laugh at him. "I knew girls farted."

I laugh, shaking my head. "They do," I say, and his eyes light up. "Not as often as boys but sometimes."

"I knew it," he says as if he just found out a national secret. "I told Caleb that."

The rest of the meal is spent with idle chitchat until Manning looks over at me. "I'm going to drive Jaxon to his mom's place. Do you want to wait for me here?"

"I'm not going to let your mother clean up this whole mess by herself," I say, getting up and getting the plates. He just smiles at me.

"Jaxon, go get your bag," he says, and Jaxon runs up to get his bag. "Okay, I'll be back in thirty minutes," he says to me, and I just smile. When he walks toward me, my eyes go big, and I'm mentally yelling at him not to do what I think he's going to do. He puts his hand on my hip and bends his head, giving me a soft peck. "See you soon."

I look at Jaxon to see how he reacts, but he couldn't care less. He slips on his running shoes and opens the door. "Go," I say to him when he just looks at me, and I make the mistake of looking up at him, and he bends his head again to kiss me.

I watch him walk out and then turn to look at his mother. "I told him not to kiss me in front of you," I tell her, and she laughs.

"It's funny that you think he will listen to you," she

says as she turns on the water in the sink and fills it. "I have never seen him like that before." She grabs some Tupperware to pack the leftovers. "When he called to tell me about Murielle, I was not shocked per se. God knows it was a long time coming. I was more scared for him." She starts saying while she rinses the dishes before putting them in the dishwasher. "Scared he wouldn't have anyone here in his corner."

"I'll always be in his corner," I tell her. "I know we just met, and I know it's not the most conventional way to meet, so I can just imagine what went through your head." My mouth is literally having diarrhea and won't stop. "Who gets involved with a married man? How can someone do that?" I finally place the last plate on the counter. "When I found out he was married . . ." I shake my head, and she puts her hand on mine.

"You don't have to justify yourself to anyone." She smiles. "Anyone. Do you know that I used to talk to my son monthly? Every thirty days, he would call, or I would call, and it was so tense. I didn't want to be rude and not ask about Murielle, and he didn't want to be rude by not telling me anything. For five years. It was the hardest thing in the world as a mother to watch your kid go through so much and not say anything. But now." She taps my hand before going back to washing the plates. "Now he has light in his eyes. His shoulders aren't slumped, and he stopped making excuses."

"I don't understand," I tell her.

"We would have a family gathering, and I would invite him, knowing that she didn't want to come, and he would have to make an excuse. His father was over it and was ready to fly out here, but I wouldn't let him. I had a lifeline with him, and I would not cut it. So I would give him the invitations, and he would try to let me down slowly. He did come a couple of times, but each time was without her. It put a strain on us all."

"I'm so sorry," I say, and she just smiles.

"I see it now," she says, looking at me. "When I saw you, I could see why Manning would be drawn to you. You're gorgeous, but you are genuinely a nice person." She looks down now. "It's about time someone put my son first."

I don't say anything to her as I clean up the kitchen. "I'm going to miss them," she says, looking around when we finish as we sit down with another piece of cake. "After being here with them for two weeks."

"Well, I think you'll just have to visit more," I tell her. "Nothing will stop you now."

She smiles at me, and we both hear the front door open and close and then see Manning walking in. He sits down in the empty chair beside me. "Did it go okay?"

"As good as it could go," he says, leaning over and kissing me. "I get him on Wednesday for dinner and then back on Friday."

"He'll be okay," Rachel says. "Now," she says, getting up, "I'm going up to shower and pack. I get to sleep in my own bed tomorrow."

"We'll be here to pick you up tomorrow at ten," Manning tells her, and she smiles at me.

"It was a pleasure to finally meet you," I say and

look up at Manning. "You did good with this one," I say, making her laugh. I look over at him, seeing him smile. "What are you smiling about?"

"Tonight, I had dinner with my woman and my son. My mother sat at the same table. It doesn't get better than that." I cut a piece of cake and hold it out for him. "Actually, it's going to be better." I raise my eyebrow. "I'm going to go to sleep beside you, and I don't have to run out of your bed."

"I can kick you out of my bed." I wave the fork in front of him.

"I'd like to see you try." He laughs, leaning over and kissing me senseless.

THIRTY-FIVE

Manning

"How long will it take you?" I look over at Evelyn, and she just stares at me. "What?"

"You just told me that we are going out to dinner with your friends at seven." She turns her back toward the car door. "I've spent all day out of the house."

"I know. I was there," I tell her. We woke up together for the first time ever, and it was even better than I had imagined. Sliding into her at five a.m. and then leaving is nothing compared to sliding into her at seven and then making coffee with her while she wears my shirt. Needless to say, she was bent over so fast we forgot all about the coffee.

We had to rush out of the house and get my mother to her flight. I was shocked when Evelyn threw a fit that I was going to just drop her off. No, my girl made us park, and we walked my mother in. I could tell that it even got to my mother when she got teary-eyed and whispered,

"Don't let this one go." I knew that already. I didn't need my mother to tell me that. We walked her as far as we could before waving good-bye, and then we set off on our day.

"It's five thirty," she tells me, and I look over at her. "We have to leave at six thirty."

"Yeah, about that," I say, and she just shakes her head.

"What are you shaking your head about?" I ask. "Do you not want to meet my friends?"

"I have to take a shower," she says, throwing up her hands. "And fix my hair. First impressions are every-thing."

"They sort of already met you," I say, looking over at her, and I grab her hand and pull her to me. "They were at the restaurant that night."

"Manning." She tilts her head back and looks at me. "Next time, you need to give me at least a twelve-hour warning."

"It's going to be fine," I say, parking my car in her driveway. "It's just the six of us."

"What's the dress code?" she huffs as she gets out of the SUV, and I grab the bag that I have in the back seat.

"Casual," I say, walking with her to the front door.

"Casual dressy or casual jeans?" she asks, unlocking the door and walking in, kicking off her Nikes.

"Baby," I say softly as she rushes to her bedroom and pulls off her sweater. My cock gets hard from looking at her. "I'm wearing jeans."

"Ugh," she says, peeling the pants off her and then

going to the bathroom. I follow her, and I'm about to grab her hips when she turns around and points her finger at me.

"Don't even think about it," she tells me. I pull off my shirt, and she bites her lower lip. "We don't have time for this," she says and backs up, putting her back to the wall. I undo my belt and open the button of my jeans, my cock springing out. "Manning." She moans out my name as I get closer to her. "You have four minutes," she tells me. I pick her up by her waist, and she wraps her legs around my hips and slides down on my cock. Both of us moaning now. My mouth goes to hers as I press her back into the wall, and I fuck her hard, lasting a lot longer than four minutes.

"We are going to be late," I tell her as I slip on my black boots. "Then they are going to know we're late because we had sex."

"This wouldn't be happening if you kept your cock away from me." She steps out of her walk-in closet, and I just look at her. My mouth salivates at her tight light gray jeans with a rip in one of her knees and a snug plain white T-shirt with a gold chain around her neck. My eyes go to the sky-high leopard heels she's wearing.

"How do I look?" she asks, slipping on a short black leather jacket and pulling her long hair out of it. I bend down and kiss her lips, slipping my tongue into her mouth, but she shoves me away. "We don't have time for that."

She grabs her black purse, and we rush out of the house. We get to the restaurant ten minutes late, and she is shaking her head when we get out of the car. I look over at her as she walks to me, and I grab her hand. After we walk into the restaurant, the hostess sees us, and I hear my name being called. I look over at the fans and just raise my hand, never letting Evelyn's hand go. "Um," she says from beside me. "I forgot that you get noticed."

"And?" I look at her as the hostess asks us to follow her.

"You're holding my hand." She looks down at our hands, and I don't have time to address the question because we are brought into a private room. "There they are," Miller says, looking over at us. I look at Evelyn, who looks at me wide-eyed.

"Sorry, there was traffic," I say.

"Don't mind him," Layla says, getting up and coming over to us. "I'm sorry about my husband. He is almost like a senior these days because he eats at four, and when he doesn't, he gets cranky." She smiles at Evelyn. "I'm Layla."

"Nice to meet you," Evelyn says and holds out her hand. "I'm Evelyn."

"We apologize for our friend," Candace says. "I'm Candace," she says, and instead of shaking her hand, she reaches out and hugs her. I can see that Evelyn is taken aback. "I'm his PR girl."

"I've heard wonderful things about you," Evelyn says with a smile, and I swear I've never been as happy as I am at this moment. We would often have dinner together, but I would always be the fifth wheel.

"I've heard nothing but good things about you." She

steps away. "And from just this meeting, you got my vote."

"Really?" Evelyn says, laughing.

"Don't mind her," Layla says. "The minute you didn't throw a drink at her, you had her vote."

"Okay, can we sit and order, please?" Miller asks, and Ralph introduces himself. I wait for the four of them to go sit back down, and then I pull out the chair for her.

"You look the same." Miller looks over at her, and we all look at him. "You know what I mean. Sometimes, you meet someone, and they look one way, and then you see them again, and it's like a whole different person."

"What the fuck?" Ralph says, and I just shake my head. Evelyn takes off her jacket and places it on her chair, and I reach over, putting my hand on her chair.

"Thank you, I guess," Evelyn says.

"This guy was going nuts for you," Miller says, laughing. "Whenever we go out, he is the first person to leave, but he stayed longer than we did."

"God, Miller," Layla says, shaking her head. "What if he didn't want her to know that?"

He looks at her, confused. "They are together, so I think it's safe to say he likes her."

We all laugh. The girls ask her questions, and by the end of the night, it feels like we've been doing this forever. When the waitress comes over, Candace asks her to take our picture, and Evelyn looks at me with big eyes. "I'll go to the bathroom."

"Why?" I ask, and she looks at me.

"She's going to post the picture," she says, and now

everyone is looking at us. "And it's still, you know."

"I don't," I say, and my heart sinks, wondering if she wants to be seen with me. "Do you not want . . .?"

"I'm just saying if she posts this picture, people will see I'm here," she says, and I see Candace smile and blink away tears. "And well, nothing is signed yet, and if Murielle sees it, she might change her mind." Her voice goes low as I pull her to me and kiss the top of her head. She tilts her head back, and I kiss her lips. "It's just easier."

"I don't care," I tell her. "I don't care if she takes this picture, and she puts it on the Jumbotron during the intermission at the game."

"Well, this is brand new," Candace says. "Does this mean you are finally going to get on social media?" I glare at her. "Okay, fine, but hey, at least he is letting me post it. Usually, it's 'don't put me on there.'"

"Look here, everyone," the waitress says, and I put my arm around her and pull her to me, so people know she's with me.

When the meal is over, we all get up, and I slip her jacket on for her and bend to kiss her neck. We walk out of the restaurant with our hands together. We are stopped a couple of times, and I'm sure someone has taken a picture of us, but I literally don't give a shit. The girls hug her good-bye while the guys hold up their hand to wave good-bye.

"Did you have fun tonight?" I ask her as we walk to my SUV. I open the door for her, and she tilts her head back. I push the hair away from her face, then bend down and kiss her lips.

"I did." She gets into the car, and I walk over to my side.

I make my way to her house, and when we get in, I look at her. "Did you like any of the houses today?"

"I did," she says, and I wait for it. We went to visit four homes, and I know which one I want, but I want her opinion.

"Which one?" I ask her as she slips off her jacket, and she shakes her head.

"It's not about me," she says to me. "It's about you. It's about you wanting to come home to that house every single day. You have to think about raising Jaxon in that home." This woman never ceases to amaze me; again, she worries about Jaxon and me, and not once did she insinuate she will spend time there. Not once did she say I love this or you should get it. She always waited for me to say something before telling me how she felt.

"I think I liked the third house," I say. Her eyes light up, and I know that's the right one. "I'm going to put an offer on it."

"I think it's perfect," she says.

"Do you think you could help me make it a home?" I ask, and she comes to me now.

"I will help wherever you want my help," she says.

"Do you think you'd like to leave some of your stuff there?" I ask, and she throws her head back and laughs.

"Okay," she says, and then she steps back. "We have to talk."

I look at her, and she stands there in front of me. "I

just." She starts to say. "I don't know how comfortable I'm going to feel sleeping there with Jaxon." I'm about to say something when she puts her hands up. "Hear me out. I'm good for having dinner and even you kissing me, but I don't think what he needs now is to have me crashing your place when his life is in an uproar."

"When are you going to put yourself first?" I can't help but ask her. "During this whole time, not once did you look at me and say what about me." I don't let her say anything. "Never in this whole time did you put yourself first. In this whole thing, all you worried about was me and Jaxon or my mother or anyone else but yourself."

She throws her hands up. "Well, that's what you do when you love someone!" she yells.

"I've never had that," I tell her. "Never in my whole life have I had someone who put me before them. Besides my parents." I look down, my heart almost exploding. "Thank you." I grab her hand and bring it to my chest. "For bringing me back to life."

THIRTY-SIX

EVELYN

"I CAN'T BELIEVE we are finally getting together," Stephanie says when I sit down at the table. "It's been too long."

"It really has been," I say. The waiter comes by to tell us the lunch specials. "Sorry it has to be lunch and not dinner. Things have been just a touch crazy."

"You look different," Stephanie says, looking at me, and my eyebrows shoot together. "You glow."

"Um . . ." I put my hands to my cheeks. "Thanks, I guess."

"So tell me, what is new with you?" she asks, picking up her glass of wine.

"I met someone," I finally say, and she smiles. "I actually met him at the restaurant where you had your bachelorette party." She doesn't say anything. "His name is Manning." I wait to see if it clicks, and I see that nothing lights up on her face. "He's amazing," I say, smiling.

"So thoughtful and basically just the nicest guy I've ever met."

"You love him." She points at me, laughing. "That's what is different about you. You have that love glow."

"I must." I laugh, grabbing my glass of water.

"So tell me everything," she says, and I fill her in on everything that has been going on. "Hold on a second." She puts up her hand. "Is this Manning Stevenson?" she asks, shocked. "The one who caught his wife fucking in a car?"

"He didn't catch her, but yes," I admit, "that would be him."

"Holy shit." She slaps the table. "It was a soap opera."

"Oh, trust me, I know," I say, and we change the subject to her wedding, which is taking place in a month. I hug her good-bye and then make my way back to Manning's house.

"Are you ready?" I ask Jaxon right before we walk out of the house. He puts his hand in mine, and I smile. "Are you hungry?" Both of us are dressed in black jeans with our Dallas jerseys on.

"No," he says as I walk over to Manning's SUV that he left here for me.

I open the back door of the SUV, and I wait for him to get in and get buckled. After getting into the driver's seat, I push the button for the garage door to open. I pull out and look up at Manning's brand-new house. He did not mess around when he said that he liked this house. He made an offer on it the next day, and in fourteen days, he was in. It was a bit of a whirlwind, to be honest, but he was gone for most of it, and when he was here, he was busy with Jaxon. The three of us went furniture shopping, and in one day, he had all of his furniture picked out. Paying a rush fee, he made sure it was delivered when he got the keys to the house.

"If you are hungry, we can get something at the game." I look in the rearview mirror and see him nod. I tried to move slowly with Jaxon, but the only problem with that was his father. He was on the road for over five days, and when he got home, I was waiting for him, thinking we would have dinner together, and I would leave. Well, he did not take that very well. In fact, he didn't take that well at all. He put Jaxon to bed and then locked all the doors, arming the alarm with a code. "If you leave, you'll wake Jaxon." The next morning, Jaxon didn't even bat an eye that I was still there. He just asked who was cooking breakfast. I want to say that it has been all smooth sailing, but it hasn't. The only good thing is Murielle signed the divorce papers. That is where the good thing ends with her. She calls Manning daily to bitch at him. He listens for five seconds, and when it doesn't involve Jaxon, he hangs up.

"Is Caleb coming?" he asks, and I nod. "Yes. We are going to go by the glass and get some pucks."

I smile at him, hiding the nerves running through my body. Tonight, I'll be going to the hockey game officially as his guest. The secret that we are dating is no more. The night after the dinner party with the six of us, I woke up to the picture all over social media. My mother even called me.

I follow the instructions Manning gave me and pull into the secret underground parking. It really isn't a secret when I see that fans are there snapping pictures. "Okay, buddy, tell me where to go?" I ask, and he guides me to Manning's place. "Okay, let's go," I say, getting out of the SUV and waiting for him. "You tell me where to go."

I'm almost at the door when I hear my name being called and look over to see Layla walking over to us. "Hey there," she says, and she kisses my cheek. "Hi, buddy, did you grow?" she asks him, and he just smiles, then looks at me. "Are you ready?"

"As ready as one can be," I answer her honestly as we walk in. I look around and see people are starting to trickle in. I walk down the corridor and stop when we get to a picture of Manning on the wall. He is looking at the play at hand, and it has his number with his name. I swear I smile like a fucking fool. That is my man, and I almost want to reach out and touch it. "It's crazy, right?" I look over at Layla. "That he's just Manning at home, and then we come here, and he's a superstar."

She shakes her head. "It can be an eye-opener, that is for sure." We walk up some stairs, and you have to show your tickets to get on that floor. I open my purse to get them out, but I don't need to because Manning is there in his workout gear talking to someone.

"Dad." Jaxon calls his name, and he looks from the guy to us. He sees Jaxon, and then his smile gets even bigger when he sees me. He walks over and tells the man scanning tickets something, and he just nods his head.

"Hey," I say when I get closer to him, and I smile. I look up at him, and he bends to give me a kiss.

"Hi," he says, and every single time feels like the first time I saw him. I sometimes just sit there and look at him. "You made it."

"I did," I say. "Thanks to Jaxon, who made sure I knew where I was going." I smile down at Jaxon.

"Nico," Manning says to the guy who he was talking to, who is now joking with Layla. "I'd like you to meet Evelyn." He puts his hand around my shoulder. "Evelyn, this is my boss."

Nico smirks when he says that and puts out his hand. "Nice to meet you," he says and then looks down at Jaxon. "How is my future superstar?"

"Good," he says and then looks up at Manning. "Can I go in and get a snack?" Manning nods, and he walks into one of the doors. This floor looks like a hotel with carpet on the floor and brown wooden doors with numbers on them.

"I have to go down," Manning says. "I'll see you later."

"Okay," I say, looking at him, and he bends to kiss me again. "Break a leg."

"I'll see you later," he says one more time and jogs down the corridor, and I walk into the room where I saw Layla enter.

"Evelyn." I hear Jaxon call my name. "Can we go down to the glass?" I grab his hand and turn to walk out of the room when I see Tim and Caleb coming in.

"Auntie Evelyn," Caleb says, running to me, and I

bend down to hug him, kissing his neck. "You're wearing a jersey."

"I know," I say, getting up and kissing my brother on his cheek. "Thanks for coming," I whisper in his ear. I didn't know what tonight would bring, and I somehow felt more comfortable having Tim here.

"Box seats," he says. "It's my dream." He was shocked like everyone else when I told him about Manning and me. But for a whole different reason, and it had nothing to do with the fact he was married. Veronica, on the other hand, was thrilled that he was finally going to divorce Murielle, who I found out did not have friends anywhere.

"I'm going to go with Jaxon to get some pucks, apparently at the glass. I'm going to take Caleb. They have food and booze." I point at the room, and he nods, then sees Nico, who comes over and shakes his hand and then looks at me.

"Wait a second," he says, looking at me. "You're Tim's sister?"

"I am," I say, and he looks down. "I heard about you." And I smile at him. "I'm not going to tell Manning because well, I don't know how he would react, but your father tried to set us up."

I laugh, shocked now. "What?"

"Yeah, when you were coming back, he thought we would connect well," Nico says, and it's at that moment that I realize I don't want to be with anyone else. I don't want to go on another first date. I don't want to have another first kiss. I don't want anyone but Manning.

"Are you okay?" he asks, and I just nod and turn to walk out of the room. My head is spinning. I know I love him, there is no questioning that, but it's a forever type of love.

I walk with the kids as they lead me down to the glass, and I see the players come on the ice. Caleb and Jaxon line up at the glass, and I stand behind them as kids come over. They slap the glass, and I wait there, and then I see him on the ice, sliding on one skate as he comes over to the glass. Picking up two pucks, he throws them both over for Jaxon and Caleb, and then he looks at me. His face changes right away when he sees me. The worry forms on his face, and he nods with his chin, mouthing, "What's wrong?"

I try to play it off and smile at him as I watch the boys slap the glass. He looks at me and then the boys.

I wait until all the guys have skated off before heading back up, and I don't even know what happened in the game. I don't remember talking to anyone; I remember nothing. The only thing I'm trying to digest right now is the fact that he's the one.

Tim and Caleb leave as soon as the game is over, and Jaxon sits next to me on the couch as we wait with some of the other family members for the teams to come out. He leans on me, and I open my arm to wrap it around him as he lays with his head on my lap.

I get a text from Manning forty minutes after the game.

Manning: Coming to get you.

I don't move as I wait for him to come, and then I

see him walking into the room. He is wearing a blue suit with a white button-down. "Hey," he says when he sees me and then comes over to us.

"He's sleeping," I say, and he bends down, and I wait for the kiss. He kisses me softly once.

"I'm going to grab him." He bends over and lifts him in his big arms. "Are you okay?"

"Yeah," I say, and he just looks at me. "Just tired." He nods, slipping his hand into mine.

He doesn't say anything when we get in the car, and the drive home is suddenly awkward silence. When we get back to his house, he carries Jaxon to bed. I walk to the kitchen and warm up some food for him.

He comes back in a couple of minutes later, and he's wearing shorts with no shirt like he always does after a game. "What happened?" he asks right away, standing with his hands on his hips. "And don't tell me nothing. When I saw you, you looked pale and like you were going to vomit or pass out."

"It honestly was nothing." I try to reassure him because I'm not sure how the fuck to explain what is going through my head.

"We said we'd never lie," he says, and I shake my head. "In here," he says. "In your house, it's just us."

"Can we not do this now?" I ask, and he just looks over at me. "You are so annoying sometimes," I say, and he just continues to stare. "Fine," I say, my voice rising a bit. "Tim came in, and Nico put two and two together, and then told me my father was trying to play match-maker."

"Like fuck," he hisses out, and I roll my eyes.

"This was before I got to town. Anyway, while he was telling me this, I . . ." I look down, nervous to say the last bit. "I . . ."

"You . . .?" he repeats, waiting for it.

"I realized I don't want to date anyone else." I look up at him. "Like ever." His mouth opens. "I know, and it's not your problem at all. It's more of a me problem than a you problem or even an our problem." My mouth just won't stop. "But it's fine. If you can actually forget this whole conversation, that would be really great." I shake my head and turn, not to look at him. I'm opening the oven when I feel his hand on my back. His hand moves my hair to one side as his arms go around my waist. He brings his head down and buries it in my neck, and I feel so embarrassed. I knew it was silly to bring it up now. "Manning," I whisper.

"Baby," he says, and I turn my head to the side, and I kiss his lips. "There is no one else," he says, softly kissing me, "I would ever want to be with."

"You don't have to say that." I put my hand up to touch his face.

"I've wanted to say that to you for the longest time, but I was just waiting for the right time," he says softly, then he smiles and says the two words that I always wanted to hear. "You're it."

THIRTY-SEVEN

MANNING

I WALK INTO the house and slam the door behind me, holding a bouquet. "Evelyn?" I call her name, looking up the staircase to see if she comes out of our bedroom. I call it our bedroom even though she has yet to move in. "Baby?" I walk into the kitchen and don't see her there either. I left about an hour ago to bring Jaxon to Murielle's, and when I left, she was just walking in.

I walk up the steps two at a time and walk toward the bedroom. "Evelyn." I say her name, looking around the bedroom. The king-size bed sits in the middle of the room, but my eyes go to the picture of the two of us beside the bed.

"Yes?" I hear her voice coming from the walk-in closet. She comes out and has her hair tied on top of her head. "What's with all the yelling?" she asks, and I sit on the bed looking at her. All she is wearing is my T-shirt, and I can tell she isn't wearing a bra, which causes my cock to wake up.

"I thought we were going out?" I ask. She walks over to me, and I spread my legs for her to stand between them. I wrap my arms around her legs, rubbing my hands up and down them. She puts her hands on my face. "I said I wanted to take you out."

"Manning," she says. "You were just gone for ten days." She bends and kisses my lips. It was the longest road trip I've been on, and she stayed over to watch Jaxon. Jaxon asked her if she would be watching him. The minute he asked, she answered she would love to. So instead of going back to her house this time, she stayed here.

"But we haven't been out on a date," I say, and she looks at me.

"Manning." She kisses me again as my fingers trail up her leg. "I want to stay at home with my man." She smiles when she says that. "I want to sit on the couch and make out with him."

"Hmm," I say, pushing the hair away from her face. Turning my head, I kiss her, opening my mouth for her tongue.

"This," she says between kisses. "This is what I want." My hands roam up to her ass, finding it bare. "Just the two of us."

"Always," I tell her. This woman blows me away every single day. She loves spending time at home like I do. To her, the perfect day is just us being together. She puts Jaxon and me before herself all the time. She pulls my shirt up over my head and tosses it on the floor behind her.

She puts her knees on the bed beside my hips. "Ten days," she says, kissing my neck. "I missed you." My hands move up to cup her tits, rolling her nipples between my fingers. "It was so lonely without you." She settles over my cock and then pulls her shirt up over her head. I see the little love bite I gave her this morning after Jaxon left for school.

"Baby," I say, leaning down and taking a nipple in my mouth. Her hands find the button on my jeans.

"I need you," she says, and after I love you, those are my three favorite words. I pick her up around her waist and place her on the bed as I take off my jeans.

My hand strokes my cock as she watches me. "How do you want it?"

"Hard and fast," she says, and I know that afterward, she'll want it slow. I flip her on her stomach, and she moans when I pick her up by her hips and squat down just a little to attack her pussy with my mouth. "Fuck," she hisses out, and when I know she's wet enough, I straighten and slam into her.

We both still. "So fucking good," I say as I pull out of her and slam into her again. I swear the sex with us just gets better. She is never shy in asking me for what she wants. If she wants to suck my cock, she will fall to her knees and take me out, not caring. If she wants me to fuck her on the counter, she'll walk by me and rub herself on me until I pick her up and have my way with her. When Jaxon isn't here, you can catch us having sex anywhere from the kitchen to the garage.

"Can't get enough," I say as she arches her back. I lean over, grabbing her tits in my hands, and fuck her while holding them. "I'm going to come," she pants out, and I see her hand slip between her legs. "Right there." I don't stop until she comes on my cock, and only then do I come in her.

I release her, and she lies on her side and looks at me as she tries to catch her breath. "See, this is so much better than us going out," she says, and I hold out my hand for her.

"Time to shower," I say, and she looks at me.

"I've already taken a shower." She grabs my hand. "But if you want to wash my back, I'm not going to say no to that." She looks over her shoulder and gets into the shower while I walk to the sink. When I open the shower door, I find her sitting on the bench with one leg propped up, playing with herself.

"You were gone ten days," she says, and I smile at her. We stay in the shower for over an hour because every time we get the soap and wash each other, it leads to another round.

She finally gets out, and I find her downstairs in the kitchen with her hair wrapped in a towel. "Did you want anything to eat?" She looks over at me, and I know that if I told her I was starving, she would make me a meal without hesitation. She grabs the orange juice out of the fridge, and she pours a glass, handing it to me and going to get a second one. "By the way," she says, taking her glass of juice. "Nice flowers."

I smirk at her. "It was a part of the date," I say, and

she smiles.

"This is much better than a date," she says. "I have to go home tomorrow."

"I was talking to Jaxon tonight while I drove him to Murielle's," I say. "We were thinking about how it would be if you moved in with us."

"What?" she says in almost a whisper.

"Well, you see . . ." I walk to her and pick her up, placing her on the counter in front of me. "We like having you here. I love having you here."

"But . . ." She places her hands on my chest.

"I want to share my closet with you," I say, and she laughs.

"You have two closets," she reminds me, and I chuckle.

"Okay, maybe that wasn't a good thing," I say. "I had this whole speech planned," I tell her. "I want this to be our house. I want you to get up and get ready here every day. I want you to come home here. I want to share this house with you and make it ours. I don't want to have just some of your stuff here. I want it all here."

"Manning," she says.

"The first time I walked into your room, I saw that saying on top of your bed. *You will forever be my always.* I remember reading it and thinking how amazing it would be to find someone who would be forever my reason. To find someone to share my life with, to laugh with, and to fight with. More loving than fighting."

"Always," she says, kissing me. "But don't you think it's rushing things a bit with Jaxon and stuff? His whole life has been . . ."

"There." I point at her. "That right there, you putting everyone else before you. That's the reason. You will forever be my always." She looks down, and I can see she's blinking away tears. "Take the leap and move in with me. We can even do a trial run."

She looks at me, and her eyebrows go up. "You would do that?"

"No," I say, laughing. "Once you're here, I'm not letting you go."

"There is just so much to think about," she says. "I don't want anyone to think—"

"Fuck what they think," I say. "I lived my life for too long worrying about what people were going to say." I pick her face up. "I hate when I leave, and I know you aren't here in our bed," I say.

"One night," she says to me, smiling. "It was supposed to be a one-night thing."

"The minute I locked eyes on you and our hands touched, I was a goner," I tell her, thinking back to that day.

"I walked in and sat at the table, and I looked around for you," she tells me, and I'm shocked now. "I tried to downplay it, but every single chance I got, I looked around."

"I was watching you," I say, and she looks at me, her mouth hanging open as she smiles. "I saw you get up and walk to the bathroom."

"You did not," she says and pushes me away.

"I did," I admit. "I didn't mean to run you over, but .

. . ." I shrug as she puts her head back, and I kiss her lips. "I hate clubs. I hated going there, yet watching you, I couldn't leave."

"I was hoping you were watching me, and then when I caught you, I took my chance. I didn't know what was going to happen, but I knew I had to jump off the cliff."

"I will forever be in debt to Becca for getting me a room that night," I say. "Forever."

"Yes," she finally says and looks down. "If it's okay with Jaxon, then I'll move in here, but . . ." She holds her hand up. "But if it gets to be too much for him—" I crush my lips on hers to stop her from talking.

Picking her up, I carry her upstairs, never leaving her lips. All that keeps running through my head is that one chance meeting, one touch, one kiss, and especially that only one night has led us here.

EPILOGUE ONE

Evelyn

LOOKING DOWN AT my watch, I make my way over to the restaurant. My heels click on the sidewalk.

The hostess gives me an up and down look when I tell her I'm meeting someone. She doesn't even bat an eye when I walk in and head to the bar. The lights are dim, so I know I'm right on time to surprise him.

He's having a meeting with Ralph and Miller along with some equipment people. I sit at the bar, and I have the perfect view of him in the glass room. The same room where he was on the night we met. "Can I get you something?" the bartender asks once I sit down.

"I'll have a vodka cranberry," I say, and the music is playing. I look over and see the guys laughing, and I send him the first text.

Me: I miss you.

I press send the same time the bartender puts down the glass. I see the waitress circle next to Manning and lean over a bit too close for my liking, but he doesn't even notice. He picks up his phone, and he smiles. I see him typing while I take a sip of the cold drink, and then my phone beeps.

Manning: Miss you more.

My hands get clammy, and my heart starts to pick up speed. Maybe this was a stupid idea. I mean, in my head, surprising him at the restaurant where we met was a brilliant idea. I pick up the phone and send the second text.

Me: I wish you were here.

I finish off the first drink and order a second. The music gets louder and the tables slowly start to disappear as more people enter the club.

The bartender sets me another drink down, and he leans in. "From the gentleman at the bar." He points at the end of the bar, and when I see him standing there, I throw my head back and laugh. Putting my phone in my purse, I walk over to him. "Hi," I say to him, and he sees my outfit. The same outfit I wore when we met.

"Hi." He leans on the bar the same way he did when we met, and my stomach gets the same butterflies, if not more, knowing I get to go home with him tonight.

"You ruined my game plan," I tell him, and he just smirks.

"And what was that?" he asks as someone bumps into me, and I have to move closer to him. Unlike the first time when he put his hand on my ass to bring me closer to him.

"I was supposed to bump into you at the bathroom," I say, and he laughs now. "Then I was supposed to lead you to the bar."

"Really?" he says. I tilt my head back, and unlike the first time, he leans forward and kisses me out in the open. "I like my plan better," he says, and I look at him now. Standing, he takes my hand and leads me to the closet right next to the bathroom. He opens the door and pulls me in.

"Is this your plan?" I ask when he pushes me against the door.

"No," he says. His hand goes to the door handle, and he locks the door. He pushes my skirt up. "That night, I was dying to touch you." His hands go to my bare ass.

"Show me," I say as his mouth crashes to mine. His tongue slips into my mouth, and my stomach goes in every single direction. My skirt is bunched around my waist now, my hands at his button, and in three seconds, his cock is in my hands. He lets go of my mouth to attack my neck. He picks me up and presses me into the door. He rubs himself across my slit, and my head hits the door. "Manning," I say as he slides himself all the way in me.

He buries his face in my neck as he fucks me hard. My arms are wrapped around his neck, and my fingers are buried in his hair. The sound of us panting fills the room. "I'm going to." I start, and he knows. He knows my body better than I do. I thought the sex would lessen a bit as we got more and more involved, but it just grew. We still have sex every single morning when he's home. It's like his body is an alarm clock, and he wakes up with just enough time before we really have to get up.

Every single night when we slide into bed, we reach for each other. I close my eyes, and I come all over his cock, when not more than three hours ago, I did the same. He plants himself all the way in me, and my name's on his lips as he comes in me.

"Hmm," I say, ready for a nap. "You know what someone wise once told me?"

He takes his head out from my neck and looks me in the eyes. This gorgeous man makes my heart flutter every single time he walks into the room. The man who has the biggest heart and will do whatever he needs to do to make sure I'm happy and his son is happy. The man who is so quiet, yet with just one touch, I know what he's thinking. "What's that?" he asks with his cock still in me.

"There is never a third without a second," I tell him, and he laughs at me. "I have a surprise for you."

He slips out of me, putting me down on my shoes. "I thought this was a surprise," he says, tucking himself back into his pants. I pull my skirt down and fix myself.

"You ready?" I ask, and he nods as I unlock the door. "Text Miller and Ralph that something came up."

He smirks at me. "Something is coming up right now," he says, taking out his phone and sending the text. I slip my hand into his, and I walk with him out the door and toward the hotel. "Where are we going?"

"You'll see." I pull him to the elevator, and it is very much different from the last time where he waited for me. This time, there is no mistaking we are together. The elevator is there, and we get in, and I press the number to the floor. When we get off on the floor, I look over at him. "One year ago, my life changed." I take the key out of my purse and open the hotel room.

"This is the room where . . .?" he says, stepping in and seeing the soft lights on and a bucket of champagne on the table with strawberries and whipped cream. I toss my purse onto the single couch and look over at him. He stands there wearing his black suit, similar to that night.

"It's in this room one year ago where I gave myself to a man I didn't know. It's in this room I woke up and looked over and was awestruck with how beautiful he was," I tell him, and I smile. "I walked out of this room the next day, and my heart was heavy, thinking that I would never see you again."

"Evelyn," he says my name softly.

"But fate had other plans for us," I tell him. "I can't imagine this life without you in it." I walk to him, and he shocks me by getting down on one knee. I stop in my tracks as my hands fly to my mouth in shock.

"One year ago, I met a girl, and she brought me back to life. I didn't know at the time that I was drowning. I thought this was the best I could do," he says. "But then I kissed her, and it's like my heart started beating again. Evelyn, you've shown me what unconditional love is. You've shown me that love can be sweet, and it can be fun, and it can be beautiful. It can make you a better person." He reaches into his pocket. "I was going to do this tomorrow," he says. "I picked it up today, but I guess just like us meeting, things don't always go as planned." He opens the ring box, and I don't even care what is inside because my eyes never leave his. "Evelyn, will you be my wife? Will you stand beside me, holding my hand forever? Will you have babies with me?" I don't answer him. I can't answer him. The lump in my throat turns into a sob as I nod my head. I walk over to him and put my hand on his cheeks.

"This is so much better than my surprise," I say to him, and he laughs, picking me up and spinning me around.

"Before you ask," he says, putting me down. "I asked your father and Jaxon." I throw my head back, laughing because that would have been my next question. "Now, can I put the ring on you"—he takes the ring out of the brown box—"so I can use that chocolate syrup on you?" He motions his head to the table.

"Only if I get to use the whipped cream first," I tell him, and in the room where we lost ourselves one year ago, he slips a four-carat square diamond ring onto my finger.

EPILOGUE TWO

MANNING

"WELL, LOOK AT who showed up." I hear Evelyn say, and I look up laughing.

"I get the whole playoff beard." She comes into the room now, and I look at her, and my heart fills. She brings her hand up to my trimmed beard. "There he is." Her eyes light up. "Hi." She bends down and kisses my lips. "You were looking a bit too much like the *Duck Dynasty* bunch."

I laugh now. We went to the third round of playoffs and lost game fucking seven. To be honest, we never thought we would get past round one. We just rode the wave, and what a wave it was. We have the itch for it now, so there will be no stopping us next season. "If you don't put her down, she is going to expect to sleep in your arms every night." I look down at our one-week-old daughter as she squirms in my arms.

"We really timed it well." I kiss her cheek, and she

squirms even more. Victoria was born three days after we were eliminated, a full seven days late, and weighed in at nine pounds. "You knew, didn't you, baby girl?" I look up at my wife. *Yeah, my wife.* The single gold band on my finger shines. When she found out she was pregnant, something was missing for both of us. She would never tell me, but I knew that it bothered her we were not married. My girl was traditional that way, especially with the baby coming. I knew she didn't care what kind of wedding we had, so with the help of our mothers, we got married on Christmas Day.

"Why are you out of bed?" I ask, and she smiles at me.

"I missed you," she says and looks down at our daughter, "and I wanted to check on her." She rubs down our daughter's face, and my daughter blinks her eyes open.

"Did you eat?" I ask, and she nods.

"Your mother just put the leftovers away," she says, smiling at me. "I'm going to miss her when she goes." Just another reason I love her. She has welcomed my family with open arms and even had my parents stay here during Christmas while we planned a wedding. She didn't even bat an eye when my brother and sister came. The only thing she did was order more blow-up beds for the kids. Our house is a home and is open to everyone.

Victoria starts to squawk, and I look up at Evelyn. "Is it time?"

"She ate about an hour ago," she says, and I get up so she can sit down. Instead, she looks at me and tilts her head back, and I lean down and kiss her. "I'm going to go lie down."

Following Evelyn to our bedroom with Victoria in my arms, I place her in the bassinet beside the bed. "Where is Jaxon?" Evelyn asks. She has become his second mom, embracing her role with everything she has. And he is thriving because of it. She didn't force it down his throat like Murielle tried to force Thomas down his throat. They are now married and in the middle of getting divorced. It seems Thomas isn't as nice as I am with people fucking his wife, but I couldn't care less. I try to respect her in front of Jaxon, but that is where our relationship ends.

"He is at your brother's house with Caleb." I laugh, getting into bed with her. "He is over his baby sister and her nighttime routine."

"He isn't the only one," she says, closing her eyes just as Victoria yells. "I swear it's like she feels my body relaxing."

She sits up, grabbing our daughter from the bassinet to hold her. "You are more beautiful than the first time I met you," I say, and she looks over at me.

"Then I think you need to get your eyes checked." She laughs, grabbing the pillow and lifting her blouse to feed our daughter.

"Are you done watching?" She looks over at me, and I lean over to kiss her.

"Who would have thought that after only one night, we would be here?" I say, and she looks down at our daughter. I look up at the frame that was over her bed and now hangs over ours. "You will forever be my always."

The phone on my nightstand starts to ping, one after

another, and I look at her. "What in the world?" I say, and then her phone beeps three times.

I pull up my phone and read the headlines.

Dallas Oilers Owner and Most Eligible Bachelor is no more. Nico Harrison marries oil heiress Laurene Christy.

"Oh my god," Evelyn says from beside me. "Where's Becca?"

I pick up the phone and dial Becca, who doesn't answer. "Becca, it's me." I can only imagine what she's going through. "Call me. Come here. I'm here."

"They were just here together," Evelyn says, and I look down at my phone, hoping someone can answer the question on everyone's mind.

Where is Becca?